MINDY HAYES

Me
After
You

Cover Image by K Keeton Designs
Cover design by ©Sarah Hansen, Okay Creations
Editor: Madison Seidler
www.madisonseidler.com

ISBN-13: 978-1979562812
ISBN-10: 1979562814

Other Books by Mindy Hayes

The Faylinn Novels
Kaleidoscope
Ember
Luminary
Glimmer (a Faylinn novella)

Willowhaven Series
Me After You
Me Without You

Individual titles
The Day That Saved Us

Co-written with Michele G. Miller
Paper Planes Series
Paper Planes and Other Things We Lost
Subway Stops and the Places We Meet
Chasing Cars and the Lessons We Learned

To my Poppy, for giving me hope

Prologue

I STARE AT his casket, completely numb. I know I should feel something. My heart should be shattering, but the space where my heart should be is hollow. My chest rises and falls, but I don't know what's powering it. I haven't been able to breathe for days. The air is locked in my lungs with no escape. How have I not suffocated?

I don't understand. Why is he in there? He's supposed to be standing beside me. With me. He's supposed to be holding my hand, comforting me the best way he knows how, with the brush of his thumb over mine. But no one takes my hand. No one says a word to me. They skirt the edges of my existence, as though sorrow were contagious.

They told me it would be a closed casket. They couldn't put him back together to make the man I know. The man I knew.

Knew. I hate that word.

I can't even look at his perfect face one last time. The last image I have of him is not the way I want to remember him.

Bloodied.

Swollen.

Broken.

He wasn't supposed to die yet. He wasn't sick. He wasn't old. It wasn't his time. How could it have been his time? I don't understand. *Why was it his time?*

They lower him into the ground, and I hear an excruciating sound. It's piercing. Guttural. Desperate. My hands cover my ears to block it out, but it doesn't help. Not even a little bit. *Please make it stop!*

Someone wraps strong arms around my body, struggling to hold me still, shushing gently in my ear. It's then I realize it's me.

"Sawyer, breathe," the voice soothes. I don't know who it is. "C'mon, Soy. Breathe with me." The voice is so calm. How can it be so calm? I can't put a name to the person, but my brother is the only one that calls me Soy.

I gasp for air that doesn't exist. I keep screaming *no*, but no one asked me a question. Is that really going to be the last thing I say before he's officially out of my sight? There's a wet film over my eyes I can't see through. I can't see them lower the casket with my husband inside.

"I love you, Grayson," I choke. "I'm sorry. I'm so sorry."

The voice softly repeats my name over and over, telling me to breathe. But I can't. The emptiness strangles me.

There's nothing they can say. Nothing can calm me.

He's gone.

Nothing else matters now.

TWO MONTHS LATER

CHAPTER ONE

Sawyer

THERE'S A KNOCK at my bedroom door, but I don't answer.

I stare at the two-tone yellow wall of my childhood bedroom, white chair rail separating the pale yellow from the bright. I feel nothing when I look at the wall, so I continue. Feeling nothing is better than feeling everything. My body can't handle feeling everything anymore.

It's been five years since I've been back here. When I left home, I promised myself I would never come back. I needed to create a new life away from Willowhaven, a place that didn't include everything I couldn't have. There were too many memories, too many raw wounds that only added to the already gaping void in my chest. But when plans fall apart, there's only one place to start: square one. Plus, I didn't have much of a choice. He didn't give me much of a choice.

Grayson and I weren't saving. We didn't get a chance to start. We were hugely in debt from his medical school loans. He was three and a half years in. We were so close to the end. So close to the pay off. We didn't plan for this. Why would we? There was no way he could have known to stay away from the parking garage that night.

There's another knock.

This town doesn't feel like home anymore. Home is with Grayson. And I can't go where Grayson went. No one will let me. So, I no longer have a home. I may have spent the first eighteen years of my life here, but I want to bury those eighteen years, bury the memories they hold. I'm damaged enough as it is. That's what I am now, isn't it? Damaged.

The door creaks open. "Sweetie," Mom speaks softly as she peeks around the door. I lay on my side, facing the wall, with the cream bedspread pulled up around me and a pillow clutched to my chest, blocking out the world the only way I can. My eyes stare at the buttery paint as it blurs in and out of focus.

I've been home for five days, eight hours and thirty-seven minutes and haven't moved from this spot. You'd think I would have lost track of time. But time doesn't move quickly when every part of you aches. It lengthens, making minutes feel like hours and hours feel like days. Time drains you until you have nothing—nothing left to give.

"Sweetie, it's two in the afternoon. Do you think maybe you should eat something?" she asks. I hear the rasp in her voice as if she's been crying.

I don't want to answer. The idea of letting her believe I'm still sleeping is so tempting, but I know that will only encourage her to come into the room and touch me. I don't want to be touched. I want to be left alone. "I'm not hungry," I mumble.

"I know, but I'm worried about you. You didn't eat yesterday. At least drink something. You need to put *something* in your body. I'm going to bring you some hot chocolate."

I don't respond because I know she will do it whether or not I want her to. She won't stop until I leave this room, and I don't plan on leaving this room any time soon. If I lay here long enough maybe the ache will go away. Maybe my body will go numb.

My heart pulses his name in rhythm with each beat. Grayson. It would be so much easier if I could breathe. Grayson. If someone could remove the vise latched onto my heart. Grayson. The pain is so consuming, so relentless. Grayson.

It's been sixty-one days since he was taken from me. The empty space next to me emphasizes his absence, emphasizing how alone I am in this foreign place. My hometown. Sixty-one days and not one day feels better than the last.

My bedroom door opens, and she shuffles into my room. The mug of hot chocolate clinks as she sets it down on my nightstand. "I'm going to leave it here. Take little sips at least. I promise it will make you feel better."

The sweet chocolate smell wafts over to me. I bite the inside of my cheeks to keep in the whimper. She says nothing more, and when she's gone the floodgates open. *Of course she had to bring me hot chocolate.*

Four. That makes four jobs I've lost in the six months I've lived in Seattle. Whether it's because of budget cuts or the economy or my attitude, they all found a reason to kick me out on my butt.

As soon as I walk out from the restaurant where I lost my serving position, it starts to rain. Not a sprinkle, or a mist, but in buckets—a torrential downpour. Awesome.

I scowl at the sky for choosing the perfect time to open up and cascade its troubles down on me. "I have enough of those in my life, thank you very much!" I almost shout when I'm startled.

"You know, you really shouldn't blame the weather." I turn at the

nearness of a new voice. "It's just doing its job."

He stands about a foot taller than me, looking all hipster in his black-rimmed glasses, plaid flannel button-down, and form fitted jeans. Completely the opposite of what I'm used to—which is exactly what I need.

"Its job must be to ruin my day."

"So hostile toward the rain." He smiles so easily, as if it's a permanent fixture on his face. "You must not be from around here." He holds his umbrella up to try and cover me as well, but it's impossible to keep personal space under an umbrella, so I feel his warm breath on my face and take in the freshness of his scent, like newly cut grass.

"No, I'm not." I sigh. I obviously stick out like a sore thumb.

"What brings you to Seattle?"

I don't want to tell this handsome stranger my life story. I want to create a new one—one that doesn't include all of my losses. I chose to leave them behind. This is supposed to be a life that doesn't include... I shove his name out of my mind.

"A change," I say, swiping the wet strands of hair from my eyes.

"Change is good. I like change. I didn't catch your name."

"I'm Sawyer. Sawyer Hartwell."

"Hi, Sawyer Hartwell from..."

"Willowhaven."

He extends his hand to me. "I'm Grayson Jones from Seattle. How about a coffee or hot chocolate to warm you up from the weather's cold shoulder?"

I chuckle. "Hot chocolate?"

"There are a surprising amount of people in this world who don't drink coffee. On the off chance you were one of them, I thought I would leave the option open."

I allow myself a smile, and even if it's only for a moment, I want to spend a little more time with him. Maybe it will numb the pain chasing me

8

down thousands of miles from home.

"Hot chocolate sounds great."

"She's like a zombie, Phil. I don't know how to make it stop." I hear Mom and Dad talk quietly in the hallway outside my room. "It's been almost a week, and I can't get her out of that room."

"Nora, it's going to take time. She needs to do this on her own. No one can force her to become herself again. She needs to rediscover that."

They must think all I do is sleep. I wish. When I sleep, Grayson is more than a memory. In my dreams, he's there. He's there, and he's real, and we walk hand in hand into the sunset of our happily ever after with his dark-rimmed glasses perched perfectly on his nose. But most of the time sleep doesn't come. It stays at bay, obscuring my only escape from the gnawing ache.

"Maybe I shouldn't have convinced her to come home," she lowers her voice more. "I know she left here for a reason, but I thought coming back would give her familiarity and support. She won't even go outside and sit on the front porch, Phil. She can't handle being here."

"She'll get there, Nora. C'mere."

"I can't lose my baby again." I hear her muffled cries.

"We won't, honey. Not this time," he tries to reassure her.

But he's lying. My heart will never be the same.

CHAPTER TWO

I REALLY DON'T want to get out of bed this morning. My head's killing me, but the garage can't run itself. I groan as I drag myself out of bed. Nothing a little Tylenol and coffee can't fix.

My phone rings from on top of my nightstand, and I instantly know who it is.

"Good morning, sunshine," Lily says. I repeat it in my head right along with her because it's the phrase she's been waking me up with every day for the last year.

"Morning." I clear my throat as I sit on the edge of my bed, rubbing my hand down my face to wipe away the sleep.

"You sound so sweet when you wake up with your gravelly voice."

I grunt, get out of bed, and head toward the bathroom. The hallway is too narrow. I feel my way along the wall to keep steady. I must have stood up too fast.

"I won't keep you. I just wanted to say have a great day and make sure we are still on for tonight. Dinner at my place?"

"Yeah. I'll be there around seven." I pop a few Tylenol in my mouth and cup my hand under the faucet before bringing it to my lips to wash them down.

"Perfect. Can't wait! Love you."

"Ditto," I reply and hit the end button. I set down my phone on the sink and feel an ache in my knuckles. Flexing my right hand, I look down at the scars on the creased skin of my fingers. There's a scar for every one of my mistakes. I peer up at my bloodshot eyes in the mirror and wish I could go back to bed. Sleep wasn't on my side last night. Not that it ever is, but it would be nice to get one good night's rest every once and in a while. I don't even know what a good night's rest means.

After I finish showering, I dig around my sock drawer for a fresh pair. My fingers graze over the small velvet box in the corner. I pick it up and spin it between my fingers before opening it. The single solitaire shimmers up at me. My lips turn up on one corner at the thought of her, and then I snap it shut before burying it again. I'd hate for Lily to find it now.

When I'm done filling up my truck at the gas station, I head to Moment in Thyme to get my morning coffee. As soon as I walk in Haley offers a smile. "Hey, what can I get ya this morning, Dean?"

"You should know this by now, Hales." I lift a crooked smile.

She pushes her red-framed glasses on top of her head, brushing her frizzy hair out of her face. "Yeah, but I like to think one of these times you'll surprise me."

"I'm a creature of habit." I shrug.

She smirks, leaning against the counter, and points her pencil at me. "You know you could change it up every now and then. There are a ton of options."

"I prefer it black, but I can't make it at home as good as this stuff."

11

She nods. "All right, all right. I'll make an extra delicious cup just for you. Just give me a minute."

I stuff my hands in my pockets and wait beside the counter as she walks away.

"…what happened to Sawyer's husband?"

My heart jolts in my chest. I haven't heard her name in years. It plays in my mind like a broken record, but no one ever says her name anymore. Especially in front of me.

"He was murdered," a voice whispers behind me, but it's such a loud whisper I'm almost positive the entire café heard her.

"Sawyer Hartwell?" I hear disbelief in another's voice.

"Yes, Dotty. That's what I said."

The air in my lungs is compressed. I can't breathe. If I thought my headache was bad before…

"Oh, that poor thing. How will she ever recover?"

"You don't ever recover from something like that."

And I hate the way she says it because it sounds so wrong, and yet so right.

"Bless her heart. Do they know who did it?"

"I've heard that it was a random act. I'm not sure if they found the suspect or not."

"What a wretched thing to happen."

I turn to see the women seated at a table behind me. "Nora says she can't get her out of bed. The poor girl won't eat. Been lying in that bed for almost a week straight, she said. Probably longer now. I haven't talked to her since last week."

"Would *you* be able to get out of bed?"

"No, I don't suppose I would."

Ms. Dotty gets up to leave and sees me. Her hand darts to her chest in surprise. *Busted.* She forces a smile as if she doesn't

12

know I heard every bit of their conversation. "Oh, hello, Dean."

"Morning, Ms. Dotty," I mutter after clearing my throat. The shock must be written all over my face as much as I try to hide it.

Haley has apparently been repeating my name because she says it with more force than necessary. When I turn, her eyebrows are scrunched together in concern and she says, "Your coffee." I take it from her hands, dropping some cash on the counter—who knows if it's the right amount—and walk out as quickly as I can manage without actually running.

I don't want them to see me lose it. My brain can't decide what to process first. It spins around and around so fast I feel like it might burst into a million pieces.

Sawyer is finally back.

But her husband is gone. And this should alleviate the heaviness that has been weighing on me for years, but it wasn't supposed to happen like this. The heaviness spreads completely through me as the painful realization sets in. Sawyer must be devastated. And there won't be a thing I can do about it. She hates me.

CHAPTER THREE

Sawyer

I DON'T REMEMBER much about the funeral. Grayson's parents and siblings took care of everything. Flashes of lilies and roses and photos and blurred faces flicker in my memory, but nothing sticks. It's all a haze. My mind must be trying to protect me.

Everyone tells you that a funeral will help give you closure. *You'll feel more at peace once it's over, and you can begin the healing process,* they say. It's been over two months since the funeral, and I want to tell everyone they can shove their closure down their throats. The sadness never ends. I fear it will burrow into every nook of my heart and fester there forever.

The problem is that I yearn for anger. Being angry at least brings out bearable feelings inside of me. Feelings I can fight and let out. Scream into a pillow, and I'll feel some relief. Now, though, all I feel is sad—deep, dark sadness. The type of sadness that wakes me up at four in the morning and crushes my chest as if Goliath is standing on my heart, squeezing out tears I didn't think I could possibly have left.

I want it to end. I want some relief. I want to know that someday I'll be okay.

I'm preparing for the look I know my mom will give me when I walk into the kitchen the following week. She's been bringing me food and setting it on my nightstand throughout the day, hoping I'll eat a little bit of it. Eventually it crusts over and is thrown away. It's been too hard to find an appetite.

When I amble through the walkway she stands up swiftly from the kitchen table, and I'm pretty sure I hear her gasp.

"Morning," I murmur.

"Hi, baby, can I get you something? You want me to make you some breakfast?" She moves toward the cupboards to take out pancake mix. I made pancakes for breakfast on Grayson's last morning.

"Cereal is fine."

She reluctantly nods and watches my every move as I make my way around the kitchen to pour myself a bowl of cereal and eat. I feel like the star exhibit at a freak show. Her eyes follow me as I bring each spoonful to my lips, as if she's not sure I'll actually eat it. *Maybe she'll pour it down her throat and throw it back up.* I swear those are her thoughts.

When I finish eating and put my bowl in the dishwasher she obviously can't take it any longer. She wraps her arms around me in a tight hug. I'm having a hard time breathing because she won't let go.

"Mama," I prompt.

She pulls back and holds my shoulders. "You want me to run you a nice bubble bath? It might help relax you a little bit."

A bath actually sounds amazing so I take her up on the

15

offer, and you would think I told her she won an Academy Award. She smiles wide and her eyes beam.

"Do you want some company?" she asks as the tub fills and she puts in the bubble bath. The white foam begins to grow.

Would I like you to stare at me as I sit naked with only a layer of bubbles to conceal me? "I'll be okay. Thanks, Mama," I say instead.

She makes a face as if I've hurt her feelings, but she doesn't dispute it. "Okay."

Once the tub is filled to the rim, she slowly backs out of the bathroom and finally allows me some privacy. With the scent of the lavender aromatherapy and the warmth of the water, my body relaxes against the porcelain, and I shut my eyes.

"I never realized how invested people get in their dogs." We curl up on Grayson's gray couch, his arm draped along the back. His cozy studio apartment is meant for one person. An accordion divider separates us from his double bed with the side of the couch lining the wood floor of the kitchen.

"Are you kidding? Haven't you ever seen Best in Show? *These people are nuts." He chuckles. "These people mean business. Their dogs are their lives. They don't mess around."*

"That Great Dane is pretty glorious, though," I say. "You have to give the owner props." The Great Dane stands impressively still as they examine him, invading his personal space.

"Imagine what he's thinking. 'Hey, get your hands out of there!'"

I laugh. "What are they even examining? He must feel so violated."

Grayson's hand gently squeezes my shoulder. His fingertips graze the bare skin beneath my sleeve. I feel his eyes on me before he speaks. "You know you're beautiful when you laugh. I wish I could make you laugh more often."

I tilt my head up to look at him. "What are you talking about? You

16

make me laugh all the time."

He narrows his intense hazel eyes. "I've made you smile. You rarely laugh."

It's been hard to find things to laugh about over the last several months, but Grayson somehow discovered that switch. I don't know how, but a flicker of hope makes me believe that maybe, just maybe, he could fix me.

His penetrating gaze drifts to my mouth, lingering for a few moments before lifting back to my eyes. He's going to kiss me, isn't he? I've only kissed one other person in my life—a person who I kissed for two years. What if I'm not any good at kissing anyone else? What if my lips were only meant for him? What if Grayson doesn't like kissing me?

He lowers his head, leaning in, asking without words if it's okay. My eyes lift to his and I nod once, subtly. His lips brush softly against mine, touching, learning how we fit together. When he feels more confident I'm not going to pull away, he presses more firmly, and this kiss brings warmth and peace and relief. We're not perfect at it, but it doesn't matter. His lips lock around mine. Grayson might be the key to putting me back together.

A knock on the bathroom door brings me back. The water is suddenly cold, and the bubbles have faded away. My fingers feel like they've shrunk when I lift them out of the water. They've been in the water for so long I wonder if they will stay permanently pruney.

"Sawyer? You okay in there? It's been a few hours." I hear the conflict in my mom's voice. She doesn't want to bother me, but she's too concerned to leave me alone for long.

"I'm alive." *If that's what you were evasively questioning.* "I'm getting out."

"I made some sandwiches if you want one."

I sigh. The thought of food makes me nauseous. "Okay. I'll

17

be there in a minute."

I can still feel his arms around me. I know how his lips would form to mine and how we would fit together. His fingers would grip my waist and brush my sides. I would almost feel unbroken in his arms. If I stay in the tub any longer I'll slip under and drown myself, so I burst out of the water to sever the memory.

It takes several weeks, but I finally let Mom push me out the door to grab a few things she says we need. She thinks I could use the fresh air. I don't doubt she's right, but it doesn't change the fact that I don't want to get out. I tell her she needs to mind her own dang business, but it's a losing battle, because here I am at the local grocery, putting milk in my basket alongside the bread and eggs.

Valerie rings up the few items Mom asked for, and I scan the candy section behind me. I'm pretty sure I deserve a little something for getting out of the house. I pause on the Reese's Pieces and contemplate it, but the knot forms in my stomach when I go to reach for them. I can never bring myself to actually buy them anymore, so I settle for an almond Snickers instead.

I know Valerie's name because her nametag says it, but I do recognize her. We used to adjust her sprinklers so when she turned them on they would douse her instead of her lawn. She didn't find it nearly as hilarious as we did.

When my mind shifts to the *we* in the situation, the unintentional smirk on my lips falls. I haven't thought about him in weeks. I wish I could say years, but he isn't the kind of person one can easily forget, as much as I desperately want to—have tried to. And being back in this town floods my mind with too many memories of him.

Her expression turns slightly confused. My smirk probably looks more like a grimace than a smile. I haven't smiled in weeks. It's hard to remember what a real smile feels like.

"You okay, dear?"

I nod automatically. "Yeah, thanks."

I grab my bags and walk outside. Mom is right about one thing. The fresh air does feel much better than the stagnant air in my room. People nod and wave kindly when I pass them. I may acknowledge them, but my mind is too focused on getting back home to curl up in bed and sleep for a few more hours.

Some people stare and whisper to each other. As much as I absolutely hate it, I can't really blame them. I've been MIA for five years, and now I'm back because my husband—I stop myself from thinking it—and I have nowhere else to go. That's prime small town gossip.

Nothing changes in Willowhaven. I thought maybe five years would alter at least a little bit, but I was wrong. Mr. Rochester still owns the local grocery—been running it for the last forty years. I worked there for about a year during my junior year and vowed never to work at a grocery store ever again. Ms. Pearl has the only floral shop in town and Moment in Thyme seems to be as hopping as ever. Henry Adler probably still works at Art's hardware. He's been working there since our sophomore year.

I don't know what prompts me to look across the street, through the row of trees, as I walk. Maybe it's to avoid the eye contact of every person walking toward me, but as soon as I do,

I regret it. My eyes have to be deceiving me. When my heart recognizes him it stops.

He waves behind him as he walks out of the hardware store, carrying a brown bag, and then squints at the sun. It can't be him. He's not supposed to be here, but yet, there he is. Six years older, but every bit the boy I fell in love with in high school. Could I actually call him a boy? He doesn't look much like a boy anymore. Thick stubble lines a much more prominent jawline. He even looks taller.

What is he doing here? I agreed to come back because I knew there was no way he'd ever show his face again. He promised me that. Through our screaming and tears, he told me there was no way in Hades he'd ever consider staying in this town with me.

I'm standing on one side of the street as if the sidewalk has formed around my feet, cementing them in place. I can't move until his eyes drift in my direction. When he sees me, I can't decipher what's going on in his head. On days when we used to lay underneath the willows and talk for hours, I learned what every expression meant. I had years to memorize them, but now he's a stranger.

His features freeze in disbelief. It's as if he can't believe *I'm* here, as if I'm the one who left without a trace. I want to scream at him and ask him why he's looking at me like that. He doesn't have the right to feel incredulous.

He takes a step toward me and I bolt. This can't be happening. I can't handle any more bombs right now. And Dean Preston is a bomb with the power to decimate my entire world.

What's left of it, anyway.

CHAPTER FOUR

Dean

"TINA'S BEEN GOING on and on about that new restaurant in the city." Henry swipes my tools at the check out. I smile and nod as if I'm interested in what he's saying.

"Yeah, Lily's mentioned it to me, too."

"If you and Lily ever want to double, have Lily give Tina a holler. We could use a night out. Tina is always talking about how I never take her anywhere."

I swipe my card to pay and chuckle. "All right. I'll have her do that. It'd be nice to get out of Willowhaven for a night."

"I hear ya, man."

I walk out of Art's, throwing a wave behind me at Henry and blink back the sunlight. As summer approaches, the sun gets brighter. And hotter. *Dang, it's hot!* My eyes adjust and wander across the street. I'm not sure why. I know where my truck is parked, and it's parked in the opposite direction. But it's as if my eyes know she's there.

Sawyer stands motionless on the sidewalk outside of Pearl's with an expression full of everything I never want to see on her face—disbelief, hurt, sorrow—and it's all trained on me.

She's back. Full force. The whirlwind that makes up Sawyer

21

Hartwell is a few feet away from me. But she's not Sawyer Hartwell anymore. She'd gone and taken a common name like Johnson or Brown. An ordinary last name doesn't match up with this extraordinary woman.

It doesn't matter that I knew she was back. Knowing she's here and seeing her face before my eyes are two very different things. She's been here for almost a month, but I wasn't sure if I'd ever see her.

She's just as beautiful as I remember—if not more—even with the sadness straining the features on her face. I feel myself gravitating toward her, and the look on her face as I take one step says it all. I'm not allowed to go any farther. Not that it would have mattered, because she takes off before I can say a word. I watch her retreating figure grow smaller and smaller as she runs down the concrete until she's completely out of sight.

I don't know what I planned to say to her. 'I'm sorry' doesn't encompass all that I feel. I'm sorry for so many things. For not listening. For not trusting her. For lying. For being so dang stubborn. For leaving.

For her sudden loss.

I maneuver into my truck, tossing the brown bag on the passenger seat. My tools fly out and hit the floor. Before I realize what I'm doing, my hands feel bruised from beating the steering wheel over and over. Leaning forward, I rest my head over the top of the steering wheel to catch my breath.

My mind plays back an image of Sawyer I've been holding onto for the last six years. An image that isn't so foreign, that looks nothing like the expression I just witnessed. When she sees me, she smiles warmly, brightening her entire face. When she looks at me nothing else exists.

"Hey, Sawyer," I call.

As she's walking down the hall, she turns her face to look at me, and her eyes beam. They always seem to shine, and I wonder if it's possible that she's part angel. Not in the cheesy pick-up line kind of way. Literally. She's too sweet to possibly want anything to do with me. And yet, whenever we pass one another in the hallway she never ceases to smile. She should look the other way or pretend I don't exist, but she never does.

"Dean… Hey. What's up?"

It's possible that this is the first time I've ever heard Sawyer say my name. Though we've lived in the same town our entire lives, we always mingle in separate circles. Her circle doesn't accept mine, not that I deserve to be in her circle anyway. She's so out of my league. There has never been a reason for us to ever talk until now.

If it weren't for my buddies, would I ever have dared to approach her? Never.

Her long ponytail falls over the front of her right shoulder. She's heading to volleyball practice so I should make this quick to keep her from being late, but as soon as she says my name I lose my train of thought.

"Dean?" Her left eyebrow lifts, and she smiles out of the corner of her mouth as if she knows she makes me lose my mind.

I clear my throat, hoping that will buy me time to find my balls again. "Would you wanna hang out this weekend?"

Her entire mouth smiles now, though she's a little shy as she says, "Okay. I'd like that."

"Really?" I didn't actually believe she would say yes. I wanted her to. I wanted her to so badly, but the odds were stacked against me. Remain cool. "Sweet. Can I pick you up around seven on Friday?"

"Okay." She nods then ducks her head timidly with a shrug and begins walking backward. "I've got to head to practice now. Coach doesn't give any leniency for tardiness."

23

"Right. Yeah. Have fun. I'll see you tomorrow."

"Sounds good." She lifts a hand, curling her fingers forward in a small wave, and with that little wave, I know there's no turning back.

Hook.

Line.

Sinker.

I start the engine of my truck, but I can barely think straight so I wait in park, my engine idling. I'm in no condition to drive. The garage would probably clear my head. Working on my bikes always helps, but Lily is probably waiting at my house now. *Freak.* I forgot all about Lil. I shift my gear into drive and take off down Main Street, heading for home.

CHAPTER FIVE

Sawyer

I HEAR MOM call my name when I walk through the garage door, but I don't stop as I throw the groceries on the countertop and dart for the safety of my bedroom. The stairs seem a mile high. I stumble and whack my shins on the edge of the landing, but continue on. I don't feel the pain, or maybe I welcome it at this point. When the door shuts behind me, I fall against it and release every emotion I've been bottling up for the last six years.

But this time, not one tear is shed for Grayson.

As I stand at my locker exchanging books, I hear Dean Preston's voice. It's probably a little strange that I know the sound of it when I've never hung out with the guy. But he has one of those distinct gruff voices that can make any girl's heart flutter.

"So he needs this to happen today?" Dean asks.

"Yeah. It's nothing you haven't done before. This should be a piece of cake for you. Just do what you do best."

Oh, I know what Dean does best. It's not a secret that he's a good fighter. But I never realized it was ever more than fights out of provocation. Was he organizing one?

"I've got this. It won't be a problem for much longer."

I peer out of the corner of my eye to see him talking to Aiden Ballard a

25

few lockers down. *They stand with their heads together, devising the plan.*

"Just meet Joe in the alley by Art's Hardware. He'll have everything you need. I'll meet you there to make sure the job gets done right." Aiden smirks. "And I know you'll be compensated."

"I don't want the money. I'll do it for free."

What in the world are they talking about? *Dean catches me staring. He's caught off guard at first, looking a little nervous. Maybe he realizes I heard every word of their conversation, but then he flashes me a smile, releasing the butterflies in my stomach, before they walk away.*

I'm too curious not to follow Dean after school. I park my car across from the alleyway Aiden mentioned and wait for him to show. It doesn't take more than five minutes before he pulls up on his motorcycle across the street. He hitches up his backpack and looks around. A man comes out of a side door and motions for Dean from down in the alley. They talk for only a minute, but it looks shady. What kind of deal has he gotten himself into? Dean comes back tucking a crowbar in his backpack. Umm... what would he need a crowbar for in a fight? A sinking feeling settles in my stomach. Maybe it wasn't going to be a fair fight. I don't really know what's going on here, but now I've gone too far.

I try to remain inconspicuous as I follow him halfway across town to an older looking home. He walks to an old, rundown shed by the side of the house, takes the crowbar out of his backpack, and leans it against the side. Aiden comes into view and nods. They talk for a few minutes, waiting, and I wish I could hear what they're saying, but if I get out or try to get any closer I'll be discovered.

An elderly gentleman comes out from the behind the house and walks over to Aiden and Dean. Maybe they aren't supposed to be here? *Aiden gets closer to the man and Dean reaches for the crowbar. Wait a second. He's not going to... He wouldn't actually...*

Dean raises the crowbar, and my heart stops. He can't! My hand is on

26

my car door handle, ready to leap from the car to stop whatever is about to go down. But then he swings the crowbar up and rests it against his shoulder as he walks over to Aiden and the elderly man. He reaches out his hand to shake and the man pats him on the back with a smile on his face as if they're old friends.

Aiden stands, resting his elbow on the elderly man's shoulder as they talk with Dean. He gestures toward the shed, and Dean nods, taking in whatever instructions he's given. I'm thoroughly confused until it dawns on me. This is probably Aiden's house. I remember hearing someone say he lives with his grandparents now.

There's no fight. The guy in the alley was probably trying to help Dean out with cheap tools or something.

I misjudged Dean. Horribly.

Dean spends the rest of the afternoon using the crowbar to tear down the metal paneling on the roof of the shed. I watch as Aiden helps him out where he can, but Dean is clearly the brains behind the project. Every day after that I follow him here. Now that I know where he's going, I can be less conspicuous. I don't stay most days—just simply drive by to watch his progress. He comes back day after day until he's completely restored the shed. After two weeks, the once rundown shed looks brand-new.

I learned something that first day I followed Dean Preston. He's not what people think. There's so much more than meets the eye. And I want to know more.

If only I hadn't wanted to learn more that day. If only I'd kept my distance and not given into the lure of Dean Preston who no one else understood. There would be no painful memories to haunt me at every turn. I could live peacefully in this town.

I believed him when he told me he would never come back.

Years ago, I pleaded with God to bring him back to me. I tried bargaining in my mind. I would do better. I would be better. I would give up anything, anyone else… just not him. But nothing worked. He didn't want me anymore. He made up his mind. So why did he come back? I don't need this. I can't heal in the same town that holds Dean Preston. He's going to capsize my barely floating ship.

I don't want you. Those were his last words before he walked out of my life completely.

You don't realize what damage those four words can have until you hear them aimed at you from the person you love most in the world.

My heart screamed out his name for hours after he left, begging and pleading for it to be some sick twisted nightmare. It eventually turned into a silent plea. My heart must have known before I did that he was really gone. My brain tried to suppress it. I didn't want to believe that it could possibly be true. When you think something will always be, it's not easy to let it go and watch as it slips away.

"Sawyer?" I don't think I fell asleep, but my brain feels muddled when I hear my mom say my name. My face is stuck to the tan carpet. I shift to sit up and feel the divots left in my cheek. She tries opening the door, but my body is blocking it. "Honey, what's blocking the door?"

I don't answer, just move out of the way, but don't get up. I lean my back against the wall and wait for her to enter.

She searches the room for me when she walks in and then

sees me on the floor up against the wall. I feel questions I don't want asked hovering on the tip of her tongue. So many questions that would open the ultimate can of gigantic worms to ever crawl the face of the Earth. And yet, I do want them asked. I want answers. I want her to know how much she hurt me.

We've been here once before. Six years ago she watched me curl into a ball of emptiness and rejection. Before, she told me I had a week to wallow, and then I needed to get over that stupid boy. But today she knows better. She knows exactly what I discovered and is too afraid to ask because what she did is unforgiveable. She knows how wrong she was to lie to me.

Finally, I hear her swallow and ask, "Do you want to talk about it?"

I don't look at her. I stare forward out my window. "Did you know Dean was back?" I question. His name sounds unfamiliar coming from my mouth. It's been so long since I've said it out loud.

"Yes," she answers meekly, and without my response she knows to leave me alone. She knows she deceived me with the deepest form of betrayal.

The door closes quietly behind her, but I don't move. I don't make a sound. The tears weigh on my chest, but they don't escape. They push harder and harder until my heart feels like it could stop beating at any second from the pressure. I remain on the floor for the rest of the day, praying my heart will give out and put me out of my misery once and for all.

But the reprieve never comes.

CHAPTER SIX

Dean

LILY IS SITTING on my porch when I pull into my driveway. I grab my tools from the floor and get out of my truck. Wearing jean shorts and an off-the-shoulder t-shirt, she smiles her slow, sweet smile and stands up as I approach. Her thumbs tuck in her belt loops as she sways from side to side.

"I thought you forgot about me."

"No. Sorry. Just got caught up in town."

She shrugs and offers another smile. "I was thinking that maybe tonight we could grab a pizza and stay in, watch a movie."

I lean in to kiss the corner of her mouth. "Sounds good." She takes my hand and I motion for her to follow me to my garage so I can put away my new tools.

I shake my head, but I can't wipe Sawyer from my mind. For the last six years, I've dreamed of Sawyer showing up. I dreamed that she would somehow find me during my hiatus from Willowhaven, though she wouldn't have known where to start to look. Hiding my tracks was my number one priority. I dreamed of what I would say, what I would do. Every possible scenario I could imagine ran through my mind. Yelling. Smiling. Anger. Hugging. Sarcasm. Shyness. Awkwardness. But the way it went down definitely wasn't one that played out in my mind.

My garage door squeals as it scrolls up.

"How was work?" Lily perches herself on my tool bench with her hands gripping the edge of the tabletop.

"Work."

"Did you have a lot of customers?"

"Yup."

"Sounds busy," she remarks.

"It was."

I wonder who else has actually seen Sawyer. Have Aiden or Josh seen her yet? If one of them had they would have mentioned it. Josh wouldn't be able to help rubbing my mistake in my face. Aiden would look at me with hope and confidence. He'd tell me to pick my life up off the floor, win back my jackpot.

"Congratulations, man. You got to keep your luscious locks." Josh pats me on the back.

I chuckle, running my hand through my hair. "I wouldn't take a bet I knew I couldn't win." I'm talking through my teeth, but I keep that insecurity from them.

"I can't believe you actually got her to go out with you, dude," Aiden says.

"Oh, ye of little faith. I can't believe you guys really doubted me." Truth was, I didn't feel that confident. But I wanted to ask her out so badly; the bet merely gave me the perfect opportunity. She was worth the risk. They never would have let me live it down if I asked her out on my own. And if she had said no, all I had to lose was my hair.

And my manhood.

"Did she blab about volleyball and her hair the entire time?"

31

"I bet you couldn't get her to shut up. Did you at least get a good lay out of it?"

I nearly punch Josh, but I shake my head instead and give him a look. They won't understand. Sawyer is more than that. Sawyer is different. Little do they know with this one, I found gold. I definitely struck the jackpot.

I hear my name in the distance. "Dean," Lily repeats loudly.

"Huh?" I blink, peering over at her.

"Where were you?" Lily pauses for my answer, but I don't reply. I stupidly keep blinking because I have no response. "Is everything okay?" She rests her hand on my elbow as I walk past her to put the wrench in my toolbox.

I almost shrug off her hand. I don't know why. Was I being that obvious? I probably look as if I've seen a ghost. Sawyer nearly looked like one. Though she did look older, that wasn't why she looked so different. There was no warmth in her eyes, no pink in her cheeks, and no smile on her unforgettable face. Everything that made Sawyer, Sawyer, was gone.

I debate on mentioning it at all, but Lily's going to find out sooner or later. This town can't handle keeping big news like Sawyer coming back to themselves, especially considering what she's going through. The small town girl who left and made something of her life, marrying a doctor, and living the big city life in Seattle, only to have her husband brutally murdered. I've heard bits and pieces over the last couple weeks. I don't know what to believe. I heard everything from a gang attacked him to a drug deal gone wrong.

The news might as well come from me. "I saw Sawyer," I say gently.

Lily's face falls, and her hand clenches the material over her

32

heart. "Sawyer's really back in Willowhaven? She actually came back? You saw her?"

"Yeah, for like a minute, and then she took off."

"You didn't talk to her?"

"No, she literally ran when she saw me." Bolted faster than I'd ever seen her run back in high school, and she was an athlete.

Lily bites her lip. "Are you going to go see her?"

I step out of Lily's grasp to put the rest of my things away. This is the last thing I feel like talking about with Lily. We don't need this kind of strain on our relationship. "Lil, she shot off like a firecracker on speed. I don't think Sawyer wants to talk to me." Based on the look I saw in Sawyer's eyes, she might have run all the way back to Seattle.

"But you *want* to talk to her." There's no question in her voice, and she's right. I don't have it in me to deny it. Lily and I keep no secrets. She went to high school with Sawyer and me. She knows what we had, what I threw away, and yet Lily loves me anyway.

"I haven't talked to her in six years, Lil." I at least make my voice sound apologetic. "But she just lost her husband. She needs space." I don't want to give Sawyer space, but I will.

Lily nods like she understands, but she doesn't. Now she'll question everything. I can see it in her eyes, the fear of losing me already setting in. She's going to second-guess what we have, which is pointless. I love Lily. And if today is any indication, Sawyer will never look at me again. Not that I expect anything more.

"Do you still want pizza? We don't have to—" Her hesitant voice makes me cringe.

"Of course I do." I wrap my arms around her waist,

bringing her tightly against me, and kiss her on the forehead. She moves forward on the bench and wraps her legs around me, cradling my waist. It feels so normal and yet unnatural. Does that make sense? "Portabellas or Jeff's?" I ask.

She chooses Jeff's because she knows how much I like it— cheesy greasy Chicago-style as opposed to the thin crust Italian crap.

"I don't mind Portabellas," I offer, still holding her waist, hovering my lips over hers.

"But you would rather have Jeff's." She smiles sadly, and I feel like we are talking about more than pizza. So, I kiss her and try to make her forget. But more than that, I try to make myself forget and get lost in Lily. Concentrating on her mouth and her hands tangling in my hair, I focus on the woman I'm with, on the woman who has stood by me through some of the hardest times in my life.

CHAPTER SEVEN

Sawyer

THERE'S A KNOCK at the front door and neither of my parents are home so I choose to ignore it. I stay wrapped up in the blankets on my bed as I stare up at the swirls in the plaster on my ceiling.

The knocking continues, but they will eventually have to stop. I'm not about to give in because they think repetitive pounding will get my attention.

In some parts of the plaster, I can make out parts of Grayson's face. I can see Grayson's thoughtful eyes behind his glasses, the curve of his full lips, his ruffled, curly, unkempt hair. He's watching over me. *I'm going crazy, aren't I?* The features are sporadically placed on the ceiling, but if I stretch my imagination far enough… but the longer I look, the more it looks like white crap smeared on the ceiling.

The knocking won't stop, so I'm forced to throw back my covers and get up to answer it, or I might kill the person on the other side. When I do, there stands my best friend since birth, Alix Fink.

The red in her chestnut hair shimmers in the midday light. Her bob is something I wish I could pull off as well as she does.

She owns that blunt cut.

"You know, when I heard you were back in town I thought they were crazy. Never in my wildest dreams did I imagine you'd set foot in Willowhaven again. And I've had some pretty wild dreams."

"Looks like I'm the crazy one." I shrug and offer a small smile.

She smiles back and grabs me in a hug. I hug her just as tightly because I finally grasp how much I have missed her.

"It's really good to see you," I say into her neck. "I've missed you so much."

"Girl, why didn't you call me? I had to hear from my mom who heard it from Valerie. You've been here for almost three weeks without telling me. It's not as if I saw you much over the last five years. I would have been here for you." She pulls away still smiling. It's a sympathetic smile, and it says it all without saying anything.

"You could have come to see me, you know. For more than the wedding… and the funeral."

She eyes me with raised eyebrows. "Goes both ways, you know. Why didn't you tell me you were coming back when I saw you then?"

"I hadn't really thought that far yet. It took a couple months for my mom to convince me to come back after Grayson was gone. She was unrelenting."

Alix walks inside, and I close the door. "If I'd known getting rid of your husband was the way to finally get you back here, I'd have done it myself a long time ago."

I stare at her because I don't know if I should laugh or cry or smack her across the face.

"Okay. Too soon for jokes?"

I nod and humorlessly chuckle. "Maybe."

"Well, you look like crap." She eyes me up and down with her fierce green eyes. "I'm serious. When was the last time you showered?"

I look down at my crinkled pajamas and try to remember when the last time actually was. It wasn't yesterday. I don't think it was the day before. It must have been the day before that... when I saw Dean. She's shaking her head when I look back up at her.

"This isn't you. Go shower. You'll feel better, and I'll be here when you're done."

I nod because she's right, and I can't deny it. She's not going to treat me like I'm fragile, even if I feel I might completely shatter at any moment. She knows what I need without asking. And if she has to jump on the train and ride to hell to bring me back, I know she'll do it.

When I walk back downstairs after my shower, with damp hair dripping down my back, Alix is searching through the cupboards in the kitchen.

"See, now don't you feel better?" She gets up from squatting down.

I want to laugh at the irony of that question. I feel clean, but I don't feel better. To appease her I nod anyway.

She starts rummaging through the drawers and compartments inside the fridge. "You got anything to eat around here? You look like my anorexic cousin, Georgia. And that's not a compliment to your waist size."

"I saw Dean." I hate that it's the first topic of conversation, but she had to know he was here, and I want to know why I'm

37

the last to know.

Alix turns back to me coolly, closing the fridge behind her. "Yeah?"

"How long, Alix?"

"How long what?" I don't know why she bothers with the innocent act.

"Cut the crap. How long has he been back?"

She sighs and leans against the refrigerator. I see in her eyes how much she wants to avoid this answer, but I won't let her. I level my stare to let her know I'll use force if I have to. It wouldn't be the first time.

"A few years," she answers unapologetically.

I nearly choke. "A few years? What's a few years?"

She shrugs. "Three years, give or take."

"Alix! Are you freaking kidding? Three years! Three *freaking* years! Why didn't you tell me?"

"What would have been the point?" she counters. Her voice doesn't match my level of vehemence, but she's confident in the decision she made to keep it from me. "You were moving on in Seattle. You were finally finding happiness away from here. Dean didn't deserve you. Bringing up Dean would have stirred up old issues that didn't need to be rehashed. He's your past, and that's where he should stay."

"I had every right to know." I step forward to enforce my point. "I never would have come back if I had known." *Or maybe I would have come back sooner.*

"Exactly! Don't you see? You can't let that douchebag dictate your life forever, Sawyer. He left you. He left you with the weight of the world. He *crushed* your world. And this is *your* home." Her voice softens. "This will always be your home."

38

"It doesn't feel like home anymore, Felix," I say her nickname quietly.

A smirk crosses her lips. "I know," she says, and that's all it takes for me to start crying again. She pulls me into her, but I don't know if it's for my benefit or for hers, because she's crying with me.

"I hate it. It never stops." I sniffle.

"It will."

"It doesn't feel like it."

"I know." Her hand rubs up and down my back. "I miss hearing you call me Felix."

Calling her Felix brings me back to happier, simpler times. When mean girls were the worst of my worries.

"Sawyer?" Lily questions with a prissy attitude, her hand on her hip. "Isn't that a boy's name?"

"Does she look like a boy to you?" Alix steps forward, arms crossed, daring this new girl to mess with her.

Lily steps back, but only slightly because the sandbox is stopping her from moving farther away. "Just because she doesn't look like a boy doesn't mean she doesn't have a boy name."

"I like my name," I say proudly.

I can tell Lily doesn't know how to respond to that, so she huffs and turns on her heel to join some other girls on the swing set, her blonde ponytail swinging back and forth as she walks.

"My mom always tells me that girls can be really mean," Alix says and rests her hand on my shoulder. "You can call me Felix if it makes you feel better."

I giggled. "It does. Thank you, Felix."

CHAPTER EIGHT

NEW MOTORCYCLES LINE the front of my garage, waiting to be ridden. A new Ducati Streetfighter was shipped in today and stands front and center. I hang out for a while, leaning against the brick, admiring it. I'll have to test her later today to make sure she runs well. It's the most logical thing to do.

"Dean! My man!" Josh hollers as he saunters toward me. His eyes are bloodshot, and his hair probably hasn't been washed in days. He looks like he's been hit by a freight train.

"What's up, Josh?" I sigh. I try to sound like I care, but he wouldn't be able to tell if I did.

"Not much, bro. I just wanted to come say hey." He holds out his fist for me to pound. "It's been a while."

I bump his fist and head for my office, waiting for the punch line. *It's been maybe two weeks.*

He follows closely behind me. "Sweet new Ducati out there."

I nod. "Yeah. She came in this morning. I'm going to take her for a test run later today." He hovers along the back wall of my office, nodding. He's probably hung over. "What do you need, Josh?"

His hands run through his hair, making it stand on end. "I need a place to crash tonight, bro."

I rub the back of my neck. I know his old man. I'm very familiar with the kind of man Josh doesn't want to—or can't—go home to. Jared may have kicked Josh out for good this time.

If I say no, Josh will end up sleeping on a park bench or behind some dumpster, or worse, never make it through the night. If I say yes, he'll show up at my house at three in the morning completely plastered. He'll sleep it off on my couch, then eat all my food when he wakes up at one in the afternoon, and I won't hear from him until his two weeks are up, and he repeats his process.

"Sure." I sigh. "Whatever you need."

"Thanks, bro. You're a lifesaver. I won't be late. Just leave the back door unlocked. You won't even know I'm there."

I grunt, but smile. I'll hear him stumble through my house, bumping into walls and slamming doors, but it won't do any good to tell him that. "Don't mention it."

"Dean." Aiden appears in the doorway. "Duncan just brought by his—" He stops when he sees Josh leaning against the wall inside the door. The silence that fills the office suffocates me with awkwardness.

"Hey, Aiden." Josh tosses a nod.

"Hey," Aiden says shortly and meets my eyes. It's clear that's all he's going to say. He doesn't want to stick around.

"I'll be there in a minute, Aiden."

He nods and walks out of the doorway without another word.

"I've really got to get back to work, Josh. We good here?"

"Oh, yeah. Sure. I understand." He begins backing out. "I'll

41

get out of your way. Thanks again. Later, bro."

"See ya, Josh."

I watch his wiry figure leave through the garage and feel a twinge of worry.

Nothing I say makes a difference. I stopped trying a year ago after the third time I bailed him out of jail. I told him he needed to sober up because I wasn't going to bail him out again, and he hasn't asked since. But he's one of my best friends, and I can't do anything to save him, because he doesn't want to be saved.

I meet Aiden by Duncan's black and white Kawasaki. "Dude. Why is he still coming around?" There's a scowl on his face.

"He needs somewhere to stay tonight so I told him he could sleep at my place."

"Dean—"

"I know, Aiden," I cut him off before his rant can begin. "But he used to be your best friend once upon a time, too."

"Yeah, until he bled my bank account dry after stealing my credit card for booze and who knows what else."

"It was lousy, I know. But all he needs is somewhere to crash. I'm not giving him more than that."

"I know you feel for him, man. You understand where he comes from. You wanna save him or whatever, but he doesn't deserve it. I won't pretend that I'm okay with it."

I nod. "I know, and I won't ask you to. " I motion to the bike. "Tell me what's going on with it."

Aiden sighs, but agrees, and we forget about Josh and get on with what we do best.

Lily and I sit down on my couch and pop in a movie for our Friday night in. She snacks on the popcorn in her lap, rambling during the previews.

"Tina was saying that Julie will be setting up a game booth at the Sole Festival again this year. She wants me to help her with the booth, and I know that's probably the nice thing to do, but I really wanted to relax this year and go to the festival with you."

"If you think you need to help out, I won't be offended."

"But …" She's clearly disappointed. "Don't you remember what happened at the Sole Festival last year?"

How could I forget? It was my first Sole Fest without Sawyer. But I know what Lily means.

The lights string across from booth to booth lighting up Main Street. Sawyer's face shines in every light. Her eyes reflect back in everyone's eyes as they meet mine. She appears at every game: throwing beanbags in wooden holes and tossing metal rings over glass bottles. She winks at me as she shovels down a corndog and devours five clouds of cotton candy. Her body sways from side to side as she drinks in the music.

She's everywhere.

I've got to get out of here. I don't know why I thought I would be able to handle this.

"Dean!" I hear my name hollered and turn to see Lily flagging me down. She's perched on a stool behind the counter of the booth lined with the wooden pin towers. She tosses a rubber ball up in the air before she catches it again. "Come play a game!"

I'm about to say, "No thanks," when it dawns on me that when I

43

look at Lily, her long blonde hair waving all around her, I don't see Sawyer in her eyes. And it occurs to me that every moment I've spent with Lily since I've come back has been a Sawyer-free zone.

I blink, taking a moment to answer her. In the two and a half years that I've been home, I don't think I've actually really looked at her. She radiates excitement and mischief and simplicity. I could use a little less complication in my life. When I take a step toward her, her pink lips smile wider. Sawyer is the last thing on my mind. And it's the first time since I've returned to Willowhaven that I feel it could be possible to live a life without the one person I never thought I could live without.

"After you won that giant stuffed bunny for me, there was no turning back." A small smirk lines her lips as she nuzzles under my arm and blinks her big blue eyes at me.

"I think you rigged the game so I would win."

"Oh whatever, you show off," she says, eating more popcorn. "It's a little difficult to rig that game in your favor. Now if I wanted you to lose, I'd have glued the pins together so you couldn't knock them over. But what would have been the fun in that?"

"I would have been trying to knock down those pins all night." My determination would have gotten the better of me.

"Which would have been much more amusing. You know, I still have the bunny."

"Do you sleep with it every night?" I tease.

"So what if I do? It reminds me of you."

I smile, but I know it's strained. "Oh, Josh will be staying over tonight, so if you show up in the morning, don't be startled."

Lily sighs and peers back at the TV screen. "When are you

44

going to tell that deadbeat that he's got to clean his act up and quit living off everyone else?"

I run my free hand down my face. I'm so tired of having this conversation with everyone over and over. "That *deadbeat* is one of my best friends, Lil. You know life hasn't been easy for him. I'm doing my best by him."

She looks back up at me from under my arm. "Dean, I know the life he's had, but so do you. Don't act as if he doesn't have a choice in how he lives. *You* did. And look how you choose to live yours. You stopped fighting. You stopped drinking. Now you need to stop enabling him."

I pinch the bridge of my nose. "We're not talking about me right now. I just wanted to give you a heads up."

She nods with pursed lips, taking in my irritated expression. She softens and reaches up to kiss my cheek. "Thank you. Just let me know when he's gone."

If she knew that I spotted him a few dollars here and there, she'd have a freaking conniption.

The movie starts, and my mind wanders. I wonder what Sawyer is doing with her Friday night. Is she still hiding away in her room? If I were to show up on her doorstep would her mom let me in? It's already apparent that Sawyer would slam the door in my face. When her husband was around did they spend their Friday nights going out to dinner and bowling? I could rarely convince her to do anything else on our date nights, but I wouldn't have wanted to spend them any other way.

I wait at the end of the lane and watch the bowling ball fly down it. I'm sure this one will give me a strike. It was a perfect set up. It smashes through the pins, scattering half of the wooden pegs. Four pins stand

45

untouched, mocking me.

I knock my head back. "Ugh! You've got to be kidding me."

"You could still get a spare," Sawyer taunts. "With three or four more strikes you might be able to beat me."

I look up at our scores on the screen above our lane. This is the third weekend in a row that I've let her convince me to go bowling. Sawyer is up by nearly forty points. She's had a strike almost every frame. She's chalking it up to talent. I say luck.

"You're getting way too much joy out of my pain." I smirk back at her over my shoulder.

"No joy." She shakes her head innocently. One leg is tucked up to her chest and she rests her chin on her knee. "Okay. Maybe a little bit."

I chuckle and grab a ball, sticking my fingers in the holes on top and cradle it with my other hand. The only way this is going to work in my favor is if I throw my signature curve ball.

"You're going to regret saying that," I caution, eyeing the pins at the end, lining up the perfect plan of attack.

"Am I now?" she retorts. "I doubt that."

I flick my wrist and send the ball spiraling, except it's all wrong. It curves too wide. So wide, in fact, that it slides into the gutter and rolls down to the end, not making contact with one single pin.

"Aww... gutter ball." I hear her false apologetic tone. She's sitting in the seat behind the computer with a fake frown on her face. "That's a shame."

"You," I say with a laugh, pointing my finger accusingly at her and pouncing.

She laughs loudly as I tickle her sides and kiss her neck. "Stop," she begs between giggles. They aren't your typical giggles. It's throaty and charming. It makes me want to throw her over my shoulder and run away with her where no one could bother us ever again. "Stop! Please!"

46

"Take it back," I order, squeezing her waist, taking pleasure in the sound of her laughter and knowing I'm the one causing it. "Surrender!"

"Never!" She defies me through her amusement, and I dig in deeper, burying my face in her floral scented hair. She smells amazing. "Okay, okay!" She chuckles. "I surrender! I surrender!"

I stop and kiss her cheek before sitting in the seat next to her. With a contented sigh, I peer over at her smiling face. "You surrender to me, huh?"

She presses her lips together, trying to prevent a smile. I reach over and rub the pad of my thumb across her bottom lip to get her to stop. I never want her to stop smiling.

"Always," she says.

"Dean," Sawyer says my name, but it sounds nothing like her. It's too high pitched. "Dean, I'm going to head home. Go sleep in your bed. You'll be much more comfortable there."

I pry my eyes open to see Lily's face hovering over mine. Confusion and disappointment set in before I comprehend where I am or what year it is. Lily runs her fingers back through my hair. I feel it stand on end. "And you'll regret it if Josh is the one to wake you up in the middle of the night on this couch." I blink a couple times and shift to get up. "For more reasons than one," she says, helping me to my feet and kissing me. I weakly kiss her back. "He'd probably try and take your bed."

I take a deep breath and shake away the thoughts of Sawyer. Never have they felt more vivid. Never have I missed her more, and guilt washes over me. I walk Lily to the door.

"Do you want to just call me when Josh leaves in the morning? We can do lunch or something?" Her eyes glimmer with cheerfulness.

I nod and she stands on the tip of her toes to kiss my cheek.

47

"Goodnight, sweetie."

"Night," I mumble and make sure she gets into her car safely before she takes off.

I run my hand down my face as I watch her taillights disappear down my dirt driveway.

I'm so screwed.

CHAPTER NINE

Sawyer

MY CELLPHONE HAS been off since the week after Grayson was taken from me. It kept chiming with text messages and emails and phone calls from people wondering what happened and trying to lend support or send their condolences while all I wanted to do was throw my phone across the room. I realize people wanted to let me know I'm not alone, I understand that. But the only way I won't feel alone anymore is to have Grayson back.

I talked to my in-laws a couple times, but it was too hard—for both of us. I probably can't call them my in-laws anymore. There is nothing left to tie us together. Is my last name even Jones anymore? When the one person who makes me a Jones no longer exists, can I still claim the name as my own?

Alix made me turn my phone back on a couple weeks after she stopped by my house. She told me it would be used as a communication device solely for her because she felt like we were in elementary school again when she had to call the house and ask to speak to me. I couldn't blame her for that one.

When my cellphone rings and her names flashes across the screen with a picture she obviously took to make me laugh, I pick up. "Hey—"

"I'm picking you up in an hour," Alix cuts me off.

"Are you now?"

"Yes. I am. You've been cooped up in that house for over a month now, Sawyer, and it's not healthy."

"It's worked fine for me so far." I can avoid curious eyes. I can avoid nosey questioning. I can avoid *him*. *Gah*. Above all, I can avoid Dean. Seeing him on Main Street was more than I could handle. There were so many emotions coursing through my body that I could have spontaneously combusted. I'm not ready to experience that again.

"Well, it's not working anymore. It's time you got some sun to thaw out that cold, black heart of yours."

"I like my heart charred, thank you very much."

"We're going to the Sole Festival," she counters.

"And if I say no?"

"I'll come there and drag your butt out of that house, looking as you are in your wrinkly pajamas and rat's nest hair."

I touch my hair self-consciously. It might not be styled, but it doesn't look like a rat's nest, and my yoga pants are comfortable.

"Fine. But only because I believe you, and I don't want to terrify the rest of humanity."

She chuckles and hangs up.

As soon as we get out of the car I regret letting Alix sway me into coming here tonight. It's crowded and loud. There are too many people, too many faces who know my story and stare

50

at me with pity in their eyes. I feel so much pressure to pretend like I'm fine. If I were to show on the outside how I feel inside they'd either lock me up in a psych ward and medicate me beyond recognition or, worse, try to hug me and console me. I want to punch every single one of them in the face. Everyone in their perfect relationships with their perfect lives. They don't know me. They don't know anything about me anymore.

We get closer to the crowd and I suddenly feel claustrophobic. I stop. "Alix, I can't do this. It's too much."

"Oh c'mon, yes you can." She skims my appearance, eyeing the messy bun on top of my head. "You could use a little more makeup, but you've got that 'I don't care' vibe going, and it's working for you."

"I don't care about the way I look. I'm not ready to be thrown back into society. It's too soon."

"I'm not asking you to hit on the next hot guy you see. I'm asking you to dip your toes in and socialize. Just be around people. Your parents might not want to push you. They might think time is what you need, and they're right, but you don't need time alone any more. You need time to learn how to be human again. He's been gone for almost four months, Sawyer. Life is going on without you. It's time."

I sigh with closed eyes and nod. "Okay."

"Good. Okay. Let's grab a bite to eat, listen to some songs, and then we can go. Baby steps." She smiles. I take her outstretched hand begrudgingly, but smile back because I love how much she feels like home.

We grab a couple of corndogs and sodas and head toward the crowd around the stage with the live band. It's a little bit country, but I'm okay with that. The lead singer swings his hips, his cowboy hat propped on his head, dipping it to every girl who calls out to him. I bob with the music and watch Alix sway and raise her arms in the air, carefree. I don't remember what that feels like.

After a few songs she leans into my ear, and I'm ready for her to tell me we can go. I've done my time. We've been here long enough. I deserve the reward of my warm bed.

"I need to pee. I'll be right back." Before I can register what she said and protest, she's gone. I breathe and tell myself I'll wait until she gets back and then leave. She can stay if she wants to. I've spent my fair share of time among the living.

My eyes drift over the crowd and immediately lock with green eyes that are so easy to get lost in. My mind draws a blank before it registers we're staring at each other and have been for who knows how long. *How long had Dean been looking at me before I saw him?* He's coming toward me and running seems like the best option, but there's not enough time before he's standing in front of me. My heart reacts to him before my brain does, and it aches for me to throw my arms around him and feel his body close to mine like we've done so many times before. His gentle smolder hooks me like it's done so many times before.

After following Dean to Aiden's house and watching him take care of Aiden's grandparents week after week, I couldn't get him out of my head. It turned out to be more than restoring the shed. He helped Aiden with yard work and worked on their cars. Nearly every time I passed Aiden's house Dean was there, taking part in some way to help them with things Aiden's grandparents could no longer do for themselves.

Dean's not the popular hotshot who every other girl fawns over, or the all-star athlete. If anything, people avoid him. Though he's not free of trouble, he's not like his friend, Josh, who I know has been suspended more times than I can count for drug possession or bringing weapons to school. It's understandable when people move from one side of the hall to the other when Josh walks down it.

Dean is different.

There's a subtle tenderness behind Dean's rough exterior. I've watched him for years. He has a gentle smolder. That may seem to be contradictory, but it's the only way to describe the gaze in his eyes. It's as if he has a secret that he holds dear, and will do everything in his power to keep it safe. Yet, he screams for attention, for someone to notice he actually exists.

I notice. I notice every day.

Dean passes me in the hallway and I offer a smile. I do that whenever we make eye contact. I can't help it. He makes me smile. He nods and life goes on as we pass one another. If we're being true to our normal routine, he'll keep walking, the same as every other day, and I will make my way to volleyball practice, but this time, after I'm halfway down the hall he calls my name. It's the first time he's ever said my name. His voice is somehow raspy and gentle at the same time.

When I turn and our eyes meet, I know in the pit of my stomach that whatever he is about to say is going to change everything. And I couldn't be more ready.

In about five seconds I will hear his raspy voice. He will say my name and that voice will caress every letter. I want him to take away my pain, but that doesn't make any sense. He was the one to create the pain in the first place. My fingers curl into fists to gain control of myself. Then my brain kicks in, and the feelings of sadness and betrayal burst to the surface all over again in a volcanic explosion. When a hesitant smile rises on his lips, the sadness and betrayal is masked again by nostalgia and

53

longing. How can someone change so much and somehow look exactly the same?

He's no longer a young, rebellious boy riding up on his motorcycle to sneak me out of my house after midnight. He's incredibly handsome with his muscular arms and facial hair. It's not quite a beard, yet a little more than a five o'clock shadow. But rather than the look I'm so familiar with—dark fitted pants and a t-shirt displaying his favorite rock band—Dean wears washed out jeans and a blue striped button-down with rolled up sleeves. His black feather tattoo peeks out below his sleeve on his left forearm. That's the only thing about him I recognize.

Somewhere in the last six years, Dean grew into a man.

His hair is different than I remember, not quite as long. It doesn't swoop across his forehead anymore. It stands on end as if he doesn't care what it's doing, but somehow looks right. It's still long enough to run my fingers through. I mentally cringe, kicking myself for the unexpected image that runs through my mind. I shouldn't like the sight of someone else this much when I'm so torn up over Grayson. The real man. The man who left me because he didn't have a choice. The man who would be by my side if it hadn't been for the men who took his life.

"Hey, Sawyer." His voice hasn't changed a bit. The smallest of words and my knees nearly give way. If he's paying attention, he'll see my knees wobble slightly.

"Dean." His name chokes me. I've missed the sound of his name. I've thought it so many times over the last six years, but not once said it out loud until I got back to this town. If I said it out loud, he became more than a memory. And I wanted Dean to stay a memory. I needed him to stay a memory.

"It's good to see you." His eyes are hopeful, sad, and

54

somehow hold the same mystery that lured me into his life before.

I attempt to smile in response. I have no words. I can't talk to Dean. He left me. And I know it's been six years, and I should let it go, but I can't. I see his face and it brings back every tormenting recollection I've been trying to suppress. I can't go there. I wrap my arms tightly around myself. Maybe it's for comfort. Maybe it's to attempt to hold what pieces I have left together. But somehow, when I have my arms wrapped around my torso, I feel as though I have a chance at shielding myself from any effect he still has on me.

The fact that he left me shouldn't matter now. I got married. I had over four years with a man I loved more than life. So why, when I look into Dean's eyes, do I feel as if the gaping hole in my chest is getting bigger? I know the answer, but I bury it away. I bury it down deeper, into nonexistence. If a memory is nonexistent, it never happened. I need those memories to be nonexistent.

His hand rubs the back of his neck, possibly contemplating his next move. "How are you?" He says a little louder to be heard above the music.

It's a stupid question, and he knows it as soon as he says it. He gives an embarrassed smile, but he doesn't know how to recover. I can tell he wants to say something else, something more, but I can't stand here for one more second. A magnetic pull draws me to him, and I have to fight it. I refuse to give in.

"I'm gonna go," I say.

He wants to stop me, but he doesn't know how. There's too much between us. Too much left unsaid. Too much pain. Too many lies. Too much betrayal. Too much time passed.

Too much.

I turn and maneuver around the crowd, sensing his eyes on me as I go.

"Sawyer," he calls urgently as if it's the last word he will ever say. I look over my shoulder. The stage lights hit his eyes with a twinkle. Looking into his eyes hurts. It's such a familiar place, but I let that place go. There was no other way to live if I didn't let him go. "See you around?" There's hope there, and I want to squash it like he squashed mine.

I can only nod once.

At first, I didn't believe him when he told me he didn't want me. How could he suddenly not want me after two years of spending nearly every waking moment together? After every kiss and glance, every laugh and smile. How could all of our little moments of something suddenly mean absolutely nothing to him?

Then days turned to weeks, and weeks turned to months, and finally, months turned to years without so much as a text from him. And I knew the boy I loved, my Dean, would never have done that to me. He never would have completely abandoned me. So, I did what I had to do. I cut him out of my heart the best I could.

At least, I thought I had.

CHAPTER TEN

Dean

THERE'S A MOMENT, when you first catch someone's eye, where true feelings are revealed before they get a chance to fade away and be replaced with an expression they want you to see. I've learned that throughout the years. My dad was my first lesson. When our eyes met every day there would be a distant sadness, but it would last for only a fraction of a second before his eyes would harden and indifference would glaze over them, exactly like the alcohol always did to him.

When Sawyer first looks at me there is light and reminiscence as if she forgets that she hates me. I get a glimpse of my Sawyer and her sunshine eyes. Then, slowly, like oozing molasses, the resentment and pain conceal her face. I don't know what's worse, knowing that she might actually miss me or that she wants so badly to hate me.

I move through the crowd, stepping around people to get to her. I have to be closer to her. It doesn't matter that her expression could kill me with one glare. Sawyer brings back feelings I haven't experienced since high school—feelings I thought I was somehow immune to.

"Hey, Sawyer." I say the words hesitantly, and it's so surreal

I can't help but smile. She's standing in front of me. There was a time when I thought I'd never get a chance to say her name again. The urge to hug her is crushing. I have to put my hands in my pockets to keep them from reaching out and running my fingers down her soft cheek. If I stretch my memory, I can almost remember how it feels.

She says my name, and it sounds tainted coming from her lips, as if she swallowed poison, and yet it's the best sound in the world because it's coming from her.

I begin to say stupid things. Everything coming out of my mouth is nothing I really want to say. I know I have a smile on my face, and it shouldn't be there, but I can't stop it. She's here, and she's talking to me.

Sawyer attempts to smile at me, but it's so sad it makes my heart hurt. I can see how uncomfortable she is, and I want to grab her and hug her and make her forget every bad thing that has happened to her. I hate that her discomfort actually looks painful. I have to say something to keep her talking. I have to say something so she won't walk away.

When I ask her the first thing that pops into my head I want to smack myself for not coming up with something better—something that won't make her think of how she's really doing. I don't want to scare her away. I know she won't tell me the honest truth anyway. But I truly want to know that she'll be okay. I want confirmation that all of the rumors circulating around town are exaggerations.

"I'm gonna go," she says hastily.

Don't go. I can't say that, but nothing else I say will make her stay. She spins away from me, escaping as fast as her feet will take her. I'm not oblivious to that fact. *Am I really going to let her walk away?* I need to see her face one last time.

I shout her name to be heard over the music. She turns her head over her shoulder and looks at me reluctantly. Everything inside of me is pushing me to go to her, to grab her and hug her and kiss her and beg her to join me in erasing the past—letting us start fresh.

I need to see you again, I think. "See you around?"

She nods detachedly and disappears into the crowd.

Though things could have gone a lot better, they also could have gone a lot worse. At least she didn't bolt away from me instantly. That's progress.

"Where did Sawyer go?" I turn at the sharp voice to see Alix. Though we've crossed paths occasionally over the last few years, we've done our best to avoid each other as much as possible; me, because of my shame for disappearing without a trace, and her, because she obviously hates me. Most likely more than Sawyer does, if that's possible.

"What did you do, Preston?" She jabs my chest with her pointy little finger, a pinprick to my sternum. "I leave her alone for *five* minutes—*five freaking minutes*—and you somehow run her off in less than that." I open my mouth to speak, but she doesn't give me the option. "Do you realize how long it took me to convince her to finally get out of the house? Ugh! She doesn't need you making this any harder than it already is. She's trying to heal from losing her *husband*, Dean, and I barely pulled her out of that dark ugly hole. She's scarcely on the rise, and all you'll do is make things worse. So leave her alone, or so help me, I'll make sure she never forgives you."

Before I get a chance to defend myself, she's already stalking away.

59

Yup. Alix sure hasn't changed.

"Was that Alix?" Lily appears by my side with a Coke and cotton candy in either hand.

"Yeah."

She nods and takes a sip of the Coke. "She was in true Alix form. What did you do? She was chewing you a new one."

"I said hi to Sawyer."

Lily chokes on her drink. "Sawyer was here?"

I nod, staring toward the parking lot where Alix stormed off to find Sawyer.

She follows my line of sight and doesn't ask any more questions. There's a silent conversation. She knows I have regrets, and she knows if she doesn't want the honest truth she shouldn't ask. So, she doesn't.

I unlock my gaze and snag the cotton candy from her hand with a grin. "You came with the goods." Leaning in, I kiss her cheek. "Thanks."

"Your sugar addiction is going to make all your teeth fall out before you're forty," she scolds, and I know she's trying to be playful, but there's condescension in her voice that I can't stand.

"Good thing veneers look better now than they used to."

She shakes her head. "Or you know… you could try cutting back on sweets."

"Never." I shove a wad of pink fluffy cotton candy in my mouth with a smirk.

"Hey, pass me the Laffy Taffy, would you?" I gesture to the bag near Sawyer's feet on the ottoman.

"Only if you stop holding the Reese's Pieces hostage." She eyes the bag

60

resting between my legs. "I realize we share a love for the same candy, but there comes a time when you have to put your desires aside and think about mine."

One of my eyebrows lifts when she says *desires*. "Now these are sacred, but I might consider it if..." I tap the side of my chin with my index finger.

"If?"

"If you promise me you'll love me even if I lose all of my teeth before I'm thirty."

"Who would I be to judge? I'll probably lose mine at about the same time." She takes a bite of the apple Laffy Taffy in her fingers, and the corner of her mouth turns up. I love that half smile.

"Good answer." I crawl on top of her, leaning her back into the pillows on the couch. Before I remember to move them, the Reese's Pieces spill all over her.

She giggles and picks some up from her stomach. As I lean closer to her, she places a few in my mouth, and I kiss her fingers. I reach for a couple of strays hidden between us and return the favor.

"Maybe I should talk about my body deteriorating more often," she says, chewing the candy I placed in her mouth.

"Yeah, it's so sexy," I murmur, hovering over her with one hand on the side of her face, tracing her delicate jawline with my fingertips. Her skin is so smooth.

Sawyer's laughter is muffled when my mouth devours hers, and she no longer finds the situation funny. Her fingers find the hairs on the back of neck, and she latches onto them, pulling me closer. She tastes like chocolate and peanut butter and makes the kiss that much sweeter.

61

CHAPTER ELEVEN

Sawyer

"THIS IS WHY I didn't want to come. I knew he would be here. Why did you make me come?" I ask, slamming the passenger door behind me. Every feeling I've been trying to suppress for him over the last few years uncontrollably rises to the surface. While I still feel the hurt, he somehow brings a comfort I've needed for the last three months. But I don't want to feel it. I know better than to let that sensation in, so I push it back down.

"I'm sorry," Alix says as she turns the ignition. But she doesn't sound sorry. "I didn't think he would have the balls to actually talk to you, but don't worry. He won't do it again."

I exhale heavily and look up at the roof of the car. "Felix, what did you do?"

"Exactly what you would have done for me."

I drag my fingers across my eyebrows and massage my temples, trying to breathe as I look out the passenger window.

"You okay?" she asks quietly.

"Oh, I don't know. The once love of my life spoke to me for the first time in six years—someone who, mind you, I never thought I'd ever see again. You tell me how you think I'm doing." *I'm losing my freaking mind.*

She is silent for a moment before responding. "He looked just as shaken if it makes you feel any better."

I nod, chuckling without humor. "It does actually. Thank you."

"How about some frozen yogurt to cool you down?"

"I really want to go home, Alix. I'm tired and not in the mood to see anyone else."

"But it's so creamy and delicious. You know you want that sweet goodness in you," she practically sings.

My instinct is to say no, but I decide it's one step in the right direction. At least I know we won't run into Dean there. "Fine," I relent with a reluctant smile. "You know my weaknesses."

"And I will never cease to use them against you."

When we get our yogurt Alix doesn't hold back after we sit down to eat. "How much did Grayson know about, you know?"

"Why don't you ever talk about Willowhaven?"

I shrug, keeping my eyes on the TV. "There's nothing to talk about."

Grayson hops on the couch next to me. "Why does that sound like a bunch of B.S.?"

"Because you're reading into it."

"But it's not like you don't talk about it because there's nothing to say. You flinch whenever you hear the word. It's seems to me you don't talk about it because there's a lot to say. Willowhaven—" He stops. "See you did it again."

"I was shrugging my shoulders." I keep from looking at him.

"Quickest shrugger I've ever met. Do they give out awards for that kind of thing?"

I glare at him with a smirk on my face. "Yeah, I'm a gold medalist.

Why are you pushing this, Gray?" We have a good thing going right now. Why does he want to taint it with the ruin that is Willowhaven?

"Because I hardly know anything about your past, S."

"Why do you need to know anything about my past? You know me now. You know who I am. The past doesn't matter."

"The past means everything. The past defines us."

"We don't have to let it." I stare earnestly into his eyes.

"It's involuntary."

I look away back to the television because with every word he speaks, it rings true, and I can't let him see in my eyes that I know he's right. "I'm not going to talk about Willowhaven with you, Gray, so drop it please."

"Okay," he relents. "But only because I love you." My eyes jerk to his again. "Yeah. I said it. I love you, Sawyer."

I realize then that Grayson might have mended my heart, because it's beating abnormally fast. I blink.

"You don't have to say it back. I just thought you should—"

"I love you, too." He looks at me skeptically, as if I've only said it because he said it to me first. But I do mean it. "I do. I love you, Grayson."

I'll never forget the smile that grows on his face if I live until I'm a hundred years old. He doesn't hesitate. He grabs my face and kisses me so ardently that it seems as though he's trying to breathe his love into me. I could get used to this.

I know I don't answer because she rephrases the question. "Did you ever talk to Grayson about Willowhaven?"

I involuntarily flinch and pick at the yogurt and fruit in my cup. "Not really."

"So he didn't know about Dean?"

"I mentioned it once or twice, but I never made it a topic for open discussion." I shrug.

64

She nods like she understands, but she disapproves. "Did you worry that he would think you loved Dean more?"

"What kind of a question is that?" I sputter.

"I take that as a yes." She purses her lips and points her spoon at me. "The question now remains: do *you* know the answer to that question?"

"What question? There is no question."

"Who did you love more? Or who *do* you love more? It's possible to be in present tense."

I'm about to rip out her throat when her eyes shift over my shoulder as someone walks into the yogurt shop. I look back to see Aiden Ballard and some girl I don't know walk through the door.

"Her, really?" Alix hisses.

"What?" I look between Aiden and Alix. "What am I missing?"

Aiden notices us then. When he realizes I'm the one with Alix his eyes jump with surprise, and then he smiles his big goofy grin.

"Sawyer?" He begins to walk over and Alix stiffens.

I stand, and he reaches for me to give him a hug. "Hey, Aiden."

He pulls me in tight for a classic Aiden hug, leaving no breathing room. "Wow. It's been a long time. You look good."

"Thanks."

He must be lying through his teeth. I pull back to offer a tiny smile. His eyes drift up and down my body, but not in a seductive way. He looks as though he barely recognizes me. I feel that way when I look in the mirror, too.

"You, too," I say. He's filled out. Once the scrawny acne-faced one of the group, Aiden has transformed into an incredibly good-looking grown man. I hardly recognize him without his long blond hair. He's keeping it cropped short now.

"What's up, Alix?" Aiden says playfully, as if he's toying her with his words.

"Aiden." Alix tries to sound bored, and I know there's a story that I must pry out of her as soon as he's gone.

"So, you ladies just grabbing some yogurt? Why aren't you at the Sole Fest?"

"We stopped by already, conquered, and left," Alix says, saving me.

He nods. "After we grab some yogurt we're headed over." The blonde with him steps forward. "Oh, man, sorry. Priscilla, this is Alix and Sawyer—some of my good friends from high school. Ladies, this is Priscilla."

I reach out my hand because I can see Alix is not going to make one smidge of effort. "It's nice to meet you."

"You too." She smiles, but I see the uncomfortable lining in the way her lips form. Her face looks pinched.

There's an awkward pause before Aiden says, "Well, you ladies enjoy your evening. I'll see you around. Sawyer, it's really good to have you back."

"Thanks, Aiden. It was really good to see you." After I say it, I realize I actually mean it. I've always liked Aiden. On days when Dean had to miss school, Aiden would step in to open my doors and escort me from class to class. Sometimes he'd carry my books for me. He'd tell off Josh Duncan when he'd make catcalls or inappropriate comments about me and threaten Josh with what Dean would do to him if he knew what went on when he wasn't around. He was the overprotective brother when my own couldn't be there.

"Alix." He dips his head forward as if he were tipping a hat. She responds with a smug smile.

Priscilla and Aiden wave and head over to the yogurt machines.

"Priscilla?" Alix mocks under her breath. "What kind of a name is that anyway?"

"Shhh…" I say with a chuckle, widening my eyes at her. Alix's quiet comment wasn't exactly as quiet as she thought. Priscilla glances over her shoulder at us with a confused expression.

"Whatever," Alix mumbles.

"You better spill," I whisper, scraping the bottom of my yogurt cup. "Or I'm going to pry it out of you with my bare hands."

She shakes her head once, signaling that she won't tell me while they are within earshot.

After a few minutes, they walk out with their frozen yogurt and one last wave. Aiden lets Priscilla leave first and then winks at Alix.

She grunts and rolls her eyes as she pointlessly scrapes an empty yogurt cup.

"What in the world have you been keeping from me? You and *Aiden*?"

Alix sighs exaggeratedly and gets up. I smirk, following close behind and throw away my cup.

We're in her car before she answers me. "Aiden went away to college for a few years. When he came back he looked like *that*." Her eyebrows rise. "Don't act like you don't know what I'm talking about." I nod, agreeing. He's really handsome now.

"We ran into one another a few months back at Dallas's. We hung out. Then stopped. And that's about it."

"Oh shut up. That is *not* about it."

"So we kissed a little bit and whatever. It's over. Onto the next." She lifts her shoulders, and I know it's far from over.

"*That* did not look over. He was totally messing with you."

"Exactly. Acne-faced Aiden grew a cocky confidence in college and Grounded Alix isn't having any of it."

"Grounded?" I laugh. "*Oh. Come. On.* And Aiden is anything but cocky. So he's grown some facial hair and confidence. He was the same old Aiden. I could tell he likes you."

"Yeah, well, he's also a two-timer. So, there's that."

"He cheated on you?" My anger rises and disappointment in Aiden flourishes. "You guys were that serious? You guys were exclusive?"

"Well." She rolls her eyes. "Technically, no. But we went out to lunch one day, and *that* night I saw him with Bridget Dalton. He couldn't pick a separate day to take her out?"

I bite my lips to keep from laughing. Alix couldn't stand Aiden in high school, and here she is consumed by thoughts of him with another girl. "You like him, Felix. Why didn't you tell him you wanted to be exclusive?"

She rolls her eyes again and exhales. "I shouldn't have to ask. He shouldn't want to be with anyone else when he's with me."

I laugh, but rein it in when she shoots me a death glare. "I won't dispute that, but I will say men are idiots. Sometimes you have to beat them upside the head before they know what you want. Maybe he didn't think you would want to be exclusive. You're Alix Fink. He couldn't get you to look his way for anything in high school."

"Shut up," she mutters. "That is so untrue."

She pulls into my driveway. "Just a thought," I say.

"Well, it's a stupid thought," she mutters again.

I shrug and hop out of the car. "Truth sucks, don't it?"

Her exaggerated eye roll nearly plows me down. "He'll have to get over himself before I ever give him the time of day again."

"Or maybe you'll have to hop off your high horse. It'll hurt a lot more to fall from it."

"Who says I have a horse to get up on in the first place?" Her attitude shines through her eyes and I laugh, but then I catch myself. It feels disrespectful to laugh, to be happy.

"Bye, Felix."

She smirks as if she knows why I stopped and pulls out of my driveway.

CHAPTER TWELVE

Dean

"HEY," AIDEN SAYS when he walks into the garage early Monday morning. It's not a greeting. It's an intro to a conversation I know I want to avoid. I don't get a chance to reply before he's already diving in. "Why didn't you tell me Sawyer was back in town?"

Yup. I knew that was coming. Exhaling, I shrug and avoid eye contact, polishing the chrome on the Harley I've been working on. "I figured everyone had heard by now," I lie, but it isn't far from the truth.

"That's a huge load of dookie and you know it. I can't believe you knew she was back and didn't say anything."

I laugh. "Did you really just say 'dookie'?"

"Yeah. I did. Why didn't you say something?" he presses.

I rub my eyes with my clean hand. "I have yet to really talk to her. She takes off every chance I get. I didn't know what to tell you."

"You could have said, 'Hey, Aiden, Sawyer's back in town.'"

He knows exactly why I didn't say anything. I have nothing to say about it. I shake my head and return to polishing.

"Is it true what everyone is saying about her husband?"

I suck in a breath and nod without looking up. "I don't know exactly what happened, but yeah, he died. I know that much is true."

"That's messed up."

"I know." I can't look at him, though I feel his eyes burning holes into the side of my head. He won't be finished with the conversation until he's asked every last question, and I don't want to talk about it with him. I already know what he's going to say.

"So what's your move? What are you going to do?"

And that's exactly why I didn't tell him. I level a stare at him to keep him from going there and then return to brush in circles. Of course, my glare isn't enough to keep him from touching the subject. "She's back, and you're not going to do a thing about it?"

Dropping my hand from the bike, I sigh heavily. "What am I supposed to do, Aiden? She just lost her husband and, as far as she knows, I left because I didn't want her anymore. We're not going there. Forget it. Don't even try."

"That's such a wuss move."

"Respecting my relationship with Lily is a wuss move? Being a gentleman and giving Sawyer space is a wuss move?"

"Fine. Give her a little bit of time, and then make it right. She's *back*, man. Are you really telling me you're going to let her slip away again? I've seen you moping around ever since I moved back home almost a year ago. A *year*. So, it's obviously been going on for a lot longer. Make it right, Dean."

"I've got Lily now."

He snorts. "You and I both know Lily is only a replacement." I glare at him because she's my girlfriend, and I

71

care about her. His hands rise in surrender when he knows he's being a thoughtless prick. "I don't mean any disrespect, but you can't sit here and tell me that you can stay with Lily knowing Sawyer is finally back home."

I shake my head. "I'm not going to break things off with Lily because Sawyer has returned, dude. It may not make sense to you, but I love Lily. I know you're not completely wrong, but it's not right to hurt Lily like that. I won't do it. And, c'mon, even if I did do that, Sawyer's husband has only been gone for a few months. She's not ready."

"So you'll stay in a hopeless relationship because you don't want to hurt Lil?" he says.

I shrug because I don't want to get into this with him right now. I don't want to have to explain myself, or the relationship I have with Lily, to him.

"You've got to work out your crap, bro." His index finger is pointing at me and I'm *this* close to reaching out and breaking the dang thing off. "I'm not going to sit here and watch you lose Sawyer again because you're too scared to finally take what belongs to you."

"Let it go, Aiden," I answer sharply. "I'll figure it out."

"Good. Because I'm tired of seeing your sulky, sorry face. It's getting pathetic." I chuck my rag at him, and he bats it away with laugh. "Win her back, my friend. You two were made for each other."

I grunt out a laugh, but earnestly ask, "What if I can't?"

"Then at least you can say you tried. You didn't brood in your garage while she found someone else to bring her back to life."

My chest sinks at the thought. "She looked different to you, too, huh?"

Aiden nods his head solemnly, looking toward the ground. "I hardly recognized her, man. She's still just as gorgeous, but that spark that made her the Sawyer we both remember is gone."

I nod knowingly. "Every time I see her it hurts. Not just because she's not mine. It hurts to see that the life in her eyes is completely gone."

"So, bring it back," he urges, as if it's that easy. As if nothing could be simpler.

"She hates me, Aiden."

"Then give her time. Doesn't time heal all wounds? Just don't wait too long. Before you know it, some other Grayson is going to sweep in and steal her all over again, and you won't get a second chance this time. You're not going to be able to replace that one, Dean."

"Trust me," I grunt. "I'm well aware of that fact." I tried. *Several* times.

"I'm sure you are. I forgave you for walking out on all of us all those years ago, but you didn't see what it did to Sawyer. If you want to make it right, you've got to start now. It's going to take a lot of time."

"I had valid reasons for leaving."

"I understand why you left, but she doesn't. I don't think it was the right decision, but that doesn't matter now. None of that changes the fact that you have to make it right."

Everything he says makes sense. I get it. But the loyal side of my heart knows I can't disrespect Lily. She's stuck around for everything even though she knew the reason I came home in the first place. How could I be so cold and drop her? I care too much about her to be that heartless.

73

My dad's grave is bare. Headstones surround his, filled with flags and flowers and pinwheels left by loved ones, while his remains as lonely as his life.

I kneel down in front of it, running my fingers over his full name—Joseph Dean Preston 1961-2009. That's all it says. Did anyone go to his funeral? Did they have one, or was he simply buried? I break down. It's the strangest feeling—mourning the loss of someone I never even liked. But he was my dad. He was the only family I had left. Why did you leave me all by myself? *Now I'm officially alone. The finality of it hits me and sends me spiraling. I did this. I brought this on myself. My fists pound the headstone settled in the soil until they sting.*

"Dean?" A voice shoots me up onto my feet. "I'm sorry. I didn't mean to startle you."

I spin around to see Lily Jamison standing behind me with uncertainty in her shoulders. Her eyes turn down with concern. Swiftly, I rub my hands across my cheeks. Embarrassment flushes my face as I exhale and look away with my jaw clenched.

"Hey, Lily," I murmur.

"I'm sorry. I didn't mean to interrupt. I couldn't believe it was actually you. I was visiting my grandparents' grave and saw you. You're back." She pauses, but when I don't say anything, she continues cautiously. "It's okay to be upset, you know. It must suck to come back to find everyone you love is gone."

My gaze shoots to her. The look in my eyes must scare her because she flinches.

"I'm sorry. I didn't meant to overstep," she mumbles.

"It's fine." I shake my head and run the back of my hand under my nose. "Stop apologizing."

She nods. "Okay."

"He's been gone for three months, and I didn't have a single clue. I

74

didn't even come back because I heard about his death. Makes me a pretty lousy son, huh?"

She presses her lips together and shakes her head. "No one knew how to get a hold of you. How would you have known?"

"If I hadn't left in the first place," I mutter under my breath. It's more for my benefit than for hers.

"You obviously had a reason for leaving. You wanna talk about it? I'm a great listener."

Shaking my head, I begin to walk away without saying anything else when she reaches out to touch my arm. Her fingers latch on to me, stopping me. I lift my gaze to hers, and the compassion in her eyes keeps me in place. "It's probably the last thing you feel like doing, but I'm here if you want. I wouldn't mind."

I consider her words, but I have no intention of talking to her about this. When I asked Alix for help, she didn't want anything to do with me. Why would Lily? "Thanks," I say, stepping out of her grasp and walk away.

"I mean it, you know?" she calls out.

I nod without turning back.

CHAPTER THIRTEEN

Sawyer

ALIX TOLD ME my nails were atrocious. Yes, she actually said atrocious. So she made us nail appointments and told me to meet her in town since she was already running errands. I wait for her on a wooden bench near Timberpond Park downtown.

I spent another couple of weeks holed up in my parents' house after the Sole Festival. It probably would have benefitted me to get up earlier this morning to search for a job since I'm obviously not making any progress, but the motivation isn't there. I don't know where to find that motivation. How do people ever move on after things like this happen? Where do they find solace? I don't want to do anything but lay in bed and sleep. Sleep is painless. The problem with sleeping is waking up.

It's not that I'm unaware of the pity party I've been holding for myself. I get it. It's probably time to work on moving forward and picking up the pieces I've left in my wake, but how? How am I supposed to know when to let go? When is it too soon? How do you know when it's been too long? Who determines those kinds of answers? When it hurts so much to think about him, how can I possibly let it go?

The foliage in the park looks fuller than I remember. My

eyes wander around and find the willow along the pathway that curves around the pond. It hasn't changed much. I can still picture our blanket stretched on the bank below the slender branches like it was yesterday.

We watch the clouds drift above us, pointing out patterns and shapes. Dean has an eye for boats and turtles, while I find flowers and bunnies.

"When do you think a wish is more likely to come true? When you wish on a dandelion or a shooting star?" I bring the dandelion up to my face and examine the white fuzz flickering in the breeze.

Dean breathes a husky chuckle. "Well, in my professional opinion of wish granting, I believe it depends upon the wish. Dandelions are much more common than shooting stars, so if you have a big wish you want to come true, I think you have to wait for the shooting star."

"So I can wish a simple wish on a dandelion and have it come true?" I feel my lips turn up.

"Yup." His lips pop on the "p."

I close my eyes and blow the dandelion fuzz away.

"A simple wish, huh?" His eyebrow lifts as he tosses some Reese's Pieces in his mouth.

I nod, tilting my face to look over at him. "Should be simple enough."

"You think it will come true?"

"It's possible."

He leans closer to me. "Is there something I can do to make it come true?"

"Maybe." I smile shyly and feel the blush rise in my cheeks. He scans my face and the look in his eyes makes me so giddy and nervous I have to look away.

His finger finds my chin and turns me back to him. "Please don't look away from me, Jack." And then his lips find mine, and my wish to finally be kissed by him is granted. It's gentle and slow and absolute perfection as his lips form around mine. Our breathing is shaky and though we're lying down, I feel myself falling.

I blink and shake my head to clear thoughts of him. I don't know how Alix convinces me to go out with her. It's so much easier to stay home. There are no curious eyes, and the possibility of bumping into unwanted company is less likely.

Alix should be here any minute, but she doesn't come fast enough. An all too familiar figure catches my eye, walking the path around the other side of the pond and he's not alone. Lily Jamison is walking next to Dean, but it doesn't click. None of it clicks like it should until she stretches up on her toes and kisses his cheek. It's as if it all happens in slow motion. He turns and smiles down at her before kissing her lips. Betrayal hits me on a whole new level.

But that can't be right. I love Grayson, and I don't own Dean. He was obviously never mine. Lily might have been one of my best friends in high school, but I always knew she had a thing for Dean. I shouldn't be surprised, but I am, and it churns my stomach like a rickety winding roller coaster.

I don't have time to turn or hide my expression before Dean somehow finds me. It's not as if he was looking for me. He's looking down at Lily, and then his gaze lifts, and he's looking at me. We're both caught by surprise. I see the guilt that passes across his eyes as if he feels he needs to explain, but he doesn't owe me anything. We are long past over, and I have no right to stake a claim on him. He's not mine. He's clearly no longer mine.

Isn't there a saying? If you love someone, let them go. If

they return, they were always yours. If they don't, they never were. But what happens if they return and they still aren't yours? Was he ever really mine? Or was he always meant to be with Lily? Was I always meant to be with Grayson? Did I lose my only hope at happiness?

Lily doesn't see me. She's oblivious to this silent staring contest. She grabs his hand and starts to haul him away on whatever adventure they have planned for this sunny summer day.

He breaks eye contact first, and I hate that it wasn't me. I don't want to give him the satisfaction that this caught me so off guard that I can't look away. My eyes can hardly comprehend what I'm actually witnessing.

"Hey, you ready?" Alix pops up at my side, placing a hand on my shoulder. I'm staring at them, and I can't stop. I don't respond so her eyes locate where my gaze is held, and she says, "Yeaaaah..." as if she was waiting for me to finally find out about them.

"Are you still friends with Lily?"

"We hang out sometimes, but she's a different person. I'm a different person. We drifted apart."

"And she ended up with my ex-boyfriend." It didn't feel right calling him that. I never referred to him as my boyfriend before. It never seemed to encompass everything he was to me.

"And she turned to the dark side, so yeah, we aren't BFF's anymore."

"Wow." I exhale. "Things just keep getting better and better." I squeeze my eyes tightly to squash the tears before they can make an appearance. Ugh. *Why can't I shut off this freaking fountain already?*

79

"Hey… Hey… She has your old trash. That says a lot about her. And him for that matter."

I want to tell her not to call him trash. He's not trash. He crushed my heart, left me broken, but he isn't trash. He is something else entirely. "I hate that the sight of him with someone else makes me feel like this."

"Like what?"

As if my heart has somehow been ripped out. I don't understand how that's possible. Sometimes I feel like my heart is still missing. "Like I've lost him all over again."

"Sawyer, he was your first love. I don't think that's something you'll ever be numb to. You shouldn't beat yourself up over it. It's normal."

"Is it?" I ask, but I'm not really expecting an answer.

"So I've heard. C'mon, we've got a nail appointment to get to and then some cupcakes to devour. Polly just made a fresh batch and I know you're going to die when you try her raspberry and white chocolate cupcake. I die. Seriously."

"I can't believe she's still breathing, no less baking cupcakes every day."

"She's actually getting ready to turn the bakery over to someone else. You're looking for a job. Why don't you see if she could use some help? I know how much you love baking."

"At Sprinkles?" I'd never thought about it before, but somehow it sounds like the perfect place for me.

"Yes! My plan is falling into place. You can get me free cupcakes any time I want. That's it. Settles it. You're going to work for Polly."

CHAPTER FOURTEEN

LILY HOLDS MY hand so tightly it's as if she saw the exchange between Sawyer and me, but I know she didn't. Unless she knew Sawyer was there, and that's why she kissed me, to remind me I was with her. Even I know it's not necessary. Or is it?

Sawyer is back. My hopes of that happening died the day she said *I do* to Grayson, but I can't deny the hopefulness that formed in my chest the moment our eyes met today. And I know it's selfish, and I shouldn't hope that this could be my saving grace, that this was a second chance gifted to me, because honestly, I know I don't deserve it. It's that no one has made me feel the way Sawyer did. The way Sawyer does. It hasn't changed. Though those six years were long, they changed nothing.

But the hurt I saw in her eyes today was different from the day I saw her outside of Pearl's floral shop. It's different from when I saw her at Sole Fest. Today it's not related to Grayson or my disappearance all those years ago. This hurt looked more like jealousy. But she couldn't blame me for moving on. She got married. What was left but learning to get over her?

Then it hits me.

"Is there something going on between you and Lily?" she asks. Her face is so serious, but the question is so ridiculous I nearly laugh.

"Lily? Lily Jamison? Your best friend, Lily?"

"Yes, my Lily. What other Lily would I be talking about?" Sawyer glares at me from the driver's side of her car.

I lift my hands in surrender. "I just want to make sure we're on the same page here. Are you insane?"

"Excuse me?" She looks disgusted, and I almost laugh. It's so hard to take her seriously when she's mad. She's like an angry kitten.

I'm shaking my head in disbelief. "Why would something be going on between Lily and me?"

Sawyer shrugs, but it's not because she's unsure. She expects me to understand what she's talking about.

"Jack, where is this coming from?"

She exhales. "The way you two were flirting today made it seem as if there was something that I've been missing, and I don't want to be one of those dumb girls where everyone knows there's something going on behind my back, but no one wants to say anything, and so I'm left in the dark looking like an idiot. I want you to be honest with me."

I chuckle, shaking my head again. This is crazy. "I don't know what you saw today, but it wasn't flirting and if it was, it didn't mean anything."

"Do you think she's prettier than me?"

She really is insane. I gently tuck my finger under her chin so she'll look me in the eyes—really look at me. Her skin is so soft I stroke my finger back and forth. "You're joking, right? Of course she's not prettier than you. Why are you so worried about this?"

Her eyes soften, and I see my Sawyer coming back to life. "I see the way she looks at you. And all of the guys in school think she's so gorgeous, as if she's the Holy Grail of hot girls. And I realize she's my best friend, and friends don't do that to friends, but you really never know."

82

I can't help it any longer. I laugh. "Well, she's not ugly, but you're the only one I see, Jack. I think you're gorgeous. I don't want Lily. I want you. That's why I'm with you. And I'm lucky to have you."

"But if she wanted to be with you, would you want to be with her?" Her voice is quiet, so unlike the Sawyer I know. I don't understand why this is bothering her so much. There's nothing for her to worry about I could never want anyone but Sawyer. Not Lily. Not Scarlett freaking Johansson. Okay, maybe Scarlett Johansson. Who am I kidding? I love Sawyer.

"Never," I say, taking her face in my hands to kiss her. To kiss away any thoughts that could be clouding her mind. I want to be the only thing on her mind. When she gasps I know I have her complete attention, and I take full advantage of it.

"You know I was thinking we could make you a key today," Lily says.

I look down at Lily—and her hopeful expression—and feel like crap knowing where my mind had wandered. She wants to move forward, which makes sense. I was nearly on the same level as her until recently. My love for her hasn't changed. But is it the kind of love she deserves?

"I mean we're always at one another's houses," she continues. "It would be convenient, you know?" she says casually.

It would be harmless to do it. It wasn't as if we ever stayed the night. I set that rule. That was crossing a line that caused more drama than I needed. But I cared for Lily. I did. I could give her this. I didn't have to use the key. And I didn't have to offer her a key to my house. Yet.

"Okay." I offer a smile.

"Really?"

"Really." I nod. Though, as soon as I agree, the regret sets in, and I know I can't take it back. But maybe this is the direction we're supposed to go. What if I've been so selfishly stuck on Sawyer lately that I haven't been giving my relationship with Lily a fair enough chance?

She squeals, and I internally cringe at the sound as she urges me toward Art's Hardware. *Ugh, what did I just do?*

Our bags swing at our sides as Lily and I make our way back to my truck after our day out. My keys weigh down in my pocket, reminding me of the extra one that I've added to my key ring.

"I've got this delicious pasta recipe I discovered that I've been dying to try out. We can make that tonight. I think you'll love it. It's alfredo-based."

"Sounds good to me." I nod.

"Do you have sundried tomatoes at your house? Oh, who am I kidding?" She giggles. "Let's just do it at my house. I know I have everything I need there."

"Okay," I agree with a shrug.

I peer across the street and see Sawyer and Alix leaving Sprinkles. Sawyer laughs at something Alix says, and it makes my heart lighter. I haven't seen that face in far too long. It doesn't matter that I'm not the one eliciting that sort of reaction from her. She appears to be happy—for the moment—and that makes me happy. She takes a bite of a cupcake and nods at Alix, like she's telling her how good it is. Alix's eyes bulge in agreement when she takes a bite of hers. Sawyer and Alix back together again. It's such a natural picture. They're missing one person from that equation though. She's walking next to me.

"What are you smiling about?" Lily asks, pulling me out of my stupor.

I peer down at her, and her cheerful face slowly falls as she places where my eyes were plastered.

"Oh." She pauses. Even through that one small word, I can hear the bitterness. "Well, she looks a little too happy for someone who just lost her husband."

I scowl. "That's a little judgmental, don't you think? For lots of reasons. She lost her husband barely five months ago. You don't think she deserves the right to have one moment of peace? I doubt she has them very often."

That shuts Lily up. "You're right. But I guess I gave up that right to be in the know when I chose to be with you."

The fact that she throws that at me makes me want to walk away right then and there.

She continues, "I just mean I chose you, Dean. Over anyone else, I would always choose having a life with you. It trumps any other relationship."

After she says that, my temper ebbs. I'd never really thought about it like that. From her perspective, she gave up her friendship with her best friends to be with me. I'm not sure how I feel about that. I don't want to be anybody's reason for ruining a relationship. Strong, valuable relationships are hard to come by. It's stupid to throw them away if you're lucky enough to have them. But I guess if she was willing to give up what she had with Alix and Sawyer, it wasn't that strong to begin with.

CHAPTER FIFTEEN

Sawyer

POLLY HIRED ME. I started the week after Alix and I stopped by. Though she knew I had little experience, she was desperate to have a willing hand. She hasn't officially decided to turn over her business to anyone yet, but she did need some help around the bakery. Long days weren't as easy for her to handle anymore. So, I offered to help and she said yes. The job fell into place.

I've only been working there for a few days, but I can already feel myself wearing down. It's been a few months since I've had a job, and my body isn't ready for the stress I'm putting it under. I'm doing all the heavy lifting for Polly. All the flour and sugar bags weigh a thousand pounds, I swear. I definitely won't have to go to the gym. This lifting will do enough toning.

I offered to close up Sprinkles for her today, and even though it's only nine o'clock, I could probably go to bed now and sleep for days. I slowly trudge down the hallway toward my room. I'm fairly certain my feet could fall off any second. I'm passing the family picture hodgepodge my mom has created over the years when I notice something different. The wall is filled with old pictures of my brother, Blaine, and me from birth up until... Grayson. In the middle of all our old family pictures hangs a collage of Grayson and me. Pictures I must have mailed to her while we were dating circle around a picture of us on our wedding day.

Grayson stands in his dark brown suit behind me in my fitted, cream lace dress. His arms encircle my waist as his cheek rests up against mine. I remember my mom taking this picture. I'm smiling at the camera, and I thought that he was, too, but he's not. He's peering at me from the corner of his eyes. There's a small tilt to the corner of his mouth. My heart clenches at the adoration I see in his eyes. I should walk away now, but I can't.

I take the picture frame off the wall. My fingers grip it tightly as our small memories cloud my mind: a picture of us in front of the Space Needle, a close up of us on the couch inside his studio apartment, one of us up against the railing on a ferry off the coast of Seattle, and one of us outside the front door of our first apartment. I don't realize how tightly I'm grasping the frame until the glass breaks beneath my hold. I see the cracks across our memories and realize that's all I have left of him—a handful of shattered memories.

A cry rips through my throat, and I throw the frame against the wall. Glass flies everywhere, but I don't stop there. My hands drag across the long wall, tearing the rest of picture frames from the wall, one by one. None of those memories matter. The glass explodes at my feet like detonating grenades. I'm screaming and crying with no regard for my actions as our past falls to the floor.

"Sawyer! Sawyer, stop!" Mom shouts as she runs up the stairs. But I don't listen. My hands swipe the other way, knocking more to the ground. "Stop it, Sawyer!" She struggles to control my outburst, reaching around me to grab my hands. Her arms snatch mine, securing them beneath her hold.

"No!" I cry. "No, no, no…"

"Baby, that's enough! Baby!" She holds me hostage until I stop thrashing, and we collapse onto the ground. "Sawyer," she whispers into my ear with a quiver. I quiet down, but the tears convulse my body as I crumple against her chest. "Oh, sweetheart," she soothes, but nothing soothes me anymore.

I lose track of how long she's been cradling me in the hallway when she murmurs, "We need to get you patched up." I shake my head mechanically to protest, but she lifts me to my feet. My eyes are dry, but I'm covered in tears. She ushers me to the bathroom with her hand behind my back, carefully guiding me forward. Sitting me down on the closed toilet lid, she gestures for me to stay put and digs through the medicine cabinet. My tears fall from my cheeks onto the skin of my hands, and I look down to wipe them away. But it's not tears. It's blood.

I wipe my hands across my wet cheeks and come away with a mixture of red and tears on my palms. My mom turns and sees me with smeared cheeks and winces. She helps me to the sink to wash my face and hands. With a white washcloth she dabs my face dry and sits me down again.

"Do you feel better?" she asks, her hand resting on my shoulder.

I answer with the shake of my head.

"Well, that's too bad. It would have made the mess I'm about to clean up worth it."

I snort a humorless laugh before she dabs a rubbing alcohol coated cotton swab under my eye. I flinch and hiss from the sting.

"Sorry."

"No, I am," I mumble and wince again when she dabs my

other cheek. "I don't know what got into me."

Her lips press together like they do when she's trying to get a handle on her emotions. "I do. You lost your husband, and you're trying to learn how to deal with it." She pauses. "I should have taken down that collage of you two. You weren't ready for those kinds of memories. I knew it could have gone either way."

I shake my head and look up at her kneeling in front of me, taking care of me like she used to when I was little. "I just snapped. Some days are better than others. I guess today was a bad day. I miss him so much, Mama."

Her face tenses, and I see tears well up in her eyes. "I know, baby."

"Sometimes I think I'm okay, and then the next second I snap back into reality. Everything comes back to drown me. I'm so tired of feeling this way." My chest feels heavy. My mind is on emotion overload, and I honestly don't know how much more I can take.

I can tell she doesn't know what to say. So, she continues treating the little cuts on my face. "You know you can always talk to me. I'll listen."

I nod. I know I can, but talking about it makes it worse. So much worse. When I talk about it I cry, and I hate crying. I want to forget. I want it to all go away.

"You know, your brother's been asking about you. Blaine would really like to talk to you."

"I don't know what he wants me to say." I've been avoiding calling him. He's the one person who can read me better than anyone else, and I can't handle a lecture right now. While I was living in Seattle after the funeral he stood by to be there for me, but he kept his mouth shut. He didn't know what to make of me.

It's been over four months now, though; he must be losing his mind. We've never gone so long without talking.

"He just wants to hear your voice and let you know he's here for you. He's worried about you."

"He could call me himself."

"He doesn't think you'll pick up." He's right. When Mom was hounding me about why I had to pick Dean of all the boys in school to like, Blaine stepped in and said 'Because she can see a future with him.' He had taken the words right out of my mouth without me knowing that was exactly what I wanted to say. Blaine knows me too well. "He tried calling in the beginning, but your phone was off."

For good reason. "Well, he could try again. And you can tell him I'm fine."

"Fine?" She quirks an eyebrow. "If you call this fine I would hate to see what horrible looks like."

I chuckle, but it falls flat.

Fine is what I have to be. I'm fine. I can handle this. I can do this. I've got this. This is my new mantra. Without making that declaration to myself, I'd coil back into my room and never come out.

So, I'm fine. I can handle this. I can do this. I've got this.

I look down at the cuts in my hands, to the wedding ring I haven't taken off yet, and I know I'm lying to myself.

I curl into Grayson's side on a city park bench. During his study breaks, I meet him here to let him wind down a little bit and we people watch. The characters we discover make for hours of entertainment. He wraps his arm around my side, brushing his fingertips from my waist up to my ribs and rests his head on top of mine.

"Thank you for saving me," he says. "I really needed this break today."

"I'm happy to be of service. You're always the bright spot in my day, so it's not completely selfless."

Grayson chuckles and tightens his arm more securely around me, lifting my left hand to rests it in his. I feel a cold item gently slip around the finger next to my pinky.

I look curiously to my hand and raise it to reveal an unmistakable ring on my ring finger. My wedding ring finger. It takes me a minute to comprehend exactly what the thick diamond crusted band on my finger is. The clustering diamonds sparkle like stars on a clear night as the sunrays sweep over each facet.

"I know it's fast, but I feel if I don't make you mine now I'll regret it for the rest of my life."

I must look like a deer caught in headlights. My brow ruffles. What did he say? "You're serious?" I laugh nervously.

His hazel eyes smile at me. "I don't want to live one more day without calling you my wife, Sawyer." He moves down from beside me and kneels down on one knee. "As soon as I saw your face I knew I needed you. It was just that. I needed you. And I haven't looked back since. I love you, Sawyer Hartwell, and I know I'll never stop." Grayson takes the hand he placed the ring on and kisses my knuckle. "Be my wife?"

If someone asked me before today if I would have said yes, I would have told them no, but looking in his eyes I don't second-guess myself. "Yes."

It's not until he has me cradled in his arms that a face flickers behind my closed eyelids. A face that isn't Grayson's. I know I should give up on Dean. He isn't coming back. I know that, but I've been keeping him saved in a compartment in my brain just in case. Today, though, I know I need to lock that compartment and throw away the key, so I say a silent goodbye and plead for thoughts and memories of him to finally leave me alone.

"Let's get married today," Grayson says.

I wake, rolling to my side and feel for Grayson on the other side of the bed. My hand reaches for his bare chest, but he's not there. My eyes open, taking in my old bedroom and I remember. Remembering is the worst part. There's a brief moment between sleeping and waking where Grayson lives. In those few perfect moments, he's not gone. He's alive, and he's sleeping peacefully next to me.

I roll back to my side of the bed and let the tears fall down my face, into my hair, wetting my pillowcase. My hand stays splayed on the empty sheet beside me, stroking the material as I imagine him there.

Over the last couple of weeks Polly has taught me a few tricks of the trade, and I've rediscovered how much I love baking. I did a lot of it in Seattle when Grayson had long days at school, which was often. Every week I'd try something new. The recipes weren't always a success, but there was something calming about baking. When I baked, I escaped. Willowhaven was the last thing on my mind. There were no regrets or feelings of loss. The unhappiness that gradually seeped into my veins was a distant memory. I zoned in on the flour and measurements and mixing bowls and lost myself.

I hear the door chime from the back of the bakery so I head up front. My stomach drops when I see him standing near the display of cupcakes. God has no mercy on me. Dean stands in a form-fitted black t-shirt with his hands tucked in the front

92

pockets of his low riding jeans. His intensely green eyes smile. He doesn't look surprised to see me behind the counter, so I don't bother being polite. He obviously has an agenda, but I don't think I'm ready to hear it. I don't know how he has the audacity to come in here after everything—after hooking up with my ex-best friend.

I must have flour on my nose because before I get a chance to say anything he smirks and taps his index finger against the tip of his nose.

I rub the back of my hand across my nose and hopefully wipe it clean. "What do you want, Dean?"

"Well, hello to you." He nods. "It's good to see you, too. I'm doing just fine. How about you?"

This sounds more like the Dean I remember. I hated his hesitation before, as if I was a caged animal who needed to be handled with care. I'm a little unstable, there's no denying that, but I can't possibly break any more than I already have. Rock bottom and I are already pretty familiar with one another.

"We're past pleasantries, Dean. I'm not going to stand here and chat with you like the last six years never happened."

"I understand that you're upset with me, but if you would just hear me out."

"Hear you out? Oh, this should be good. You wanna tell me why it was so hard to pick up a phone for six years? Or maybe why you're back, and yet I didn't have a clue?"

"Things aren't always black and white, Sawyer. Sometime decisions have to be made that we don't want to make. It doesn't change the fact that they happen, and I'm sorry."

I shake my head and look up at the ceiling. *He's sorry?* That's rich. "You know... Willowhaven might not be that big, but there

93

are definitely ways for us to run in different circles. Let's keep it that way." *Please can we keep it that way?*

"You can't really mean that, Sawyer." He eyes me, trying to call my bluff with a rise of his eyebrows.

"Honestly, yeah. I'd much rather never hear your voice ever again, so you can just turn around and walk out like this never happened. You can pretend I don't exist. I can pretend you don't exist. It's nothing new to us." As I say the words, they burn with the lie. I can't pretend he doesn't exist. I've never been able to do that. My mind has never let me do that.

But I want my words to sting. I hope he walks away. It'll make things easier, plus, he's good at it. If only he would repeat that performance. Then I could go back to my life of thinking about him in the distant past tense as opposed to the constant present, because whether he lied to me about loving me, or lied about not loving me, it doesn't matter… Either way, he's a liar, and I don't want anything to do with a liar.

CHAPTER SIXTEEN

Dean

I WASN'T EXPECTING that to hurt as much as it did. Although she may sound snarky, she also sounds completely honest. I didn't come here to fight with her. I was going to be polite and get on with my day, but her initial greeting struck something inside of me. I know she's hurting, and I probably deserve everything I have coming to me, but that doesn't mean I won't strike back in the process when it's necessary. She can hate me, but she doesn't need to be rude about it.

"Okay. I deserved that." And more. "I just had to… I just wanted to… I need you to…" I grunt, aggravated that I can't get the words right.

"Just spit it out already, Dean. I've got to get back to work."

"I need you to know I truly am sorry."

Her eyebrows raise and she laughs. It's completely without humor, but at least it's more of an emotion than I've gotten from her thus far. "A little late for that, aren't we?"

I sigh. "I'm trying here, Jack. You're not making this very easy."

"Oh my gosh, I hate it when you call me that. Please don't," she begs, her eyes on the ceiling as she swallows. She does that when she's annoyed. As if she's so irritated she can't stand to look at you for one more second.

"You used to love it when I called you that," I say quietly. The words stick in my throat. I didn't mean to say it out loud.

"No, I hated it, but I loved you, so I never asked you to stop." Her eyes meet mine again, slicing right through me.

So this is her way of telling me she doesn't love me anymore. Of course she doesn't love me anymore. I don't expect her to. I don't know what I expect. I just...

A patch of black catches my eye on Sawyer's wrist as she runs her fingers through her hair and sighs.

"Did you get a tattoo?"

She looks down at her wrist and shifts uncomfortably. I don't understand why. It's not as if I would judge her. It catches me by surprise because it's so out of character for the Sawyer I knew.

"Yeah," she answers and lifts her eyes to me resolutely, almost defiantly asking with her eyes, *What are you gonna do about it?*

"What is it?"

She narrows her eyes defensively. "Why do you care?"

"It's just a question, Sawyer. I never thought of you as the tattoo type."

"I never thought of you as the deserting type, but you proved that theory wrong. People change."

I have to give it to her. I left that one wide open. My fingers coil into a fist and rub back and forth across my forehead. I will not lose my temper. She doesn't deserve it.

"It's a dandelion," Sawyer finally murmurs. I look up and watch her peering down, brushing her thumb lightly over the small tattoo. There's a distant, sad look in her eyes, and I wonder what she's thinking about. I don't know a lot about symbolism or why she got the tattoo, but I know what dandelions mean to us.

"Look, Dean. It's water under the bridge. We don't have to make it more than it was, okay? We had a high school fling. It ended. We moved on. That's all there is to it." Her voice holds indifference, and it cuts me deep. She's brushing aside the only relationship that ever meant anything to me. I'm getting brushed under the rug like some dirty little secret.

I hold my ground. "No! Not okay! Be livid with me. Yell at me. Cry. Smack me if you have to. But don't pretend like what we had wasn't real," I snap. I hate raising my voice. I especially hate raising it to Sawyer, but I can't bear the thought of it not being real. It was real to me, even if she doesn't believe that.

"You've got to be kidding me," she scoffs. "Like you did?"

I nod and swallow the lump in my throat. "Okay. I deserved that, too. But you know what I mean." I know I threw it away. The guilt and regret of it eats at me every day. If only she knew I did it for her.

"I don't want to fight." She sighs with a shake of her head. I've never heard anyone sound more defeated. "I don't want to do this. I don't have the energy to deal with this." She throws her hands back and forth between us as if to emphasize her revulsion with the thought of us. My stomach tightens against the punch. "I'm dealing with too much right now, Dean. Okay?"

There are tears brimming in her eyes, and I know how much she hates to cry, so I lift my hands in surrender. "Okay." She's so delicate; she could crack with the softest tap. I don't want to be the one to shatter what she's working so hard to reconstruct. All I wanted was to hear her voice. I wanted her to acknowledge me again. Just once. "Okay. I'll go."

"Thank you." She sounds so relieved my ego gets knocked down a few more levels.

I leave without getting the double chocolate cupcake I went in there for, and that bums me out. I was really craving one of those.

Aiden wasn't kidding when he said I needed to start working for her forgiveness now. I know I don't deserve it right off the bat, and I may not deserve it at all, but I want it now more than ever.

CHAPTER SEVENTEEN

Sawyer

THAT NIGHT, AFTER being on my feet all day, I decide a bubble bath is exactly what I need. It doesn't help that Dean got me all riled up earlier either. I hate that the sight of him brings me back to bowling alleys and Sole Festivals and lying under the willow in Timberpond Park. I hate that I think of Reese's Pieces and motorcycles and dandelions. When my mind goes back to those places it reminds me how it felt. It remembers that he can make me feel vulnerable and adored and tongue-tied and strong all at the same time. *Why does he still have that effect on me?*

Dean has only raised his voice to me like that one other time. I'd seen him lose it on other people, but never on me. He hated showing that side of himself in front of me. As soon as he found himself losing his temper, he would walk away or breathe through it. I'll never forget the look in his eyes that night.

The music is booming through the valley of the lake. The bass echoes off the mountains surrounding us. Our entire class—which consists of about three hundred students—is partying at Coral Lake for a summer kick off, the kick off to the last summer before our senior year. A bonfire blazes orange and red on the beach under the night sky.

Dean, Aiden, and Josh are huddled together a few feet away from the bonfire and dancing crowd when I walk up to them.

"The princess herself has arrived," Josh remarks. "Stop the presses!" His tone sends an unpleasant shudder down my spine. It holds more mocking than teasing, but I smile anyway. Showing him how uncomfortable he makes me would only be providing more ammo.

"Hey, guys."

Dean puts his arm around my waist, tugging me close to his side, and plants a kiss on my temple. "Hey, Jack," he whispers into my hair. "You look beautiful."

I smile up at him and let my lips linger on his jaw. "Thanks."

"Well, that's about as much of the happy couple I can take," Josh says and pulls something skinny and white from his shirt pocket. It's probably something he can smoke. But at least it means we most likely won't see him for the rest of the night.

"I'll catch you losers on the flipside." Josh walks away, with Aiden in tow, throwing a dirty hand gesture in our direction. Dean tries to laugh it off, but I can tell he's just as uncomfortable as I am.

"I won't lie to you, Dean. I don't understand why you're friends with Josh. You're nothing like him."

Dean shrugs, but I can see my comment bothers him, so I try to smooth it out. "I just mean, he's always high or drunk or asking for trouble, and you... aren't. How did you become friends with him?"

"We get each other, Jack. He's got my back. I promise he's not all bad. Things aren't easy for him."

"Doesn't mean you have to be friends with him. He doesn't seem like the best company to keep around." I worry about Dean. He doesn't need to get mixed up with something because of Josh. Who knows what illegal shenanigans Josh is involved in?

"Life's not all rainbows and butterflies, Sawyer. Our world isn't like

100

yours." The shift in Dean's tone makes me wince.

"Well, that's a little unfair, don't you think? Just because life sucks doesn't mean he has to be such a jerk."

"You shouldn't go poking your nose into things you don't understand,"
he snaps.

"Dean, I didn't mean to make you mad. I just don't think Josh—"

"Just leave it alone, Sawyer!"

He swears and kicks the dirt. His eyes are heated. His pupils dilate, covering every green inch of his irises.

I can't help recoiling. He's never yelled at me before. Sure, we've been in fights, but they were merely mild disagreements, slightly heated debates, not knockdown, drag-out screaming matches.

In an instant, his countenance changes. His shoulders sag, and before I can say anything, he turns and walks away. I try to follow him, but he disappears into the crowd. I search everywhere for him, but he's gone.

He never did explain to me why I made him so angry. I remember when he finally came back to me after that, though. It wasn't that night or the next day. In fact, Dean ignored me all weekend. I tried texting him and calling him, but I never got a reply. I tried going over to his house, but no one answered. It wasn't as if I expected them to. His dad rarely ever showed his face when we were at his house. Why would he answer for me now?

It wasn't until Monday after school that I saw Dean. He ditched all of his classes, and I was getting more than a little worried. What if something actually happened to him? It wasn't like him to disappear. I remember worrying that I pushed him over the edge.

Dean's leaning back against the driver's side of my car in the school

101

parking lot, his arms folded across his chest. A black baseball cap covers his hair with little flips of the brunette locks resting on top of his ears. When he sees me he stands up straight and his arms drop to his sides. I think about ignoring him and giving him the cold shoulder. He put me through hell this weekend. If something happened to him, how would I have known? There wouldn't have been anyone to tell me. I should make him suffer for it. But I'm so grateful he's okay I run up to him and throw my arms around his neck.

He sucks in a deep, surprised breath and forms his soft lips to the bare skin at the nape of my neck. "I'm so sorry, Jack." He presses little kisses over and over on my skin and I tremble.

I shake my head and hold him tighter, reaching my hands all the way around to my elbows. "I don't care. I'm just so grateful you're okay." I place one hand on the back of his neck, brushing down the hair peaking out of his cap. The need to take care of him consumes me. He has no one to take care of him.

"I thought you would hate me." Dean pulls back and looks down into my eyes. The tips of his fingers stroke my waist as he holds me away from him.

"Hate you? Even if I wanted to hate you, my heart wouldn't give me that choice. You're stuck with me."

The corner of his mouth turns up in a half smile, but he sobers. "I shouldn't have freaked out like that. It was wrong of me. I didn't mean to scare you."

I nod. "I get it. I don't understand the relationship you have with Josh. I over stepped."

He shakes his head. "No. It doesn't excuse what I did. I'm sorry. I'm so sorry I yelled at you."

"It's okay, Dean."

"I've been trying to gain the courage to come talk to you for days. I

102

thought you'd never forgive me."

*The tips of my fingers brush his cheek as I cradle his face in my hand.
"Have a little more faith in me than that. It'd take a lot more to scare me
than one glimpse of a little temper." I smirk.*

*He moves the bill of his hat to the back of his head and leans in to
kiss my lips. "You know I love you."*

*"I do," I say against his lips. "But don't shut me out again, okay? I
was really worried about you."*

"Never," he whispers and forms his mouth to mine.

Lily takes care of him now. Does she take good care of
him? Is he happy? I don't know why I'm still worrying about
him. He's a grown man. He can take care of himself. But even
after all we've been through, it would be comforting to know
he's not being neglected. He's had enough of that in his life.
Even through my resentment I can still see he deserves more.

I dim the lights in the bathroom and shuffle across the tile
floor to light some aromatherapy candles, then sink under the
warm water to try and forget. The heat relaxes my muscles while
the soft music calms my mind. I let my head lie back against the
porcelain and breathe.

In.

Out.

In.

Out.

*"You know, as much as eloping sounded tempting I'm really glad we
didn't." I brush my toes against Grayson's at the end of the tub. Sinking
lower in the water, the bubbles tickle my chin.*

"Yeah? Why's that?"

"I think my mom would have killed me. Or you when she found out it was your idea."

He chuckles, and I feel it ripple down my back. "Hey now, it was only my idea because I thought that's what you would have wanted."

"It was." My head falls back against his bare shoulder. Eloping would have been easier. So much easier. But it was too impulsive. It wouldn't have been right. I didn't want to elope for the right reasons. "But today was perfect. Having our families and friends there made it feel official and… right. You know?"

"It was right. I can't imagine having anyone else by my side today but you." His nose brushes up and down the length of my neck.

A twinge lurches my heart when Dean's face flashes in my mind. I smash that box closed as swiftly as I can, but it's not fast enough. The pain of losing him and what could have been ours hasn't ebbed.

If I agree with Grayson, it will be a lie. I tilt my head back to kiss his smooth jaw. His head tilts down in my direction. His hazel eyes glide deliberately slow over my face, and I wonder if it's physically possible to melt away because his penetrating gaze paralyzes my body. His eyes end their memorization on mine, so full of love and desire. I hate myself for loving Dean. I decide, once and for all, to douse that old flame because Grayson was the one by my side today. He is the one I am with. He is the one doing everything in his power to make me happy. I will love the one I am with.

All right. Hastily, I rise from the bathtub, splashing water on the tile floor. Not even some candles, Enya, and bubbles can relax me. When it's not one, it's the other. Dean and Grayson will haunt me forever. My mind never gets a chance to shut them off. But I know that can't be right. My mind isn't on constant Grayson and Dean mode. So when do I have relief? When do they leave me alone?

104

Sprinkles. When I bake, they take a break to sit back and watch me work. As most men do when a woman is hard at work in the kitchen. The irony is not lost on me. So, I throw on some pajamas and head for the kitchen.

"Did you not get enough of your kitchen at work, sweet girl?" My dad is sitting at the kitchen table with his laptop open in front of him. I imagine, now that he's retired, he's searching for a new set of golf clubs. What is it with old guys and golf anyway? They have so much time on their hands they want to spend it doing the most boring, time consuming sport ever?

"Baking calms me. Do you have any requests?"

"Taking orders? Hmm. This works for me. I'll make it simple on you. Chocolate chip cookies?"

"I can work with that."

An hour later, I've made at least three-dozen cookies, and the kitchen is a disaster.

I don't notice Mom until I hear her talking to Dad. "She says baking helps," Dad whispers as if he thinks I can't hear him.

As I'm pulling another batch of cookies out of the oven, Mom walks over to me. "Can I help?"

"If you want to load the next cookie sheet, you're welcome to."

She nods, attempting to stifle a smile as we work alongside each other until every last cookie is baked. The only problem is, I have no idea what I'm going to do with nearly forty cookies.

Aside from eating every last one.

CHAPTER EIGHTEEN

I DRAPE MY arm over Lily's shoulder as we walk toward the movie theater in downtown Willowhaven. She leans her head in the crook of my shoulder and tucks her hand in my back pocket.

"I ran into Josh down by the post office today. I know you really care about him, so I tried being polite, but he didn't acknowledge me. He walked right past me."

He probably was too hopped up on whatever he's on to care about anyone or anything around him. I hum a response because I don't have much to tell her.

"I don't know how you can be friends with someone who has such a disregard for everyone and everything around him—someone who has such a lack of respect for themselves. I don't like him, Dean." Lily says, relieved to get the truth off her chest. "There, I said it."

She doesn't realize I already know this. I don't care what she has to say about him. I've had it with her inability to accept anyone different than her. "Lil, I know, and whatever you think about Josh doesn't matter to me. To be honest, I'm tired of you constantly shooting him down. You don't know him. He's had it worse off than anyone in this town. So, just lay off, will you?"

Shards of glass coat the kitchen floor—the mug my mom gave my dad for his last birthday before she left no longer usable. I look up at Josh, and his eyes are panicked. The TV goes quiet—my dad must have muted it. I grab a broom from the cupboard and race to start sweeping it up. I don't know if he'll be more upset that I broke the mug or that I made a mess.

"Boy!" my dad hollers from the TV room, and I shrink. "What did you break?"

I don't know what to say. I don't know how to tell him. So, I remain silent, hoping he'll let it go, but I'm not that lucky. Life isn't that kind to me.

The sound of the recliner latching back into place races my pulse. He's coming. I move quicker, sweeping the broken pieces into a pile. I feel his figure hovering behind me in the archway of the kitchen entrance so I turn. Ignoring him will make it worse.

"Is that my mug?" His voice is steely as he points to the ground littered with broken glass.

"Yes, sir," I reply quietly and swallow.

"You stupid moron! What made you think it was a good idea to get that mug? That's not yours to touch!" He towers over Josh and me. His eyes dart to the broom in my hand. "Did you think I wouldn't notice? You trying to hide the evidence?" He's shouting, and I don't know how to make him stop. I wish Josh wasn't here to listen to him yell. I'm used to his yelling. That's how he communicates, but he's different this time. Rage burns in his eyes.

His arm reels back to take a swing, and I shut my eyes, but the hit never comes. I hear his fist connect with flesh, but it's not mine. I open my eyes to see Josh hunched over in front of me. My dad's eyes widen when he realizes he didn't hit me.

My dad gasps, speechless, unsure where to go from here. He grunts but doesn't make another comment before he trudges away. I hear the slam of his

107

bedroom door and let out the breath I was holding.

"Why did you do that, Josh?" I hiss. "You shouldn't have stepped in front of me. It should have been me."

"I'm used to it." He wipes the blood from his face with the back of his hand. "Your old man doesn't normally hit you, does he?"

I shake my head. "Not a lot, no."

He shrugs. "Happens to me every day."

He always tried to protect me. "Until you've stepped in his shoes, you have no place to judge him or my decision to be friends with him."

Lily stops us on the sidewalk and peers up at me. Her hand reaches up and brushes hair from my forehead. "I'm sorry. You're right." She licks her lips, a nervous habit of hers. "I won't say anything ever again."

"Thank you," I sigh.

"I really am sorry, Dean." She's speaking as if she regrets saying it because it made me angry, not because she's sorry.

I say it's fine, but I want to be off the topic. I steer her toward the ticket line so we can get into this movie and take my mind off it all.

I've been working on getting over the past, moving past the life that my dad created for us. And it's so freaking hard to do that when all Lily does is remind me of it. She doesn't realize what she does, but if I tell her to lay off she'll question me further, want more details, so desperate to *save* me.

But I don't need to be saved. I've already been saved. The thought of Sawyer alive in this world saves me every day.

CHAPTER NINETEEN

Sawyer

"I HAVE BEEN *dying* to see this movie for months," Alix says as we walk into the movie theater lobby. "When I first saw the trailer in April it was one of those that I thought, 'I will go to the theater by myself if I have to.' And you know how much I loathe that idea."

"Good thing I'm here to save you from social suicide. Heaven forbid you go to the movies alone."

"I'm not above it," she counters. "I would just prefer not to. Watching movies alone isn't nearly as fun."

"Well, you're in luck today."

Alix and I find a couple of seats toward the middle of the theater. We've made it in time for the previews, which, for me, are half the entertainment in going to the movies.

Once we're seated, popcorn starts flying over the seat, piece by piece, like snow falling all around us. Alix and I share a look. Then one pegs her in the temple, and her head swings back so fast she almost looks possessed. I turn in the same direction and see Aiden a few rows up, grinning from ear to ear, popping the white kernels into his mouth as he smacks his gums.

"Fancy meeting you ladies here."

"Couldn't you have found another theater to terrorize?" Alix hisses.

Aiden chuckles soundlessly. "Sadly, no," he replies. "This is the only theater that allows my behavior—encourages it actually."

Someone in the theater shushes us.

I notice a new girl sitting beside him. A redhead this time. No Priscilla in sight. She's looking down at the phone illuminating her face, ignoring him and us.

"Nice date. She looks super attentive," Alix remarks.

"We keep each other company." He shrugs with mischief in his eyes, aiming his comment at Alix.

The redhead looks up at that moment, as if she just realized there's a world around her. "Shelly, do you know Alix and Sawyer?" Aiden asks.

"I don't think I do. Nice to meet you girls." She waves. She's got a strong Southern accent. So strong, in fact, that it's hard to understand what she says.

"You should probably pay more attention to your date, Aiden. You're boring her already, and the movie hasn't even started yet," Alix says.

"Who says we came here to be entertained by a movie?" I hear his insinuation. It can't be lost on Alix, and I can only imagine how Shelly must feel. Hopefully she knows he's just trying to razz Alix.

Aiden and Alix continue their quiet bickering, but my eyes zero in past Alix's shoulder, on a couple entering the theater, walking slowly down the dark aisle with the faint floor lighting revealing their faces. They both search the theater for seats. Thankfully, they haven't spotted us yet. Dean's eyes come close to our row, and I sink lower into my seat to remain undetected. Just before he's about to discover us, Lily grabs his hand, leading him to a couple of seats in the back corner.

I don't realize I'm grabbing Alix's leg until she hisses, "Ouch! What the crap, Sawyer?"

Her eyes follow my line of sight over her left shoulder and then she turns back to me.

"Is it...? We can go," she whispers. "We don't have to stay."

I hate that I want to accept her offer. Alix really wants to see this movie, but I can't stand the thought of being enclosed in the same room as them for two straight hours. Leaving, though, also means walking past them. There's only one exit.

She decides for me. "We'll go. C'mon." Taking my hand, she pulls me from my seat.

"Oh c'mon, Alix. I didn't scare you off, did I?" Aiden's not loud, but it's loud enough that Dean and Lily could have heard him.

"Shut it, Ballard," Alix snaps over her shoulder as she leads us down the row.

We walk up the aisle and out of the theater. I don't pay any attention to them. I don't let my eyes wander. I'm not sure if they saw us leave or not, but I don't care. As soon as we walk out of the theater and into the open air, I feel like I can breathe again.

"Better?" she asks.

I nod and exhale. "I'm sorry."

"Don't apologize. I would have made you stay, but there was this look of terror in your eyes. You okay?"

"I will be." My arms find solace across my chest.

111

Alix sighs as if she's trying to figure out what we should do now. "Sleepover?" she questions. "I'm pretty sure it's time. It's been over six years, and you owe me a movie. Maybe two to make up for missing that one."

"Only if the sleepover includes buttery popcorn and loads of candy."

"It wouldn't be much of a sleepover without all that diabetes."

"Then I say we have ourselves a deal."

We stop by the drug store to stock up on junk food and head back to my house. The eating starts almost as soon as the chick flick marathon begins.

"Are you ever going to give Aiden a break?"

"Pshht. He doesn't deserve a break."

"Felix, you like him. I know you do. And I can tell he likes you, too. So, he was a dumb boy. He didn't cheat on you. He didn't lie to you or lead you on. How do you know he was even on a date that night? Maybe he and Bridget were going out as friends."

"Then he should have explained himself. He saw me when he was with her, and he smiled, like hey, it was fun, but I can get a much hotter woman than you."

"Oh, Alix." I laughed. "There is no way that, number one: his smile meant that, and number two: he thinks Bridget is prettier than you. You're being dramatic."

She shrugs. "Whatever."

"You won't even give him a little time of day?"

"Nope." She shoves popcorn in her mouth and keeps her eyes focused on the TV mounted on my wall.

I leave it. I know she's scared of really getting hurt. She'll figure it out eventually.

Three movies later, it's two o'clock in the morning, and Alix is sprawled across my bed in a junk food coma. I shove her to one side and crawl in next to her. Apparently moving her was a bad idea. Darth Vader has returned. If she turned to me now and said, *"Luke, koooohhhhh heeeeeee, I am your father,"* I wouldn't doubt her to be the real deal.

Her throaty breathing makes it especially hard for me to fall asleep. I'm reminded as to why I rarely invited her to sleep over when we were younger and why I never slept over at her house. My mind stretches to remember the last time we did this, and I instantly remember why I've been trying to suppress that memory. It feels like both forever ago and yesterday.

The bathroom tile is cold on my skin. It helps to alleviate the nausea. If you want to know what slowly dying inside feels like, I could probably tell you.

"He's really gone," I choke. Alix rubs my back as I lay on the bathroom floor. The pain is excruciating. It runs through my veins, tearing them to shreds, crippling every part of my body. I didn't know it was possible for the body to survive this kind of agony. "Is it my fault? Did I do this?"

"No, it's not your fault, Sawyer," she murmurs. "You had no control over this."

"Why does it hurt so badly?" I curl further into the fetal position. But I know why. This is my punishment.

"It's probably going to hurt for awhile."

"Why did Dean leave me?" My words are hardly audible coming. It's a wonder she can understand me. I clench the front of his Blink 182 shirt that I'm wearing. I can barely smell the scent of him on it anymore. It was the last piece of him that I had. "He's supposed to be here with me."

113

"I know, but I don't know if he's coming back. You have to learn to live like he's not coming back."

I wheeze. "I don't want to live that way."

"I don't think you have a choice," Alix speaks softly, tracing her hand in a circular motion over my back and down my arm. But there is no relief. This is the kind of ache that will never die. No matter how hard I try, I know this will be the kind of pain that will stay with me forever. And no one will understand it but me.

Alix reaches over and rubs my back. I don't realize I'm crying until her shushing brings me back. "It's okay to cry, Sawyer. Cry as much as you need to."

She thinks she understands why I'm crying, and I let her believe it's because of Grayson, because I can't bear the thought of telling her the real reason. I can't talk about it. Not because she wouldn't understand. She would probably start to cry with me if she knew, and I'm tired of making people feel sorry for me. I'll get through this. I can do it on my own. I can. I've got this. I'll be okay. At least that's what I've been telling myself, but I'm still waiting for the day I will feel okay. I don't know how to fix me. I'm stuck in a whirlpool of misery that fights to drag me under, and I can't get out.

In the morning, we make pancakes. My eyes feel heavy and raw from my meltdown, but Alix leaves it alone. I silently thank her with my eyes, and she knows. My parents join us, and we eat breakfast peacefully. My mom notices my swollen eyes, but she keeps it to herself. Her eyes widen, but she forces her mouth

114

shut.

"They're so sweet and fluffy. What did you do to make them this way?"

"I beat the egg whites before whisking them into the batter."

She takes another bite and hums. "I should have you cook more often. You can be my little in-house chef."

"Just tell me when, Mama."

Alix leaves after breakfast, and our Sunday carries on much the same as breakfast. My parents and I sit quietly on our porch for a little bit with our sweet tea and enjoy the warm weather. Nothing heavy is discussed. We're all playing a part in pretending everything is back to normal when we all know it's not. Dad talks about the lives of some of our old family friends, and mom fills in the gaps that he misses. I pretend to care and listen, but don't make many comments. Everyone's lives keep on moving forward while mine stands still.

CHAPTER TWENTY

Dean

I GRAB MY jacket and head for the front door. My dad is in his recliner in the living room, but if I'm quiet enough, I might get by without him noticing me since he's got the TV blasting so loud. Unfortunately, the swipe of the lock isn't drowned out enough.

"Boy! Where do you think you're going?" he hollers.

I clear my throat and turn to see he's still facing the TV. He couldn't be bothered to turn around to talk to me. "I'm going out with Sawyer Hartwell."

"Phil Hartwell's girl?"

"Yes, sir."

My father spins the recliner around and grunts. "What does she want to do with the likes of you? Doesn't she know you'll amount to nothing?"

I shrug to disguise my wince. "We're just hanging out."

He takes a sip of his beer with a blank stare. His eyes see through me and slice into me at the same time. "I know what hanging out means." He watches me for a moment without saying a word, staring me down, scanning my body with a look of utter disgust. "Does she know what you are?"

I don't know what he means by that so I don't answer, thinking he'll finish his thought, but I guessed wrong.

"Answer me, you little piece of crap! She know what you are?" he *demands.*

"I don't know, sir," I speak up, blinking away tears that threaten to surface.

"You should tell her now before it's too late. She should know how pointless it is to waste her time on you."

I don't want him to see the tears that prick my eyes, so I clench my teeth and nod. I bolt through the door before he can call me back.

My office phone rings, starling me back to the present. "Preston Motorsports," I answer. "This is Dean."

"Hi, Dean. My name is Rob Dillon. How are ya doin' today?"

"I'm all right. What can I do for you, Mr. Dillon?"

"Call me Rob, please."

"Okay, Rob. How can I help you?"

"You are the owner of Preston Motorsports, correct?"

"Yes, I am."

"I've got an offer for you, and I'm hoping I can take a minute of your time."

"Okay," I say hesitantly.

He laughs. "Don't worry. This isn't a sales call. I'm actually trying to do quite the opposite. I've heard a lot about your garage. You do good work."

"Thank you, sir. We do our best."

"Not many motorists in a fifty-mile radius go anywhere aside from your garage."

Huh. How did he know that? I didn't know that. I mean, I know the garage does well, but... "Glad to hear it. I make sure to have the best mechanics on hand. Bikes are our lives."

"I knew I'd like you, kid. Your policy, 'We'll have it done on

117

time or it's on us,' is something I've never heard before. It's bold. Most might actually think it's a stupid move—business suicide."

"Well, we make it a point never to be late. I know that's half the issue with people going to a mechanic. It's never done when they say it will be done. It's always more expensive than they anticipate. I like to make sure we have satisfied return customers."

"You're smart, too. Jerry Drake had great things to say about you."

I nearly choke. "Jerry Drake? As in Drake Motor Industries Jerry Drake?"

Rob chuckles. "He's a good friend of mine. Apparently, he just bought a Streetfighter from you. And I've been in the market for a good investment business. He seems to think I've found the right place."

How had I not put two and two together?

"I'd like to make you an offer for your garage."

"What kind of an offer?"

"Well, I'd like to buy it. I want you working there, managing it, but I'd like to take the business end off your hands. I think you've really got an interesting concept going on and I'd like to expand it."

"I really appreciate the offer, Rob, but the garage isn't for sale."

"I'll pay you $300,000 for it. Cash."

If I had been drinking something, it would have come out my nose. "I'm sorry?"

"It's a generous offer. But I'm willing to negotiate."

I swallow. "With all due respect, sir, I've never had any interest in selling the garage. I started it up a couple years back.

It's a passion of mine, and I enjoy what it is I do. I don't think I could sit back as a manager and watch you do what you'd like with it."

"I can understand that. But I promise you, we could make Preston Motorsports more than you could imagine. I tell you what, I'll give you $350,000 for it."

I pause to think. "That's quite an offer, but I built this business up myself. It'd be very difficult to let it go just like that. I think I'm going to have to pass, Rob."

"$500,000 then," he counters again.

I run my hand down my face and sputter out a laugh. *You've got to be kidding me.* "If you don't mind. I'm going to have to think about this proposal. It's a big decision."

"I understand. I can be a patient man, Dean, but the offer will only stand for a few weeks, and then I will take my business elsewhere."

"Yes, sir. Thank you. Have a nice day."

"You too."

When I get off the phone, I lean back in my chair and sigh in disbelief. I wish I could wake my dad from the dead and tell him that someone thinks I have the potential to amount to something in this town. Someone wants to see me succeed.

CHAPTER TWENTY-ONE

Sawyer

I WAKE UP to Alix's ringtone the following Sunday. "Breakfast at Moment In Thyme?"

"It's 8:45, Felix," I groan with my eyes closed. "It's my only day off. I'm sleeping in."

"No, you're not. I want some blueberry stuffed French toast, and I'm not about to go to Haley's and look like a cow while I stuff myself all alone."

"Oh my gosh, Alix. Really?" I yawn.

"Yes, really. If you'd ever had her blueberry French toast, you would understand. I'll be there in twenty minutes." The tone in her voice leaves me no choice.

"Ugh," I grunt and throw my comforter off. "Fine. But this breakfast better be worth it."

"You know Haley's food is always worth it." I hear a click, sounding the end of our conversation before I can say bye.

There's only one table available in the very back of Moment In Thyme when we walk in, so we head that way. It isn't until we're halfway to the table that I see Dean and Lily, and I want to turn around and make Alix save me, but I'm so tired of being a coward. Alix doesn't notice them until we're almost passing their table, and she pinches my arm as if I haven't already seen them.

I flinch and hiss, "Ouch!"

Dean looks up first. His eyes jump, but other than that he shows no telltale signs that he's uncomfortable. I hope he's uncomfortable.

"Dean, Lily, how are you two this morning?"

Lily lifts her head at the sound of her name. When she locks eyes with me, she's visibly uneasy. I try to keep walking, but Alix holds me in place, enjoying watching them squirm.

"Sawyer," Lily says my name, breathless. "Hi." She gets up awkwardly, her chair nearly falling backward. "It's good to see you." She's coming at me for a hug, and I know I cringe, but that doesn't stop her from putting her arms around me as if she's still the best friend I had back in high school.

I wish I could say the same. "It's good to see you, too," I lie.

"It's been a while. Like... five years?" she asks politely.

"Something like that." I attempt to smile, but I know it doesn't look like one. The last time we talked, she was trying to tell me how Dean wasn't worth any more thought. She was trying to convince me to move on with my life. She was the one that convinced me a move out of state was a good idea. And I agreed wholeheartedly. The skank was trying to eliminate the competition, as if she knew he would come back.

"Lily couldn't make y'all some breakfast on this fine Sunday morning? Her cooking can't be *that* bad, Preston," Alix taunts.

"It's always good to see you, Alix," he says with an easy

smile as he crosses his arms and calmly leans back in his chair. It doesn't go unnoticed that he doesn't answer her question.

"I wish I could say the same," Alix repeats my thoughts verbatim.

I can't possibly stand to linger here and watch them for one more second so I say, "Have a good breakfast, you guys." I grab Alix's hand to pull her away.

"Thanks," Lily mumbles with a timid smile.

"You too," Dean says.

Alix leans close to my ear. "That was probably much more fun for me than anyone else."

We situate ourselves at the far back table, my back purposefully facing the lovely couple. "You could have kept your mouth shut, and we could have walked by with the awkward I-know-you-saw-me-and-you-know-I-saw-you-but-we're-going-to-ignore-each-other-anyway scenario."

"But that would have been too easy for them. They don't deserve to be let off the hook."

I couldn't say I didn't agree with her, but I didn't want them to see that they affected me. They shouldn't affect me. Seeing them together doesn't make sense. And every time I see them, it hurts more than I want to admit.

"She's trying so hard not to look our way, but the back of your head is obviously a magnet. I guarantee they leave soon."

As if on cue, I hear the scraping of their chairs against the black and white linoleum floor.

"Cowards," she mumbles, tucking her hair behind one ear. "Oh wait, Dean's coming this way," she hisses.

My eyes bulge and my stomach drops. "What?"

She doesn't respond. Her eyes remain glued behind me as

she watches him approach. "One woman not enough for you, Preston? I'm not sure this table can help you with that."

"Alix," I hiss. I could strangle her.

She closes her mouth, pursing her lips, unrepentant as she looks between Dean and me. She's waiting for me to tell him to get lost, and though that idea is probably the right choice, I'm not going to.

"Sawyer, can I please talk to you for a minute?" he asks, ignoring Alix. As he should. His voice is firm, but somehow uncertain. He assumes I'll say no but is determined to ask me anyway.

I rub my forehead, trying to come up with a reason why I can't. But I can't come up with anything on the spot other than simply not wanting to. But that would be a lie. I can't lie to myself. I'm curious about what else he has to say, though I know I'm probably not going to want to hear it.

"Sure," I sigh. "Alix, will you give us a minute?"

She looks at me incredulously until she realizes I'm not backing out. "Fine," she concedes. "I'll go order our coffee."

"Hot chocolate for me," I say.

She gives me a funny look, but doesn't say anything more as she walks over to the counter and begins talking to Haley.

"Hot chocolate, huh?"

That's definitely not a subject I want to breech, so I nod and ask, "Won't the Missus be a little peeved you're talking to me?" I look up at him. Every time our eyes meet it feels surreal.

When you look into the eyes of the person you loved every day for years and are forced to stop cold turkey, you go through withdrawals. My body craved the touch of his gaze on me. It was never just a gaze. It was a promise of shooting stars and infinity of dandelion wishes.

"She's the one that suggested it," he admits, sitting down across from me. I'm not sure if that makes me more irritated. No, I take that back. It definitely makes me more irritated. He wasn't man enough to come on his own this time? "She thought you should know that nothing happened between us until about a year ago. I told her you probably already know that."

They've been together for an entire year? Somehow, that makes it worse. They've had a year of stolen glances and kisses and shooting stars, and oh my gosh, I think I'm going to be sick.

"I really don't care, Dean," I manage to say. I'm trying so hard to hold his gaze and remain apathetic, but it hurts so much to look in his eyes when we're this close and feel so far apart.

"Are you sure about that." It's not a question. It's a statement—a snarky one at that. I've been caught.

I pause, stunned by his audacity. "Are you kidding me? Did you really just ask me that?"

He opens his mouth, but nothing is spoken. He obviously regrets saying the words, but he can't take them back now.

"That was a really jerk thing to say."

"I didn't mean anything by it. I'm sorry. I shouldn't have said it."

I want him to leave. Being in proximity to him is torture. I don't know how to be around him. This is such new territory for us, so I have to keep telling myself that he's not my Dean anymore. He's Lily's, and I'm Grayson's. I know I can't really say that anymore, but I was his for over four years. It's hard to think of myself as anything else right now. I belonged to Grayson longer than I did to Dean. That has to mean something.

"I'm sorry, but none of this changes the fact that we should

124

talk. You may not want to, but it has to happen at some point." He pins me with a meaningful stare that I can't decipher. *What does he want hashed out? How he left me without a trace? How he lied to me? How our lives will never be the same?* I don't want part it any of it.

"No. It doesn't." Talking would require spending more time with him than I can handle. It would require hearing him tell me how much he doesn't want me all over again. It would require revealing things to each other that should stay buried. We need to keep it in the past where it belongs.

"Sawyer, I don't want it to be like this whenever we see each other. We live in the same town. We are bound to see each other often. I can't tell you how sorry I am that I hurt you. Can we please put it behind us? Forgive me. Forget about the past?"

Forget the past? I wish I could forget about the past, but it's not that simple.

I don't know why I gave Dean the power to take every part of me, because when he was gone I had nothing left. How pathetic is that? That I gave him everything I had. It took years for me to gain a part of myself back and, when I did, I gave it to Grayson. And Grayson took that part of me to the grave.

And now, here Dean stands, asking for my forgiveness, asking me to *forget,* and all I want to do is scream, '*Not until you give me back what is rightfully mine!*' I want my soul back. I want to know I'm not a shell. I want to know I can be whole again. I want to know I haven't completely disappeared.

"Fine," I say.

"Fine?"

"It's fine. I forgive you." If for no other reason than to get him off of my back. Maybe saying it will make it true. Let him go back to Lily, let him have his happily ever after. Maybe then I can finally move on if I have closure.

"Why is it that I don't believe you?" His left eyebrow arches.

"Believe what you want, but I think we're done here."

"I didn't mean to make things worse. I don't want to make things worse, Sawyer."

"You don't? Then why come and talk to me at all? I thought we already established there's nothing left to say."

He levels his stare. His temper is rising. "I think there's everything left to say. You just won't give me a chance to talk."

"I don't care. I don't care, Dean. I don't care. Please leave."

"Sawyer…" The pleading in his voice almost has me backpedaling. There's a raging war inside me. One side wants to sit here and listen to his voice, a one-sided conversation where he tells me all the things I always wanted to hear. *Lie to me. Tell me you always loved me and that you regret leaving me.* While the other side smacks me upside the head and wants to shove him out of his seat to send him flying across the linoleum floor with only his bruised pride to carry him out the door. The conflict is weighing heavily in favor of the later.

"I think she asked you to leave, Preston." I hear Alix come up behind me.

He clenches his jaw and shakes his head, but he's surrendering. "We're not done, Sawyer. You can hide in the bakery and hide in your room and hide behind Alix, but one day you'll have to talk to me. One day," he points his finger at me, "you'll have to forgive me."

"Good luck with that, champ." Alix pats him not so nicely on the back. "Out of my seat."

He gets up and lets Alix take his place. "Fine," is all he says

126

before he walks away.

I can finally breathe when the front door closes behind him.

"They really are gluttons for punishment, aren't they?" she says, sitting back down.

"Can we stop talking about them?" I look down at the menu, not really seeing anything in front of me but splotches of letters. It takes me three tries of reading chocolate chip pancakes before it actually clicks that's what I read.

"I'm sorry. I just know how much it hurts for you to see him, and it makes me mad that I can't change that."

"I can handle myself." I shift in my chair. "I'm a big girl. Let's just have some breakfast. I think I want the spinach and feta omelet."

"Savory. Good choice. I'm still going to indulge in my fluffy, buttery blueberry stuffed French toast. You'll never touch anything else in this café once you try it."

"I'll try a bite."

"You think I'm actually willing to share?" She smirks. "Who am I kidding? You have to take a bite. It's better than sex."

We're finishing up breakfast when Alix hisses, "Code red. Code red. Or is it blue? Which is worse?"

"Blue?" I question and peer over my shoulder to see who she's peeking at. Aiden. I chuckle with the shake of my head. "And I thought I was bad."

"Oh shut it. Our situations are completely different and you know it."

"Yeah. You've got it a lot easier." I smirk, and she glares, but she knows I'm right.

"You think we can get out of here without him noticing us?"

"Not likely, but we can try."

Alix leaves some cash on the table and slowly stands, moving her chair back quietly as to not let it squeak across the floor to draw attention to us.

A thought formulates in my mind. She had her fun today. I'm pretty sure it's my turn. When I get up I purposefully knock my chair back, but make it look like an accident. It clatters to the ground, and all eyes shift in our direction. Alix darts me a death glare that could knock me on my butt if it were a physical shove. I clumsily stand the chair back up and lift my shoulders as if to tell her I couldn't stop it from happening, but she's not buying it.

She dares a glance in his direction and, sure enough, we have his undivided attention. Aiden watches us with a widening half grin as he leans over the counter, stirring his coffee with a red stirring stick. His eyes wander up and down Alix, and his grin never falters even when he meets the scowl on her face, if nothing else it seems to make his smile bigger.

"I hate you so much right now," she mumbles.

"I know," I reply.

There's no way to avoid him on our way out so we head that way.

"Care to grab dinner later, Alix?" he asks. I hear the teasing in his voice and know he's waiting for her sarcastic reply.

"In your dreams, sparky," she mutters as she passes him without stopping.

"So you like the thought of me dreaming about you?" he calls.

Her hand is on the cafe door and she pauses. I see in her stance that she either wants to turn around and smack him or retort, but neither happen. She walks out the café without waiting for me.

"Hey, Aiden." I smile.

"It's good to see you, Sawyer." He lightly punches my shoulder as I walk by him.

"I'm sorry... for her."

"No need to apologize. She'll cave eventually."

I can't hold back my laughter. "You might be right, but you've got a long way to go."

"I've got time."

I wave at him as I walk out the door. "See ya, Aiden."

He nods like he's tipping a cowboy hat.

Alix is huffing and pacing outside the cafe. "It's about freaking time. Did you talk to him? What did you say to him? What did he say to you?"

"Nothing." I chuckle. "Absolutely nothing."

"It better have been nothing, or I'll hang you by that pretty long ponytail of yours."

I dramatically grab my ponytail and gasp. "Not the ponytail!" I smirk.

"I mean it." She begins to walk, and I fall into step beside her. "He's quite the charmer. He'll charm you, too. I can see he already has." She eyes me, and my amusement continues.

"You know I've always liked Aiden," I say. "He's a good kid. Am I not allowed to be friends with him?"

"No!" she snaps then reels in her temper. "I just don't want you talking about me with him."

"Okay. I promise to stay out of it," I say. I only partially mean it.

"Thank you," she huffs. "Now we've got a busy day ahead of us."

"I didn't agree to a full day here," I contend. "I agreed to breakfast."

"Well you're already out of the house. What's the sense in going back?" She links her arm through mine and tugs me toward her car.

Alix keeps me out of the house nearly all day, running errands and shopping. I don't realize it's as late as it is until she drops me off at home and it's dark. It isn't until I walk into my bedroom and draw up my covers that I realize I haven't thought about Grayson all day. I finally didn't feel like I was slowly dying inside, but it somehow guts me with guilt. How could I have forgotten him for so long so soon? Is that normal? Am I allowed to start feeling normal again? Or at least as close to normal as it gets as a widow.

CHAPTER TWENTY-TWO

MY RUN IN with Sawyer has consumed my thoughts for days. The bikes are supposed to be my solace, but I can't find that today. I really ticked her off, which was the last thing I wanted to do. It was as if my mouth couldn't help it. It kept running, spewing out stupid comment after stupid comment.

"What do you think the odds are of Alix saying yes if I were to call and ask her out?" Aiden walks over to me, wiping a dirty rag over his oily fingers. "If I sincerely ask. All jokes aside."

"I'm going to give you the benefit of the doubt and say I'm 99.9% sure she will tell you no." I stay hunched down beside the bike I'm working on. I've got to have this bike ready in an hour or this guy's repairs are free. Normally this sort of fix would take longer than I told him, but he needed it done before leaving on a trip tomorrow. I don't know why I challenge myself like this.

"That's the benefit of the doubt? Point-one percent she'll say yes?"

"I thought I was being generous." I look around the bike to see Aiden leaning against the tool bench. "I'm pretty sure there's no way she'll ever go out with you again."

"Dude."

"No." I drag my fingertips across my lips, coming up with a better analogy, one that really depicts how I think Alix feels. "I take that back. If you were the last two people on the planet, I'm pretty sure she would find a deserted island in the middle of some gulf of some ocean where you would never be able to find her."

Aiden exhales melodramatically. "You're killing me." But he starts to nod, looking confident. "Fine. Okay. I'll get her to come to me."

I choke on my laugh. "I would love to see you do that."

"I will. Just you watch." He wags his finger at me. "She'll be begging for me by the end."

"Okay, Aide. Whatever you say."

"You know a few words of encouragement would be nice. I mean you *left* Sawyer, without so much as a text message for *six* years! She got married *and* is now dealing with the loss of her husband, and I still believe in you. You can't give me anything to work with?"

My lips press together. "I don't know why you like Alix in the first place. But if it means that much to you, man, she would be an idiot not to fall at your feet. I don't doubt that you are good enough for her. I just know how stubborn that girl is, especially after what you did to her, but if anyone can tame her, it'd be you."

"Dude, you *know* Bridget and I are just friends. It was hardly a date! I took her to get shakes at Rita's because there was nothing else to do that night. Alix took it the wrong way."

"And you never explained it to her."

"She never gave me the option," he counters. "Every time I try to have a civil conversation with that woman she either flips me off or gives me a snide comment I can't help but return."

"Well, she'd be stupid to never give you the time of day. I hope it works out for you, man."

"Thank you." He nods approvingly and pats me on the back as he walks by. "Thank you, Dean. I know you really mean that."

I chuckle and grab my torque wrench to get back to work. I look at the clock on the wall. I've got forty-five minutes. "Anytime, Aide."

Lily crawls across the couch onto my lap later that night as I'm trying to relax in front of the TV. "I missed you today." She presses her lips to my cheek. "Did you have a good day?"

I don't understand how it's possible that she missed me. I saw her last night and she called me this morning. Then she called me on my lunch break. We talked for fifteen minutes.

"Rob called me again fishing for my answer. I didn't give it to him yet. He's going to give me a few more weeks. For some reason he really wants the garage, but I think I'm going to turn him down."

"You need to do what you think is right. You know I think it's an amazing offer, but you don't want to rush into a decision like that if you don't feel one hundred percent positive about it, sweetie."

I nod. I can't stand it when she calls me that, but I don't know how to tell her not to.

It's been a week since my failed attempt to talk to Sawyer at Moment in Thyme. I've walked past Sprinkles a million times, but either she's in the back or she doesn't notice me. I walk by and watch her smile at costumers. I can see a face that isn't drenched with pain or resentment.

Lily swings one leg on either side of me, straddling my lap and blocking the TV. I'm forced to look up at her before she leans in and presses her mouth to mine. Her hands loop around my neck, tugging me closer to her. There's desperation behind this kiss, and I don't understand the sudden shift in her mood, but I respond and move my lips against hers. As her lips brush across mine, her breathing picks up. What does she feel when she kisses me? Kissing Lily is nothing like kissing Sawyer.

There is nothing like kissing Sawyer.

Sawyer holds my face in her hands, grazing her fingertips along my jawline. I can't stop kissing her. Kissing Sawyer is like being set free. The chains of my life at home can't hold me down. When she kisses me, I don't feel worthless. I don't feel like I could wither away to nothing and be forgotten. But I keep hearing my dad's words. They run on repeat. She should know how pointless it is to waste her time on you.

I touch my lips to hers lightly, tasting her strawberry lip-gloss, before breaking away. "Why'd you say yes, Jack? When I asked you out. Why did you say yes to me?"

She bats her thick eyelashes at me. "It must have been your charming smile and tousled I-just-rolled-out-of-bed hair." Her fingers find my hair and massage my scalp playfully.

I lean into her touch and chuckle. "No, I'm serious. I'm such a screw up. Why take the chance to soil your reputation?"

Her eyes pierce mine with a small turn of her lips. "You're special, Dean Preston. You just haven't figured that out yet."

There's no hint of sarcasm or mockery in her voice, and it takes a moment to set in because no one has ever said anything like that to me before. If she asked me to run away with her this very instant, I would. Then I kiss her so hard I see stars. They've come out to shine for her.

I pull away from Lily with wide eyes. Her eyes are stunned and confused. Our breathing is staggered. I can't speak. This has never happened before. I don't know what I should say.

"What's wrong? Are you okay?"

I'm speechless. What am I supposed to say? *I had to stop because in that moment I wasn't kissing you. In my mind I was kissing Sawyer.* That would go over well.

"I think you should go, Lil."

"What?"

"My head is pounding." I knead my forehead. Maybe rubbing it will rub away the images. "I'm going to take some Tylenol and go to bed." I shift her off my lap and head for the kitchen.

I know she wants to say something. I can feel the tension building. It's like a hot air balloon filled my entire living room, and it's about to explode and destroy my life as it stands. She doesn't say anything, but I feel her hovering in the archway to my kitchen. I fill my glass of water and turn to her.

"Do you think you'll be okay tonight?" The question is there. It's plastered across her face, staining her eyes, but I know she's too afraid to ask what she really wants. She's not stupid. She knows I'll be honest, and she's not ready for the truth. I'm not so sure *I'm* ready for the truth. The truth could mean the possibility of actual happiness or it could mean the ruin of me, once and for all.

I nod and debate carrying on the charade, telling her I'll feel better once I get some sleep, but I keep my mouth shut.

"Okay." She walks over to me and plants a kiss on my cheek. "Goodnight, Dean."

"Night, Lil."

Once she's gone, I slide down my cabinets onto the linoleum floor and lean my head back. Aiden's right. As much as I freaking hate to admit it. I can't keep doing this. At some point this will have to end. I just don't know how.

CHAPTER TWENTY-THREE

Sawyer

I TOLD MY mom I would go to the grocery today. She always lights up when she knows I'm going out into society and not holing up in my bedroom for the entire day. I figured I'd already be in town, and I didn't have to work late today. It made sense.

I push the cart up and down the aisles, tossing things in the cart that we might need—the essentials—butter, milk, eggs. Once I get to the cereal aisle, I amble down the lane in a fog.

Grayson pulls up beside me in the cereal aisle with an empty cart. "Do you think the store clerk would be peeved if we had a cart race?"

"Gray, you are going to get us kicked out of here, and I don't have time for that. I really need milk for my cereal." It's sitting in a bowl at home, waiting to be eaten after I opened the fridge to discover we were out of milk. My biggest pet peeve.

"Well, if someone had listened to her husband last night when it was mentioned, this predicament might have been avoided."

I keep my eyes on the refrigerated section at the end of the aisle lining the back of the store. "If someone had gone last night when I asked, this midnight run could have been avoided."

"If someone had thought about it today on her day off, she might not

feel so defensive about the situation."

"I hate you so much right now," I say, trying to bite back a smile.

He chuckles. "No you don't. You love me."

"You hope I do." I grab two gallons of milk and turn to place them in my cart.

"I know you do." He brushes a kiss against my cheek and takes the milk from my hands to place them in his cart that's now filled with at least six boxes of cereal. I give him a knowing stare. "It was buy one get one free," he defends himself. "I figured you might want more cereal to go with your milk." Grayson smirks, and one of his curls falls across his forehead.

I shake my head and brush the curl back. "You're hopeless."

"Yeah. Hopelessly—"

My metal cart hits another cart as I round the aisle.

"Oh, sorry." I'm still smiling from my memory, but when I look up to see the person I hit, my chest tightens.

"Sorry, Jack." Dean returns my smile until mine falls and then his follows suit. "Er... Sawyer. I wasn't paying attention." When he says Sawyer he sounds like he's trying to speak a different language. It doesn't sound right.

I nod and steer my cart in the other direction, avoiding all eye contact. I hate his eyes. I hate their kindness and their warmth. I hate their intensity and mystery. I thought the mystery faded, but it's still there—dominating—because when I look at him now I have no idea where his head is.

I used to love his eyes. The way they changed from green to blue depending on his mood. The way they looked at me like I was something to cherish. But when I look at his eyes now I see my past, and I see what I wanted my present and future to be. I see a person who died as I watched his motorcycle speed away.

138

It's too hard to look him in the eyes now. All it does is remind me of what I lost. What we lost.

"Just doing some grocery shopping for Mrs. H, huh?" Dean's voice is behind me.

Of course he would need to go down the same aisle as me. "Small talk, really?" I say over my shoulder.

"Whatever gets you talking."

I snort and grab some bagels off the shelf, doing my best to pretend like he's not there.

"Bagels are on sale. Smart move. I'll get some, too." I hear him toss a package into his cart.

"How convenient that you needed to go down that same exact aisle as me."

"It is convenient, isn't it? Hmm."

I chuckle, but bite down on it. I don't want him to know he can still make me laugh.

I make my way up the next aisle. The wheels of his cart squeak behind me, but I don't want to look as I put more items in my cart.

"Oooh... I've always loved Cheez-Its. Good choice."

"Are you going to follow me through the entire store?"

"It's not my fault you're going down every aisle I need to go down."

We both know what he's doing, but I decide to stop reacting. For the next twenty minutes he shadows me through the store, commenting on everything I put in my cart. I do my best to ignore him. He stays a good distance away, but close enough that he doesn't have to yell everything he wants to say.

"How is Mrs. H doing, by the way?"

I sigh and bite back a smile; thankful he can't see my face.

"My mom is doing fine. I'm surprised you need to ask since you've been living back here for a few years. Shouldn't you know?"

He doesn't miss a beat. "She tends to walk in the other direction or ignore me completely whenever she sees me, like she never saw me in the first place."

I can't stifle the laugh this time.

"You would think that's funny."

"It sounds like my mom, is all."

He chuckles. "She hasn't changed. She'll probably never like me, but I've accepted that."

"Probably smart of you."

"Blaine doesn't hate me, too, does he?"

"You really want the answer to that question?"

"Probably not," he says quietly. "He's probably joined the rest of your family."

I want to tell him that no one hates him. Hate is such a strong word. They just really, really, really don't like him. Though I doubt that will come as any consolation.

He doesn't give me the chance to respond before he asks, "Is he still living in Seattle?"

"Yeah," I say, placing some cans of soup in my cart.

"Seattle must be a really awesome city for a person to move there and never want to come back to visit."

I grit my teeth stubbornly to keep from replying. It's not so much that Seattle is this grand place as it, simply put, is not Willowhaven. People aren't in your business. It's so far from here that it makes it easier to leave behind the things you want. It makes having a fresh start attainable.

When I don't answer him, Dean takes a hint. He doesn't

140

leave me alone, but we shop in silence.

After I've loaded my items on the conveyer belt at the cash register, I turn to look at the candy section, perusing a suitable choice. I feel his eyes on me, but I try not to let it affect me. Valerie is scanning my last item when I hand her a Twix.

"No Reese's Pieces?" he asks quietly, picking up a bag and putting it with his stuff on the conveyer belt.

I hand Valerie some cash and say to him, "I haven't been able to eat Reese's Pieces without getting sick to my stomach in six years."

When I look over at him, he stands motionless with eyes so dejected I want to wipe them clear. I know I have the power to, but I can't. The guilt sets in, but not enough to take it back. I turn and walk away.

I should put on an indifferent face and make him think he has no effect on me. I should pretend like what he did to me didn't completely break my heart, but I've never been good at keeping my feelings inside. My emotions might as well be tattooed on my arms since my sleeves wear them every day.

As I pass through the automatic doors at the front of the store, I make the mistake of looking over my shoulder, back at him. He's standing at the cash register. I'm pretty sure Valerie is asking him for his money, but he doesn't respond to her. Our eyes lock as he stares. My heart is heavy. My stomach is unsettled. His eyes look so sad and lost. I blink and keep walking before I give in.

CHAPTER TWENTY-FOUR

IT'S BEEN WEEKS since I saw Sawyer at the grocery store. I've decided to keep my distance. When I try to talk to her, it makes it worse. I don't want to make it worse. I want to make it right. Every effort I make gives me less and less hope she will ever forgive me.

So, I've decided focusing on Lily is the only way I can get on with my life. Three and a half years ago, she burrowed herself into my life. I wasn't sure how I felt about it in the beginning, but as years have passed, and our friendship has developed into more, I've realized she's around to stay. There's no shaking her, not that I really want to, but I haven't scared her away yet. After everything I've shared with her—things I never shared with Sawyer—she keeps coming back for more. I owe it to her to try and make this work. She gave me a chance. I want to give her one in return.

I didn't reveal every gory detail to Lily, but she got the gist. With all my secrets exposed, I feel like I can finally breathe. I peer over at her and shrug. "That was the way my dad worked."

Lily's fingers brush the tips of mine on the back of her couch. "That doesn't make it okay. He made it impossible for you to find comfort in the one thing everyone deserves."

I shrug because that's the way life was for me. I couldn't change it now. "It's not that I'm not grateful I had a roof over my head and food in the cupboards. I know lots of kids don't even get that... I just—"

"Dean, it's okay to feel resentful. I think you've earned that. Everyone deserves the right to feel safe and loved in his or her own home. You might have had a place to sleep every night, but you didn't have a home. He was a lousy excuse for a father. Don't for one second believe you deserved anything less."

I nod, looking down at the carpet. Sawyer was always the one to tell me that I was of worth. Rolling my tongue around in my mouth, I bite it. It helps to keep my emotions under control. "I don't know where to go from here. Is it twisted that as much as I hated him, I miss him?"

When she doesn't answer, I look back up at her. Tears pool in her eyes, and she bites her lips with the shake of her head. "He was your dad, Dean." She blinks the tears away. "It's okay."

"I don't know how to handle everything I'm feeling. I'm angry. I'm bitter. And I'm sad. Devastatingly sad." My fist rubs against my forehead as I look at my lap. It's hard to look at Lily after everything I confessed. I try to focus my mind on the force of my fist on my forehead. It somehow calms the tears rising behind my eyes.

Lily's hand reaches out and stops my fist from rubbing my forehead raw. She takes my hand in both of hers and scoots across the couch. She faces me with her legs crossed Indian-style. "You're allowed to be angry. You're allowed to feel bitterness. You're allowed to mourn your dad, even if he made life a living hell for you. He was still your dad, Dean." After a moment I look over at her. "But at the end of it all, you have to let it go. It's not important anymore. Because he's gone, you are now free from his hold over you. Your potential is limitless. You get a second chance at life to go and be

143

whatever you want to."

"I'm not sure that I know how to do that."

She lets a trace of a smile form on her lips. "Well, then it's a good thing you have me."

I open my front door to see Lily with a picnic basket. "Hungry?"

"I could eat." I smile and pull her in for a kiss.

"Oh," she says against my mouth, and I feel her smile. Her arms loop around my neck, and she stands on her tiptoes to bring us closer to the same height. We break apart and she sighs. "Hi."

"Hi." I kiss her once more.

"I thought we could head to the park and have a picnic. It's a really nice day. The leaves are beginning to change."

"Sounds good to me." I nod and put her down. "Let me go grab the keys to my truck."

When we get to the park, I follow Lily with the picnic basket in my hands. Lily decides where we're going to sit and fans out the blanket. It happens to be under the willow Sawyer and I spent nearly every week under during our junior and senior year. The drooping branches have faded to a yellowy green. It stops me from walking closer. I almost ask her if we can move, find any other tree to sit under, but I don't have a good enough excuse in mind. Nothing I can say will keep her from raising suspicion. And though nothing's a secret between Lily and me, I don't need to rub her face in my memories of Sawyer.

I help her straighten out the flannel blanket, and she kneels down with a bounce. "I brought sandwiches and some fruit." She reaches into the basket and pulls out Tupperware filled with grapes and different kinds of melon. "I figured we could both use the boost with something healthy. We've been eating out so much recently."

I have to remind myself that she's trying to watch out for me, but it's becoming increasingly difficult. I like my junk food. I want Twinkies and potato chips. I want fried chicken and donuts. Toss in a bag of Reese's Pieces, and I'm set.

"Thanks, Lil," I say, because she's trying to be thoughtful.

We sit and eat in peace, watching people walk by. She starts talking about the most recent girl drama, and I immediately feel myself tuning her out, simply nodding my head when it's seems like the right time. I don't know how long she goes on. I finish my sandwich and pick at the grapes. She picks one up and holds up her hand, waiting for me to open my mouth. A smile turns her lips when she tosses it and misses my mouth completely. I tried to shift to the side to catch it, but she has horrible aim. We laugh and her rambling starts again, but this time I try to listen.

"Nicki can't figure out what James wants. One minute he's all over her, proclaiming love and marriage proposals, and the next he shuts down entirely and acts like she doesn't exist. It doesn't make sense. She thinks he's seeing someone else behind her back, but that doesn't seem like James to me, but what do I know…"

Yup. Nope. Can't do it. I don't care about Nicki. And James and I have never been friends, so I haven't got a clue what's floating around in his head. I'm not sure what she wants from me. I've got nothing.

The pond is placid today. The greenish-blue water shines like glass. It's interesting to think of what's going on underneath the surface. The top looks so calm, but underneath, creatures are

145

trying to survive. Algae festers. A whole other world exists. It reminds me of Sawyer. She tries to remain composed on the outside, but I know there's a world of emotions going on underneath the surface. Wind courses through the park and ripples the top of the water slightly.

I'm brought back to Lily when I hear her say, "Aww, look. It's a dandelion." She plucks the dandelion growing near the edge of blanket. "We should make a wish. What should we wish for?" she asks.

There are so many things I could wish for, so many things that if a wish could make them come true, my life would be set right again. I look from the dandelion to Lily with her smiling eyes. Sunlight glimmers through the willow branches, lightening the blonde in her hair that falls across her face. She really is beautiful. What could she possibly want to wish for? Life seems good to her. Anything that tries to knock her down hasn't gotten the chance to leave its mark. She won't let it. I admire her for that. I wish I could say the same about myself.

The sun flickers through the willow tree above us. The park is quiet today. We decided to come here after school because it's always less busy on weekdays. Sawyer's finger idly traces the tattoo on the inside of my arm.

"What if I don't have time to wait for a shooting star?" I ask.

"You've got a big wish, huh?" Sawyer shifts on her side to look at me. "Well, no matter how simple or complex, I think the dandelion can handle it." She peers at me from under her thick eyelashes and picks a dandelion sprouting between us. "She may look fragile, but all this white fuzz that blows away will plant its seed and start over again. Wherever it lands, a new dandelion will grow. She'll get a new beginning."

"How did you get to be so wise?" I roll onto my side to face her and

hold myself up on my elbow.

"I've wished on a lot of dandelions throughout my life." She holds up the dandelion with a smile, offering hope for something better.

I lean in to kiss her lips and then inhale deeply before blowing away the fluff. It drifts with the wind and eventually flies away, disappearing into the sky. I can feel Sawyer's eyes on me so I peer over at her.

"What did you wish for?" she asks.

"Do you believe if you tell someone your wish it won't come true?"

"That's a common misconception, in my opinion," she says with playful authority.

The corner of my mouth turns up. I want to kiss her, but I know if I do, I won't stop, and I really want to hear what she has to say. "And why do you think that?"

"I believe in positive affirmations. If you say something out loud or write it down, it's more likely to happen. You're more likely to make it happen."

"What if it's out of my control?" I ask seriously.

"Then saying it out loud can only help. If you can't control it, I don't believe saying it will make it any less possible. But, you don't have to tell me if you don't want to, Dean. I understand if it's personal or if you want to protect the sacred nature of wish making." Her eyes tease me, but hold their softness.

I pause before responding. Looking down at the short green blades between us, I pick at the grass. Sawyer's fingers push back the hair in my eyes asking with their touch for me to look at her. "I wished that my mom would come back."

Her eyes glide over my face and stop when they meet mine again. "That couldn't wait for the stars? Did you get in another fight with your dad?" she asks carefully.

I nod once and look over my shoulder toward the sky. "I know my

147

mom left for a reason. I can't blame her for not wanting to stay with him. I just don't understand why she didn't take me with her, you know?" My eyes shift back to Sawyer, and her deep brown eyes clench my heart. "At the same time, I can't say that I wish she did."

"Why?"

"Because then I wouldn't have you in my life. And you make up for what she lacked. You make everything better." I shrug.

Sawyer looks at me sadly, but with no pity. I can't pinpoint what it is because no one has ever looked at me the way she does. "I love you, Dean Preston," she says. "You know that, right?" Her fingers graze my jaw and brush my chin with tenderness.

"I know, and I don't know what I did to deserve it."

She shrugs and simply says, "You're you."

"Do you have your wish ready?" Lily's bright blue eyes sparkle under the sunrays that are seeping through the branches. Her smile widens, encouraging me to make it a good one.

I nod, and she leans her head forward, bringing the dandelion between us so we can blow on it at the same time. I think twice about this. Lily and I don't make wishes on dandelions. Sawyer and I do. I feel like I'm cheating on Sawyer, which is a ridiculous thought. I know it's childish. Adults don't make wishes on dandelions, but if I'm going to make wishes on dandelions with anyone, it's going to be Sawyer.

Lily takes a deep breath and exhales. I watch as the white fuzz flies with the breeze.

"Hey… you didn't make a wish," she pouts.

"I did," I assure her. "I just let you blow it away."

Not a day goes by that I don't wish I could go back in time.

CHAPTER TWENTY-FIVE

Sawyer

"I'VE GOT MY little brother's soccer game today," Alix says when she picks me up. "I told him I would stop by for a little bit before we go shopping."

"That's fine," I say, buckling my seatbelt. "Your mom going to be there?"

"She said she would stop by toward the end." It's apparent in Alix's voice that she doesn't think she'll show, but I don't comment on it. It wouldn't be anything new for her mom to bail on something like this. Not because she doesn't care, but because she's so flighty.

I didn't realize soccer was such a big deal in Willowhaven. Nearly every elementary aged kid is signed up. There are four different games going on. Alix and I walk to the last marked field and sit on a blanket. Alix's brother, Brooks, is with all his teammates. When he sees us, he waves with the biggest grin on his face. I peer at Alix and see her return the smile, packing it with as much love as she can.

My eyes wander around the field until they spot the last person I would expect to see there. What confuses me more is the clipboard in his hand and all the little soccer players huddled around him. He wears a dark blue baseball cap with black Ray-bans and is instructing the boys.

My forehead furrows. "Is Dean one of the soccer coaches?"

Alix shifts her gaze across the field. "Ah man, I didn't realize Brooks would be playing against his team today."

"So, you knew that he coached?" The huddle breaks and runs onto the field.

Dean shouts, "Go get 'em, boys!"

"He's been doing it for the last couple seasons," Alix mutters.

Weird. I'm more baffled than annoyed that he's here. It seems so out of character for him. I knew he liked soccer, but when I attempted to convince him to tryout for the soccer team our senior year you would have thought I asked him to commit murder. Dean and extracurriculars didn't mix. He once told me his after school activities included his bike, music, and me. I get up and find myself walking toward him before I think about what I'm doing.

"Hey, where are you going?" Alix calls, but I don't answer.

I meander through the parents and onlookers around the soccer field and wind up right next to Dean. He does a double take when he sees me.

"Hey, Sawyer," he says, perplexed.

"You coach soccer?"

"Looks that way, doesn't it?" He hollers something to one of his little players on the field, but I'm too lost to catch what he's saying.

"Since when do you know how to coach soccer?"

He peers at me from the corner of his eye, but keeps his focus on the game. "Since always."

"Well, I knew you liked to play for fun, but I hadn't realized you knew it well enough to coach it. And after the last time I saw you on a soccer field I figured you'd want to stay far away."

He grimaces, but ignores my last comment. "Learn something new every day, don't ya?" He shouts something to a player named David. "But it's a league for eight year olds, Sawyer, not professionals. I think I can handle it."

"I didn't know you liked kids."

He chuckles. "You seem to know very little about me, all things considered."

"Why do you think I'm so confused?"

"Well, as you said, people change." He calls out some words of encouragement to a few of his other players. "It's been six years, Sawyer. There are probably a lot of things about me you don't know anymore. But I'm not the one dead set on keeping the silent treatment going." He turns to me. Though sunglasses shield his eyes, I know what his gaze is portraying. It's smug.

"There's a difference between the silent treatment and knowing a pointless conversation when you see one. No sense in wasting words on something that won't change a thing."

"Is that what you think? That if we have an actual conversation about us that it won't change a thing?"

"I don't think. I know. And there is no us. That died a long time ago."

"Then why are we having this conversation right now?" he counters. I stare at him without a witty retort. He bows his head lower, near my ear and softly says, "Now, who's scared?"

I shiver. Gritting my teeth against his lure, I walk away. *How did I get myself in that conversation anyway?*

"Good talkin' to ya!" Dean hollers.

My rational thought kicks back in. Why I thought going over and talking to him was a good idea, I don't know. Carrying on a conversation with him will lead to more frustration and heartache.

"What were you talking about?" Alix asks when I drop down on the blanket next to her.

"Nothing," I say shortly.

"Looked like a lot more than nothing. Why did you go over to him?"

"I have no idea," I grumble and watch the players run up and down the green field chasing the black and white ball.

"Seems like a legit reason." Out of the corner of my eye, I see her nodding and I chuckle.

"Shut up."

I can't stay focused on the game. My eyes keep straying to Dean. Half of the time he's watching his players—calling out direction and praise—the other half he's watching me. He might be wearing sunglasses, but I can tell. His lips turn up in a small smirk every time our gazes meet and I turn away. I want to leave, but I've already made Alix do that once because of him, and I can't do that to Brooks. Alix and I are the only ones here to support him.

We end up staying for the whole game. Brooks' team wins. They jump and throw their fists in the air as they run off the field, giving each other high fives and fist bumps. I look over to Dean's team on the opposite side of the field. He high fives every one of his players as they walk off the field with their heads hanging low. As soon as they see his smile, they light up and high five him. He tells them what a good job they did and how proud he is of them. It makes me think about a younger Dean, a Dean who probably never heard those words. My heart flutters rapidly in my chest and tears start to prick my eyes. *What the crap is happening to me?* I blink to clear them, thankful my sunglasses hide my expression.

When the last player passes him, he looks up and catches me staring. I stand there for a moment in a daze. He looks so handsome, and I want to run to him and hug him for being so sweet with his little players. They lost, and he's treating them as if they've won. He lifts the corner of his mouth up in a crooked smile and my knees buckle. Refusing to smile, I set my jaw and turn to find Alix. She's hugging her brother and telling him how awesome she thinks he is. I don't see their mom anywhere in sight. It doesn't surprise me, and I'm glad we stayed the entire time, even if it meant I had to be in the same place as Dean for an extended period of time.

CHAPTER TWENTY-SIX

Dean

BRADEN IS THE last one off the field. I give him my last high five and pat him on the back. He played really hard today. I know he was trying his best to make that last goal, but it wasn't meant to be. We'll get 'em next time.

When I look up, Sawyer and I get caught in another staring match. If only I knew what she was thinking. It stung a little that she thought I didn't have it in me to be good with kids. Her surprise was a little insulting. I realize it wasn't a hot topic of conversation when we were together, but I thought she knew me better than that. And I don't know why I'm surprised she brought up the last time we were on a soccer field. That was the last mistake I ever made, and my right hand is still struggling with the aftermath. I flex my fingers subconsciously.

Dustin Hale scores the winning goal to break the tie. After the ball hits the net he turns and pounds his chest like thinks he's Tarzan. "In your face, Preston! You don't mess with state champs! We will own you!" He does a back flip and pumps his fist in the air. I exhale to keep myself in check and roll my eyes before walking off the field.

"Oh c'mon, Preston, too butt hurt to take the loss like a man? You're

just gonna walk away?"

I toss a wave, but don't turn to acknowledge him. He doesn't need any more encouragement to be a prick. "It was just a game, Hale."

I meet Sawyer on the sidelines where Josh and Aiden are drinking Gatorade to cool down. She offers a small smile. "You were really great out there. I'm impressed. You should have been on the team."

I shrug. "I just want to play for fun. I'm not much for team sports," I say and kiss her.

"Hey, Preston," Dustin hollers. I breathe to keep my cool. I can only imagine what's coming next. "Did you hear your mom is back?"

My heart leaps, but my stomach has the opposite effect. I keep my face straight, turning to see Dustin smirking, tossing the soccer ball up in the air and catching it as he walks toward us. He's always been a sore winner, but I don't know where he's going with this.

"I thought the way I scored with her last night would top this win, but she didn't feel nearly this good."

A dark fog engulfs me. I don't hear, see, or feel anything around me but my fist meeting Dustin's face. It all happens within a matter of seconds. One moment I'm standing in front of him, the next I'm kneeling over his body wailing on him. Nothing else plays through my mind expect for retaliation.

Strong arms pull me back as people shout my name. I try to wretch free, but their hold tightens. Sawyer comes into view, but I don't hear a thing that's coming out of her mouth. My sights are set on the douchebag being picked up off the ground by his buddies. He wipes his mouth and spits blood, cursing at me, but I don't hear any of it. I want another shot to tear him to shreds.

"Dean. Dean. Hey." Sawyer places her small hands on either side of my face. "Hey, look at me. Look at me," she says carefully, stroking my jaw. "Dean, you with me? Hey." With my teeth grinding, I breathe through

155

my nose and shift my stare to Sawyer.

Worry spreads across her face, and I blink away my rage.

"Hey, there you are." She smiles gently as if she didn't just see me beat the tar out of that kid. "He's not worth going to jail for. Will you breathe with me?" She inhales through her nose and exhales out her mouth. I watch her take a couple breaths and feel her chest rising and falling against my body, then I imitate the motions. Her brown eyes peer up at me with tenderness, and my anger slowly dissipates.

"I'm sorry," I say and the solid arms holding me back loosen.

"I've got this guys." She nods to the guys behind me, whom I can only assume are Josh and Aiden. They step back.

She shakes her head at me. "He said some lousy things, but you're back now." Her lips press softly against mine. "You scared me there for a minute." The tone in her voice is meant to be light, but it's laced with fear.

"I know. I'm sorry." The shame floods inside of me. She was never supposed to see this side of me. I thought I had it under control for her. It was the pledge I made to myself when we started dating—if I get to have Sawyer in my life, I'd leave fighting behind. My one clean year is now soiled. "Jack, I'm so sorry."

Sawyer takes my right hand, bringing my knuckles to her mouth and kisses around the broken skin. "Is your hand okay?"

"I just tore that kid apart and you're worried about my hand?"

"If I had the strength, I would have taught Dustin a lesson for you." That thought both worries me and amuses me. "Though I don't necessarily think violence is the answer, I see why what he said broke you."

Her understanding deepens my shame. I know she's just trying to make me feel better, and I don't understand why. She deserves so much better than me. "I promise never again. That was my last fight. Never again will I let that side take hold of me."

"Okay. I'll help you. We'll do this together."

156

Sawyer's long waves cascade over her shoulders, and it takes everything in me to stay on my side of the field. I ache to feel her hands on my face again, to have her look at me the way she used to. My fingers long to run through her hair, to brush it back from her face and take off her sunglasses so I can see all of her. My mouth turns up at the thought.

Her jaw clenches before she severs our connection and walks over to Alix and Brooks. With a sigh, I turn back to my team for our post-game talk. They hold their Gatorade, ready and waiting for some words of advice from their coach. I look over my shoulder at Sawyer once more. She bumps Brooks' fist with hers and ruffles his hair. Brooks tries dodging her hand and they laugh.

This is how it has to be—living our lives apart.

"Hey, sweetie," Lily greets when I answer my phone. "I've got a plumbing issue. Do you think you could come take a look at it?"

"Sure thing. Just let me finish up at work and I'll head over there." It's a little after six. We just closed up.

"Wonderful. Thank you! So, like seven?"

"Yeah. I should probably shower first, too, so like seven-ish."

"I'll have some dinner ready for you."

"Sounds good."

"I love you," she says sweetly.

It gets caught in my throat on its way up, but I force it out. "Love you, too."

157

When I get to Lily's the door it's locked, so I knock. She opens the door with disappointment written all over her features. "Why did you knock? You have a key now, remember?"

I didn't forget. I didn't feel comfortable using it. "Right." I nod. "Guess I'm not used to that yet."

"Well, let me close and lock the door so you can use it."

"Lil, that's silly." I step in past her with my tools in hand, placing a kiss on her cheek. She doesn't conceal her disappointment well. "What's the problem?"

She recovers and says, "I'm having issues with my kitchen sink. I think it's the garbage disposal. The water is taking forever to drain."

She follows me into the kitchen, and I take a look around. I turn on the faucet and run the garbage disposal. I hear the disposal running, but she's right. It's not draining properly.

While I do my thing, she busies herself in the kitchen, finishing up dinner. It takes about twenty minutes, but I get everything working as it should. "Good as new."

"Thanks, hun." Her arms wrap around my neck, and she kisses me. I kiss her back and search for more. I want to get lost in her touch. There have been countless times where she's attempted to make me forget—forget my past, forget my dad, forget Sawyer—but it has yet to happen. I wish it could. I wish *she* could.

After we break apart she gets our dinner together, piling food for me on my plate. We sit down and eat at the round table in the octagonal nook of her kitchen. We've done this numerous times before. It should feel like an everyday happening, but I've never been able to feel at home in her house. It's Lily's house, not mine, no matter how hard I try to imagine us together in it.

"So, I'm going to be doing a little makeover in my house." She lifts her fork like a wand and waves it around the space. "What color do you think I should do the kitchen?"

I look at the deep red walls around us and feel them closing in on me. "Something lighter, maybe?"

Her eyebrows scrunch together and then she starts to nod. "Yeah… I like that idea. Maybe a pale gray or cream?"

I shrug and take a bit of mashed potatoes. "They both sound good to me."

"If it was your house, what would you want it to be?"

She's insinuating more, but I'm not sure what yet. "Umm… I like gray. Gray's a good color. Goes with everything."

With a twinkle in her eyes, she smiles. "Maybe a light bluish gray? That could be pretty."

"Sure." It's not my house, so I don't really care.

"I want to make this a house you could call home someday."

Lily and I never talk about *someday*. I should have assumed with the key this was coming, but I never thought that far. I'm still trying to get my head wrapped around the key I never plan on using.

"I think you have good judgment, Lil. Whatever you like will be perfect." Making decisions based upon what I think could lead to disaster. I hardly know what tomorrow will bring. I'm barely entertaining the thought that she could be my future. Things can always change.

"But I want your input," she says, trying to encourage me.

"I gave it to you. I like gray, but for now, this is your house. You might hate gray. Do what you think will look best. I know it'll look good no matter what."

159

That seems to appease her a little, but I can't erase the disappointment that refuses to leave her eyes. She smiles delicately, and we finish our dinner chatting about mindless subjects that don't affect our future.

CHAPTER TWENTY-SEVEN

Sawyer

MY PHONE BEGINS to ring, but Alix is with me, so I look at the screen to see who it might be. Blaine's name flashes across the screen with a picture of him sticking out his tongue at me. I silence it and set it back down.

"Who is it?"

"My brother," I try to sound casual.

"You still avoiding him?"

"Who says I'm avoiding him?"

"The ignore button you just hit."

"He knows how I'm doing. I'm letting him off the hook. I'm doing him a favor, really. This way he can call and look like the caring brother without having to deal with the baggage. My mom tells him what's up."

"Your mom doesn't know what's up. I don't think you know what's up."

"Don't I?"

"No."

"Don't I?" I ask again, deflecting the topic.

"I'm not playing this game with you."

"I'm not playing this game with you."

"Well, obviously not, since I don't know what game you're talking about," I say, flipping the channels on Blaine's TV.

"The game of avoidance, Soy," he replies as he walks from the couch to his kitchen. "Someone moved here. She looks like my sister. She talks like my sister. But she doesn't act like my sister."

I gasp with exaggeration and turn around to lean over the back of the couch. "I'm truly offended."

He chuckles. "Shut up. No you're not, and you know why? Because you know it's true. You're merely buying more time to explain to me what in the world happened to you."

Dean happened. "You know what happened," I say evenly. *At least you know part of it.*

"Well, you've been living in my house for a few weeks now. And don't get me wrong, I love having you, but I want my little sister back. Can you please go find her?"

"Fine. But only because you asked so politely. I'm waiting to hear back from some places where I dropped off job applications, and then I'll be out of your hair."

Blaine braces his hands on his countertop, gazing at me across the open space. "I don't want you out of my hair, Soy. I just want you back to normal."

"Normal is such a relative term. I think it's open to interpretation."

"Fine. Interpret this." Blaine breaks out into a flailing modern interpretive dance across his kitchen and I burst out laughing.

"Maybe that should have been your true career path. Law doesn't really suit you, spaz."

"The modern dance world isn't ready for all of this." He continues dancing none too gracefully, and I fall back against the couch in a fit of laughter, momentarily forgetting about the past.

162

"Janna is having a Halloween party tonight. Go with me."

"Hey," I say, shooting guns at her with my fingers, "that sounds exactly like the last thing I want to do."

"Oh c'mon, Sawyer," she whines. "We'll get to dress up and have so much fun!"

If she thinks dressing up is the selling point, she's sorely mistaken. "Felix, I haven't worn a costume since we were fifteen and dressed up like the Spice Girls. And even then I thought we were getting too old."

"That costume rocked and you know it!"

I laugh, shaking my head. Those costumes were pretty legit, but that was back then. This is now. I'm twenty-five years old. That inner-child in me died a long time ago.

"Everyone is going to be dressing up so if we don't we'll look like the idiots."

"You didn't give me any notice that she was having the party, and I didn't say I would go."

"First of all, I didn't tell you so you wouldn't get a chance to mull it over and back out or last minute find something that was *obviously* so much more important that there was no way you could miss it. And secondly, I'm not giving you a choice now."

"Why do I feel like that's been happening a lot lately?"

"Because you've given me no choice but to force you into fun things since Grayson—" she cuts herself off and stares blankly at me with a gaping mouth. It's not as if she's the most sensitive person around, but for some reason, putting Grayson and died in the same sentence is too much for her. Have I mentioned how much I hate that word? Died. But I can't say he passed away. That makes it sounds like it was natural. But he didn't just pass away peacefully in his sleep. His life was brutally

163

taken from him. He did die.

"Fine," I give in to keep her from saying it and/or keep her from apologizing for almost saying it. "Ugh. I can't believe I'm agreeing to this. What am I supposed to dress up as?"

Her eyebrows raise suggestively, and I fear for my life.

Alix and I walk up the steps to Janna's house, and I'm positive someone vomited Halloween all over it. Orange and black lights decorate all the trees and bushes. Carved pumpkins line the walkway. Ghost and witch cutouts dot the lawn and peek out from behind fake rickety fences. A tall coffin leans against the corner of the entrance with Dracula inside, blood dripping from the corner of his mouth. It's all very cliché and *so* Janna.

"You're not allowed to leave my side tonight. Not like Sole Fest. And I swear if I catch a glimpse of Dean, I'm out of here. No buts about it."

"Okay, fun sucker." She rolls her eyes.

"Say that ten times fast. I doubt you'll come up with the words you intended on saying."

The front door swings open, and we're met with high-pitched squealing. Janna stands there in a skanky bunny outfit with her hands wildly waving in the air.

"You guys!" She surges forward and grabs Alix and me in an overwhelmingly snug hug. "I'm so glad you two came! It feels like high school all over again! Gang's all here!" she squeals again.

My ears are bleeding.

"Hey, Janna," we say in unison.

Janna grabs my shoulders. "Sawyer, you're simple and gorgeous as always. Cat. So classic."

Alix wanted us to relive the Spice Girl days, but I managed to convince her that a black cat was much more age-appropriate. Or rather, I told her it was cat or nothing. I wore black leggings and a black tee with black ears. She dotted my nose with a black marker and painted whiskers on my cheeks. Then she proceeded to tell me I had to wear black high heels and keep my hair down so she could curl the ends. *It completes the ensemble.* Whatever that means. I'm a freaking cat.

"And Alix, Rosie the Riveter. So you! I swear you girls haven't changed a bit!"

I'm about to tell Alix I'm out when Janna finally invites us in. "There's drinks and snacks in the kitchen and games going on in every room. I think there's poker and ping-pong, and I know a bunch of the guys started a game of pool in the basement. Dance party is in the living room. So, fan out and have fun! If you need anything, let me know!"

Janna is right. It does feel like we're in high school all over again, and I'm not a fan.

"There's a reason Janna throws parties and we don't," I mumble.

"I forgot how over the top she can be," Alix whispers back. "But we don't have to hang out with her all night. Let's go get a drink."

I nod.

I hadn't realized the town still consisted of all these people. We weave through bodies mingling and dancing. There has to be at least a hundred people in this house. Some I recognize from high school, but some must be from the town over.

Once we grab our drinks, we head for the living room. A couple of people acknowledge me with a wave or head nod, but unlike Janna, the majority of the people I went to school with are doing what they can to avoid me. They can't figure out what to say to the girl with the dead husband. 'Hey,' wouldn't be so bad. They don't even have to ask me how I'm doing. I wouldn't tell them the honest truth anyway—not that they actually want it.

Alix and I dance with a group of girls we used to play volleyball with. They acknowledge me with warm smiles and pretend like I don't actually have a dead husband. I'm okay with that for tonight. It's Halloween. I should get to be whoever the heck I want to be for one night. I decide tonight I'm going to toss my problems to the side. They don't exist. I'm not Sawyer. Tonight I'm... a cat. Okay, for name's sake let's say I'm Catwoman. I'm fierce and sexy and couldn't care less about the peons around me.

"Dang, Sawyer, you make black look good," a voice murmurs near my ear.

I turn to see Garrett Walker, a guy I went to school with from kindergarten through our senior year. I wouldn't say we were friends, but we weren't not friends. We hung out in the same crowd. Exchanged 'heys' and 'how's it goings?' but nothing more than that.

"Thanks?"

"You don't look like you just lost your husband. It's been what, a month?"

Wow. You have no social skills whatsoever. Now I know exactly why we weren't friends. "Eight, actually."

He nods like I said something really interesting. He must be hammered.

"Garrett!" Alix hollers. He bobs his head to say hey to her and she says, "Get lost."

He backs away with his hands in the air. "Just wanted to say hey to my old friend, Sawyer, here, but all right."

"I don't care. Leave," she asserts, and he does as he's told.

"Thanks," I mutter.

"Anytime."

We continue to dance and get lost in the music, until I hear Janna squealing again. I peer through the archway into her foyer to see who she's welcoming now and wish I hadn't. I was just easing back into my easy fantasy world as Catwoman. Why couldn't my fantasy world last a little bit longer? Lily walks in with Dean in tow, and my heart surges. I'm instantly back in high school.

Dean didn't do his hair. It's falling across his forehead, a mixture of shaggy and bedhead. His jeans are a little tighter, and he's wearing one of his old Blink 182 t-shirts with black converse. His wrist has a thick leather band wrapped around it, and he even shaved, leaving a faint five-o'clock shadow. He looks just as lost as he did when he used to walk through the halls of our high school.

"You're a rocker! I *love* it, Dean!" Janna's voice is only partially drowned out by the blaring music.

He's not a rocker. He's Dean from six years ago.

Across the crowded hallway our eyes meet, but it's as if no one else exists. An impish smile tugs the corner of his lips as he tucks his hands into the front pockets of his black jeans. Through the years I've only seen him with two people: Josh and Aiden. Dean doesn't easily let anyone in, but he let me in. Being his exception makes me believe that even the most seemingly

167

impossible relationships can last. If we're willing to try, we could last forever.

We meet halfway, and he takes my face tenderly in his hands, kissing my lips before I say anything. Everything else disappears. It's always that way with Dean. He has the power to make me forget girl drama and petty fights with my brother—things that don't actually matter. He gives me perspective.

"Somehow I'm lucky enough to get to kiss this mouth," he says against my lips.

"Funny. That's what I was thinking."

Dean smirks and kisses me once more. "I'm going to help Aiden with some yard work at his grandparents after school, but then I was thinking we could take a ride on my bike. It's going to be a perfect evening for a cruise."

"All right, Romeo. Just toss a pebble at my window. I'll be waiting." I wink.

"You did not just call me Romeo."

"If the shoe fits."

He barks out a laugh. "That's been my problem my whole life. I've been wearing the wrong shoes."

"Just needed little ol' me in your life to get you the right ones," I say, using my best Southern accent and trace the band logo on the front of his shirt.

His amusement continues as he shakes his head at my ooey-gooey cheesy lines. "Where do you get these lines? You're too much sometimes."

"But you can't resist me." I lace my fingers behind his neck.

His arms tighten around my waist. "I won't dispute that."

Once more, his mouth takes control of mine and I let the kiss pull me under.

I feel faint as though he's pulling me under now. My legs waver like I'm floating in water. They could give way at any

168

moment. "Sawyer." I hear the alarm in Alix's voice when she steadies my arm. "Sawyer, you okay?"

Dean's eyes drift over the crowd, landing on me, and it's a shot to my heart. His gentle smolder has me captured. I can't breathe. He's *my* Dean. *No!* But he's not. Lily's latched onto his right arm, leaning her head against his shoulder in a frilly fairy costume. It feels so wrong—my stomach churns with nausea—I'm going to throw up.

"Sawyer, you don't look so good." Alix stands in front of me, blocking my view of Dean. I let my eyes focus on her and blink.

"I think I'm gonna be sick."

She instantly links her arm with mine, resting her hand on my elbow and leads me to the front door, toward Dean. *No, no, no.* Why hasn't she seen him yet? I try to stop her, but I don't have the strength in my legs to stop with enough force. He's watching me with worry and confusion. It's almost as if he wants to take a step forward, to reach out to me. I equally want him to and know I couldn't take it if he did.

"Alix," I finally find my voice, but it doesn't matter. She's placed him lingering in the entryway and immediately understands my unease. We halt in place.

"Holy emo Preston, Batman." She mutters a few other choice words under her breath, echoing my unspoken sentiments. "I think we just went back in time."

"Alix," I warn. The churning in my stomach is making its way up, and the last thing I need is to make a bigger scene by upchucking all over everyone around us. I wrap my arm around my torso and try to keep it down.

Her head turns to me, trying to get me to focus on her.

169

"C'mon. You need air. The front door is closer. I'm sorry." She tugs my hand, and we skirt passed them without a word. Dean makes like he's going to offer his help, but he doesn't. His hand hovers outstretched by his side, the slightest effort to touch me. He watches us as we go and thankfully doesn't say a thing.

CHAPTER TWENTY-EIGHT

LILY AND JANNA continue talking at my side about who knows what. They didn't notice Sawyer stumbling out, though it was hard to miss her. Or maybe it was hard for me to miss her. There are like a thousand people in this place and the music is blaring through the roof.

I should go after her and make sure she's all right. She'll probably spit in my face. I know I'm the last face she wants to see, but I have to go to her. What if something is really wrong? I'd never forgive myself if I could have done something to help. The battle in my head ends when I make up my mind. I know she's not mine to take care of anymore, but I guess some instincts never fade.

"I'll be right back," I say to Lily.

I don't wait for her to respond before I'm out the door. I close it behind me and jog down the stairs.

Sawyer is bent over near the bottom of the stairs, puking into the bushes. At least she sounds like it. I'm not sure if anything is actually coming up. All I hear are her dry heaves. Her dark silhouette retches forward. Alix is standing over her, rubbing her back and holding her hair out of the way. I don't think. I go.

"Is she okay?"

Alix looks up, and as soon as she realizes it's me, her eyes narrow. "Does she look okay to you, Preston?"

I bite my tongue, though a million things run through my head to snap at her. "Is there something I can do? Do you need me to take her home?" Alix grimaces. "If you want to stay and party, I wouldn't mind taking her."

"I'm sure you wouldn't," Alix retorts.

"Felix, shut it," Sawyer mumbles and slowly stands up straight, wiping her mouth with the back of her hand. She takes a breath. "I'm fine, Dean. You can go back to the party."

She won't look at me. She's blatantly refusing to as she tugs on her clothes and tries to fix her hair. She fluffs it forward, letting her long curls drape over one of her shoulders. I so badly want to reach out and run my hand through those curls. She looks so beautiful. I know she was puking her guts out, and I should be disgusted, but she's beautiful. Her skin looks porcelain under the moonlight, and her brown eyes deepen in the dark.

"I wanted to check on you. You didn't look so good. Was it something you ate or drank?"

She winces and shakes her head but finally looks up at me. When she does, the frown I've become accustomed to is absent from her face. She looks puzzled, but she meets my stare. Her eyes glide over me for a few moments, taking in my appearance from head to toe, and then her eyes droop in sadness.

"Wow," she breathes. It probably wasn't something she meant to say or wanted me to hear. I don't know what she means by it. 'Wow,' like, I can't believe this idiot is still trying? Or 'wow,' like, she appreciates the way I look. She wouldn't think

172

that. Not now. Her head shakes again as if she can't believe what she's seeing. I don't get it. Then Alix bows her head near Sawyer's ear and whispers something. Sawyer nods and blinks, looking away from me.

"Thanks for your concern, Preston, but I'll take it from here." Alix reaches around Sawyer's waist to lead her to the car, but Sawyer pushes away from her grasp.

"I'm fine. I can do it myself," she mutters adamantly and puts one foot in front of the other. She's not steady, but she doesn't look unstable. I repress my instinct to go to her and lift her in my arms to carry her home. I clench my hands into such tight fists my short nails dig into my palms.

"Thanks, Dean," Sawyer mumbles over her shoulder, but refuses to look at me as they walk away.

I don't say anything else as I watch them go down the lamp-lit street and out of my sight.

"Where did you go?" Lily lifts up on her toes and kisses my cheek. "I missed your face."

I find her mingling with some of her friends on the outskirts of the living room. I can tell her the truth, but I don't want to hurt her feelings or start anything tonight. "Someone left looking pretty sick, so I went to see if there was anything I could do." It was the truth, just not the whole truth.

"That was nice of you."

I shrug and don't answer. She lets it go. Her friends continue talking, and I stand there wondering what happened. Sawyer seemed so disoriented. If I didn't know any better, I

173

would have thought she was drunk, but she's never had a drink in her life. Though, we've already established that people change.

Aiden finally shows up with some girl I've never seen before, but at least now I'm not completely alone. I seriously considered peacing out almost immediately after Sawyer left. I can lie to everyone else, but I can't lie to myself. The only reason why I agreed to come with Lily tonight was because I hoped I would see Sawyer. There was no way Lily was getting me to dress up. She finally suggested I wear what I used to wear in high school since it could pass as a guy in a band. The pants were a little snug, and so was the shirt, but Lily said I nailed it.

I wasn't planning on talking to Sawyer. I wanted to see her face. That girl is a freaking drug, and I'm going through withdrawals trying to keep away. Focusing on Lily diminishes it for a little while. I don't know why I thought it would go away completely when it hasn't over the last several years of staying away.

"You just missed Alix," I say to Aiden when his date goes to the 'powder room'. *Who says that?*

"Are you *freaking* serious?" Aiden's hands toss up in the air. "That's the whole reason why we came here."

"You brought your date to a party so you could see Alix?" I chuckle to myself and shake my head at the ground. We're horrible excuses for human beings.

"I wanted to mess with her head. It always makes her fly off the handle when she sees me with someone else. I love watching her squirm. I think I'm starting to wear her down." Aiden rubs his hands together with a wide smirk.

I release a laugh, thinking of Alix's annoyed face whenever she's in the same vicinity as Aiden. "The only expression I've ever seen on Alix's face when she sees you is irritation—like she's about to pummel your face in."

"Hey," he says, "it's better than indifference. I get under her skin. That's passion. Eventually, she'll cave."

"I really hope that, man. For your sake."

Aiden smiles, peering over at me. "Oh, ye of little faith. You say that as if you don't think I can do it."

"I know you can. I'm just not sure how long you're going to last in a ring with Alix. Even if she does finally cave to you someday, if you can make it through all twelve rounds, you'll find yourself knocked out by the very end. Alix will sit on top with her fists pumping in the air."

He hums. "You don't realize how badly I want that."

"I do actually," I say, nodding and laughing. "I really do. I just don't get the appeal, Aide. She's freaking crazy and kind of a wench."

"Just the way I like them." He waggles his eyebrows and smirks. "And she's only a wench to you. For me, it's playful banter."

I lift an eyebrow. "Lucky me."

I finish out the night at the party with Lily. The entire time I want to leave, but I stay for her. No sense in starting a fight I know she'd put up if I tried to leave. With Aiden at my side, I'm able to bear the obnoxious gossip and pointless small talk. After I drop Lily off at her house I debate stopping by Sawyer's house to see how she's doing, but I know that won't fly with anyone.

I accept my defeat and head home alone.

CHAPTER TWENTY-NINE

Sawyer

I TOLD POLLY I would lock up. She looked especially dead on her feet when seven o'clock rolled around. Today was an especially crazy day since we had an order of six-dozen cupcakes that needed to be picked up the following morning. Once the bakery closed, it took me nearly two hours to get everything cleaned and straightened up to be ready for tomorrow so it wasn't until after ten o'clock that I began turning off lights.

"Sawyer Hartwell."

I turn my head at the sound of my name as I twist the lock on the bakery. Josh Duncan is strutting toward me with a slightly clumsy stagger.

"I heard you were back in town, but if I had known that age would treat you this well, I would have sought you out sooner."

"Hi, Josh," I say stiffly. I can smell the alcohol before he's even in arm's reach.

"That's not a very warm hello." I don't get a chance to step back before he pulls me in for an awkwardly tight hug. His hands roam unwelcome up and down my back. I stiffen.

"It wasn't meant to be welcome," I say, shifting out of his leech-like grasp. Josh had a wandering eye in high school.

Whenever he would see me in the halls, I couldn't help but feel like he was undressing me with his eyes. He always given me the creeps, but since he was Dean's friend, I figured they were friends for a reason. In the past, I told myself it was probably me being paranoid, but now, with his shifty eyes and wandering hands I'm feeling uneasy on this barely lit street.

"Oh where is the love? I haven't seen you in years, and you can't pretend to be happy to see me? I'm happy to see you." He attempts to wink.

"It's good to see you," I lie. "But I've had a long day, so I'm going to head home." I step to the side to walk around him. "Goodnight, Josh."

"Hey, hey now." His hand latches onto my arm and pulls me back in front of him. "We were having a conversation. I just want to get reacquainted." He attempts to smile, but his teeth are clenched, so it's more of a sneer.

"You're drunk, and this conversation is over. Let go of me, Josh," I say as firmly as I can muster. Trying to be discreet, I search the streets around us, but it's a little late for people to be out and walking around town on a Wednesday night. Farther down the street, I see a few people, but they're walking in the opposite direction. If I scream now, they might hear me, but I could be screaming prematurely and make an unnecessary scene.

"You know if you picked me, I never would have left you like Dean did. I'm here, aren't I?"

I feel a pang in my heart. It's one thing for me to talk about Dean's abandonment. It's another for someone to wave it in front of my face like it's everyday conversation.

"You talk of picking as if you tried, but I don't recall there ever being a competition."

177

"Oh, there was plenty of competition." He doesn't let go of my arm as he leans in closer to my face. His pungent breath fills my nose. "We just settled it as men would, behind closed doors, away from the ladies."

"I should go home, Josh. It's late. I'm tired," I try again. "You should go home, too. Sleep would make you feel better."

"I can make you forget," he whispers. "I can make you forget it all."

A shiver surges up my spine. "Let me go, Josh," I press, pulling my arm back, but he won't loosen his grip.

"I just want a taste. I want to know what I've been missing all of these years. Dean was a fool to let you go."

Bile rises in my throat. It didn't occur to me that he would actually try something. We're not in some dark alley. We're off Main Street, but he's not deterred. "If you dare try, I promise you'll regret it."

"I doubt that." His hands grab my wrists, locking them behind my back before shoving me against the brick building. It's so quick I don't get a chance to scream before his tongue invades my mouth. The jagged bricks stab my arms, and the more I attempt to break free, the harder he pushes, the deeper the brick digs into my skin. One of his hands moves to my chin to hold it still, keeping me from thrashing. I try to lift a knee, but his body is flush against mine, leaving no room for leverage.

Tears pierce my eyes as I cry into his mouth. He takes my desperate pleas as encouragement and begins feeling his way up my shirt. Each inch that his fingers crawl, the more intense the fear swells in my chest. This is really happening to me. And then he's gone.

I exhale and open my eyes as someone throws a punch

178

across Josh's jaw. He doubles over, and, just as quickly, is upright and held by the throat.

"If I *ever, ever* see you near Sawyer again, I swear I'll end you, Josh."

I know that voice. I know that voice like I know my own.

"Oh c'mon, Dean. We were just getting reacquainted." Josh smirks with blood dripping from his lip. "She liked it. Didn't you hear her moans?"

Dean punches him again, knocking his head to the other side. "Don't give me that load of bull." His voice is seething as he attempts to remain calm. "You don't touch her."

"Why do you care? She's not yours," he slurs. "She's free game now. Didn't you hear that her husband got whacked?"

Dean punches Josh again so hard his head snaps to the side and hangs. Dean lowers his voice to a deadly calm. "I'm going to give you one more chance to shut your mouth and walk away because we're old friends and you're drunk, but if you so much as *think* of touching Sawyer again, I'll kill you. I swear on my life, Josh... I will end yours."

Josh lifts his head weakly and raises his hands in mock surrender. He spits blood. "Damn, Dean. I was leaving anyway."

Dean stands rigid with his back to me as he watches Josh stumble down the sidewalk. When he turns and sees me, his stone face softens. He relaxes his jaw and swallows. "You okay?"

I nod, but the tears are spilling down my cheeks. I don't know why I'm crying. He reaches for me, and I don't protest when he pulls me into his arms. In his arms, I feel safe. I feel protected. I forget that I hate him so much.

"I'm sorry, Sawyer. I'm so sorry I wasn't here for you sooner," he murmurs into my hair. The warmth of his breath

179

trails down my neck as he holds me close.

I nod into his chest and quietly cry because I know he's apologizing for so much more than tonight, and for tonight, I want to pretend that I forgive him.

After a couple of minutes, the warmth of his strong arms around me is more than comfort. An ache to be held longer and tighter forms, and that's when I know I have to pull back. I don't want to want him. I can't want him. I won't let myself ever again. He releases me, but stays close. I feel his eyes on me.

"You okay to drive?" He tilts his head down to try and make eye contact, but I can't. I can't meet his stupid piercing eyes, so I look in the direction of my car.

"Yeah, I'm fine," I brush him off.

"Let me walk you to your car."

I nod mechanically. He bends to the ground and picks up my purse. I take it from him with a quiet, "Thanks."

My hand shakes as I search for the keys in my purse.

"Are you sure you're all right to drive?"

I nod, but it's so he'll leave me alone.

"Let me take you home, Sawyer. My truck's around the corner." I hesitate. "Please?" I hate that he feels as if I can't handle myself, like I'm too weak—or broken—to handle Josh Freaking Duncan. "I really don't want to leave you alone."

"I'm fine."

"I know," he says as if he's trying to appease me. "It's for my own peace of mind."

"It wouldn't make any sense. I'd have to leave my car and then have no way to get to work in the morning."

"Maybe you should take the morning off."

"I said I'm fine, Dean."

"Okay," he gives in reluctantly. He eyes me warily, but I try to ignore him. His stare is making me nervous. Heat pools in my veins, knowing he's scrutinizing everything about me.

I finally find my keys as we reach my car. "I've endured much worse. I'll survive a little run in with a drunk idiot."

"Just be safe driving home, okay?"

"I will," I snap and then feel instantly guilty for some stupid reason. I have nothing to feel guilty for. He's the persistent one. I want to be left alone. Even as those words cross my mind, I know I'm lying to myself. I've been alone long enough.

"Night, Sawyer."

"Bye, Dean." I climb into my car without looking back.

When I get home, I'm lucky enough that my parents are already in bed, so they don't see me. I look at myself in my bathroom mirror. I look absolutely haggard. My make-up is smeared under my eyes. My hair is a mess of snarls. I splash my face with water, but then decide it's not enough. I have to take a shower. I need to wash every last ounce of Josh off my body. When I've finished rubbing my skin raw I spend ten minutes brushing my teeth. I brush and spit, brush and spit. It's not enough, but I head for bed. I pray sleep will give me peace.

Their fists come down over and over again. I don't see Grayson's body on the ground as their figures surround him. I watch, frozen, next to our car, unable to do anything about it as he calls my name, shouting for me to run.

"Run, Sawyer! Go! Run!"

But I can't, and no one notices me. They continue with

their rage. And Grayson's voice gets more and more desperate until I can't hear him anymore. Until the only sound left is the pounding of fists on flesh.

I wake up screaming, hands shaking my shoulders. "Sawyer, Sawyer! Baby, stop! Stop!"

My heart races. Sweat drips down my face as I try to catch my breath. My eyes dart around my bedroom, and the anvil on my chest disappears when I realize it wasn't real.

"Sawyer, it was just a dream," Mom murmurs, running her hand across my forehead, clearing the damp strands from my face.

But it didn't feel like just a dream. Did Grayson scream my name as he took each blow? Did he think of me as he took his last breath?

"It felt so real," I cry.

"It's over."

I nod and nestle into my pillow, but I'm too afraid to fall back asleep and dream of his cries. I'm reminded of Josh and his repulsive mouth. I'm reminded of Dean throwing punches, trying to protect me.

"Will you stay with me?"

There's a beat before she answers. "Of course," she chokes.

My mom crawls in beside me and wraps me in her arms like she used to when I was little and had nightmares about monsters and demons. These monsters and demons are so much worse.

The tears spill down my cheeks until my eyes are too tired to make any more, and I finally drift off to sleep.

CHAPTER THIRTY

I YAWN AND wipe my eyes when I get out of bed the next morning. Sleep didn't find me at all. My relief was short-lived when I drove by her house last night to see her car in the driveway. Though she was safe in her bed, I didn't save her. I wasn't fast enough.

Concentrating at work is nearly impossible. I'm lagging so much I know I won't be able to keep up with my workload.

"What did you do to Josh?"

I look up at Aiden who closes my office door behind him. "When did you see Josh?" I ask.

Aiden sits down across from me so I know he doesn't plan on letting this go. "He stopped by my house this morning, wanting to apologize for all the junk he's pulled. He told me he was leaving Willowhaven." He rests his elbows on his knees with a serious expression and levels his stare. "Dean, the guy was nearly unrecognizable."

"How do you know I had anything to do with that?"

"Because as soon as I mentioned your name he started to cry and repeated how sorry he was, then mumbled more crap. He was more of a mess than usual. What happened?"

Wiping my fingers across my mouth, I contemplate what to say, how much to say. *What would Sawyer feel comfortable with me saying?* "I found him outside of the bakery with Sawyer pressed up against the building. Let's just say Sawyer wasn't saying yes."

Aiden sucks in a breath, leans back in the chair, and exhales. "I'm surprised you left him alive."

"Me too." The image of Josh holding her to the building replays in my head. Her cry will be burned into my memory. It makes me sick to think of his hands on her. I wanted to kill him. I wanted to kill him with my bare hands.

"How's Sawyer?"

"She was pretty upset, but she wouldn't let me do much. I know she was embarrassed. I made sure she got home safely and that was that."

"Good riddance," Aiden said and stood. "Hopefully he's out of our lives for good. You did the right thing, man."

I nod, but his words leave me feeling heavy. I wish I didn't have to do what I did. I wish that Josh had tried harder to be a better person. I wish life could have been different for him.

"If you see Sawyer before I do, give her a hug for me," he says before walking out the door.

I laugh because I'll be lucky if she ever lets me touch her again.

Sawyer's humiliated, tearstained face haunts me all day. Between every invoice and every phone call, between every repair and every conversation with Aiden, her face invades in my mind. When I can't take it anymore, it shifts to the feel of her in my arms. She let me hold her. She finally let me touch her, and that small feeling of hope carries me through the entire day. It was only a step, but it was a step in the right direction. And like the pathetic guy I've become, I'll take whatever I can get, no matter how wrong I know it is.

Lily hasn't been able to stop talking about the redecorating of her house for the last hour. I'm sitting behind my desk working on invoices. It's after hours, since I couldn't manage to fit in all that I needed to with a tired, wandering mind. I told Lily she could come, but I've been regretting the decision since the moment she walked through the door.

"You know, I was thinking of painting the walls in my living room like a sunny yellow and the laundry room a calming green. But then I thought the laundry room could be whatever I want it to be. No one really goes in there but me, so I should have fun with it and go crazy. So I'm thinking maybe light pink and white stripes or lavender and cream, like…"

She keeps going on and on, and I can't listen to it anymore. I can't. She hasn't taken a breath. It's not what she's saying that breaks me. It's the thought that I know it's over for us, and I have to tell her. For her sake, I have to let her go.

"Lily, I don't think I can do this anymore."

She doesn't flinch. She doesn't even look at me with disgust. She looks at me as if she's been waiting for this day to come and shakes her head slowly. "You're not talking about paint, are you." It's more of a statement than a question.

I shake my head.

She nods, her turned down eyes shifting to the floor before meeting mine. "It's because of Sawyer, isn't it?"

I could say no. I could tell her that it wouldn't be right even if Sawyer didn't exist. But it is Sawyer. It's always been Sawyer. I don't say it. I nod. Maybe by nodding, it will hurt less. She won't have to hear me say the words.

185

"I want to hear you say it."

It didn't occur to me that Lily would know me so well. I know we've been together for over a year, and I realize we've built our lives around each other's, but I thought maybe she could see the cracks in our foundation. It's too easy to give this all up. It makes it that much more clear. I have been so unfair to Lily.

"It's always been Sawyer, Lily." I'm not talking about since Sawyer's been back. It's always been her. Even when she wasn't in Willowhaven. Even when she didn't know where I was. But I don't say this.

She nods because I don't think she can talk, but this time there are tears in her eyes, and it feels like I kicked a puppy. I've let this go on for too long. I should have ended it as soon as Sawyer came back. It was a jerk move to keep up with the charade. I know that's all this is now. Even if I don't get to be with Sawyer, I know I can never give anyone the love they deserve because I gave my heart away a long time ago.

"Lil," I say, taking a step around my desk toward her. "I'm so sorry."

She shakes her head rapidly, lifting her palm to me to ward me off. "No. Don't. That doesn't make it any better. I understand, okay?" She licks her lips and breathes for a minute. I consider saying something, anything, but I think it's better if I keep my mouth shut for the moment. "I thought maybe when you came back it was my second chance. Sawyer was gone. I knew I'd always be second, but it was better to be second to you than nothing at all." Her eyes lift up to me, and she shrugs. Her lips pucker as if she's trying to suck back a cry.

That's a blow I wasn't expecting. I swallow and remove her

key from my key ring—the key I never once used. "I never wanted to hurt you. I'm so sorry that I have."

Lily slowly reaches for the key and presses her lips together—biting them so hard I know she'll leave a mark. She nods mechanically at the ground, unable to meet my eyes. She raises her shoulders in a shrug and looks back up at me. "What can you do? You win some, you lose some, right?"

"Right," I whisper. I want to hug her, but I don't know if that will make it worse.

She steps forward, quickly pecks my cheek, and leaves me without another word.

I watch her retreat and a punch of guilt hits me in the stomach. I did the right thing, didn't I? Lily deserves more. She needs someone who is going to love her as much as she loves in return. That person isn't me. I knew that from the beginning, but I hoped that someday it would be. And maybe it could have, but not anymore.

Sawyer will haunt me forever. I know that now. No matter who I am with, Sawyer will always perch in the back of my mind, watching and judging my every move and choice. So right now I'm making a vow, whether it is a vow to me or a vow to Sawyer, I haven't figured that out yet. But I can't leave her broken. I have to see Sawyer survive. I have to see her put back together.

I have to make her mine again.

CHAPTER THIRTY-ONE

Sawyer

WITH FALL UPON Willowhaven, Main Street has shifted from lush green canopies to wildfire. The yellow, orange, and reds blaze and drift across the street when the wind blows, creating a tunnel of color for me to walk through. I'm almost to my car when my phone starts to ring. It's Blaine. Out of habit, I silence it.

When I sit down in the driver's seat, my phone buzzes, alerting me of a new voicemail. The little envelope icon flashes at me. It's sending me subliminal messages. *Listen to me. Listen to me.* Instead of deleting it immediately, I dismiss the message and toss the phone in my purse before heading home. I feel it pulsing from the passenger seat the whole way.

Once I get changed into some comfy clothes, I see my purse dangling from the chair in front of my vanity. Blaine has left me at least a hundred voicemails over the last few months, and I haven't listened to a single one. I know why. He knows why. But for some reason when I see this new voicemail flash on my screen, I decide to listen.

"Soy, you know this is getting old, right? You haven't returned my calls in over eight months. *Eight* months. Now if that's not a world record I don't know what is. So, bravo. Now you can either keep ignoring my calls, or hey, here's an idea, you can call me back. It would be the most logical choice. Love you, sis."

I stare at the ceiling with my phone still pressed to my ear and feel the tug of a smile on my face. I've really missed him. I don't let myself think about it. I turn my screen back on and press his name.

"Are pigs flying? Or maybe hell just froze over?" I hear a smile in his voice.

"Hey, Blaine."

"Took you long enough. I bet you haven't listened to a single message of mine until tonight."

"How would you know?" I counter.

"Because you can't avoid my natural brotherly charm. If you hadn't turned off your phone or listened to my first message, we would have talked months ago."

I snort. "Don't be too sure of yourself."

"You're missing out. I've left some really good material on there. I bet I'd keep you entertained for hours."

I snort. "You're so full of yourself."

"So full of *awesome*."

"Oh, right." I laugh. "Must have gotten those words confused."

He chuckles and then goes quiet. "Seattle misses you."

"I miss you, too," I say quietly.

The question hangs in the air, but I know he won't ask it so I answer him before the silence stretches on any longer.

"I'm fine, you know."

"That's what Mom keeps telling me." He doesn't sound

189

skeptical as much as he sounds like he's waiting to call my bluff.

"But you don't believe it."

"It's not that I don't believe it as much as I think it's the biggest load of BS ever spoken."

"So I've got a few things I'm working through. But I'm functioning. I've got Mom and Dad. I have a job. Alix makes me socialize."

"Oh, Alix. She's still hanging around Willowhell?"

"I don't know why you hate it here so much. I have more reason to hate it than you do."

He chortles. "I don't really hate it. I'm just glad I don't live there. It's a pleasant town, but it's not for me. It isn't big enough for all this personality."

Blaine and I talk for about an hour, not once mentioning Grayson. It's refreshing. He knows how to talk to me without needing to question every little detail of my life. He understands me without needing straightforward answers. He can pick apart everything I say and know exactly what I'm meaning without having to explain myself.

"You're jerking my chain, right?"

"That's a horrible expression, and no, I'm not. Mom really never told you, either?"

"If she had, I would have told you. You know I left that place before you did. I know about as much as you do. If I had heard he was back, I would have been there to beat the living daylights out of him that very same day."

"That's probably why she kept it from you, too," I snort. "We don't need any arrests to add to the family rap-sheet. I think I've racked up enough of a record for everyone."

He chuckles under his breath. "You know I never hated

Preston. I hate what he did to you, but he used to make you happy. Maybe that's why Mom didn't tell you he came back. She was afraid you would come back and forgive him."

"Maybe I would have, maybe I wouldn't. But she didn't have the right to make that decision. Nor did she have the right to keep it from me. After all of these years, that's what I think hurt most about coming home."

"What she did or seeing him?"

"Seeing him," I murmur. "It freaking drop-kicked me while I was down."

I can imagine him nodding on the other end. "Have you talked to him since you've been home?"

"A little, yeah."

"Have you given him a piece of your mind?"

"Enough of it." I sigh. "But, overall, I've done my best to avoid him." I know what giving him the time of day might do. My mind shifts to the other night and I swallow.

"It's your life, Soy. I want you to know that no matter what you do with it, I will love you."

My eyebrows scrunch together. "I know."

"Okay. Well I've gotta go. Kierra is waking up, and Candice isn't home from the grocery store yet."

"Go take care of your family. We'll talk later."

"You won't ignore my calls anymore?"

"If you're lucky."

He laughs. "I've got my foot in the door. I'll take full advantage of that if you decide to cut me out again."

"I'm shaking in my boots."

"You don't own boots."

"Shut up. Love you, brother."

"Love you, too, sis."

When I get off the phone with him, I feel a little lighter. I lie on my bed and fall asleep to the pitter-patter of fresh rain on my windowpane.

There's nothing but the sound of rain as it trickles down our bedroom windows. I shiver and Grayson tugs me against his chest, pulling the comforter up.

"The power always has perfect timing, going out when it's raining and freezing outside."

"I don't think the power decides to go out because it's cold," Grayson murmurs as he tugs me closer to his chest.

"I do. The weather loves to torture me." I pause and listen to the water plunk the glass like piano keys. "But I do love the sound of rain." I sigh. Thunder rattles the windows.

"I love the thunder." His cold feet find my legs.

"Grayson!" I scold with a laugh and shift to dodge the ice cubes.

He chuckles near my ear. "Oh, c'mon. My feet are cold." He follows my legs across the bed, keeping me secure in his arms so I can't escape.

"Stop it! You're so cold!"

"And you're so warm. Why don't you share?" He nuzzles his face into my neck, tickling my skin. I love and hate the torment.

"No!" I chuckle, trying to maneuver my body so his feet can't torture me. "Gray, I don't like this game."

"Oh, but I do." His husky voice takes on a sultry tone, trailing painfully slow kisses down my neck.

"I think we're talking about two different games now," I murmur.

"I like this new game," he says as he nestles me into the mattress with his face buried in the crook of my neck, pressing his lips down to my collarbone. "I could play this new game all night."

I chuckle breathlessly. "Why don't we?"
"You don't have to ask me twice."

I wake the next morning, and though I dreamed of him last night, Grayson isn't the first person on my mind. It's a startling revelation. It's been nearly nine months since he died. The pain hasn't subsided, but I've learned to live with it. It's become a part of me, and I haven't forgotten him, but I know I have to start picking up the pieces of my life. I promised Grayson I would. I failed him as a wife. I can't fail him now. It's time I started to make good on that promise. I've wasted enough time.

My decision is made before I can talk myself out of it. I hop in the shower and get ready to go see Dean.

As I slide into the driver's seat of my car, my phone rings. Alix.

"Hey."

She gives no greeting before barreling forward. "So, were you ever going to tell me that Josh Duncan attacked you the other night?"

"Who told you that?"

"Aiden, actually." She sounds more irritated by the fact that she had to say his name than by the fact that I didn't tell her. "And I don't appreciate being told by a third party for every life-altering incident that happens in your life. You should have told me."

I chuckle. "Aiden, huh?"

"It's not what you think," she snips. "Do not deflect. Sawyer, that's some scary business. Are you okay? Did he hurt you? Oh gosh, did he touch you?" She's shouting now. "I'll kill him! I swear I'll rip off every limb of his body and beat him with

193

them!"

I sigh and crank the ignition. "I'm fine, Felix. Really. I was a little shaken up, but I'm fine now."

"I heard Dean showed up like a real knight in shining armor," she says dryly.

Dean's face was far from a knight in shining armor. He was downright enraged and then regretful. "Yeah. I got lucky." I don't want to talk about Dean with Alix.

"You're dang straight you got lucky! What are you doing now? I heard you start your car. Where are you going?"

I clear my throat. Though I don't want to tell her, I do. "That's actually where I'm going right now."

"You're going where?" The tone in her voice tells me she already knows.

"I'm going to see Dean." She's silent, and her silence worries me more than anything. "Felix?"

"I'm here. Just processing. Are you sure that's a good idea?"

"I want to thank him. I may have lashed out a little that night, and he didn't deserve it after he saved me, so that's it. I'm just going to thank him."

"Okay," is all she says.

"Okay?"

"Call me when you're done." And then she hangs up without another word.

CHAPTER THIRTY-TWO

THERE ARE A lot of things I plan for during the day, but seeing Sawyer stand in the entry to my garage looking all curious and anxious was not one of them.

"Sawyer," I say, caught by surprise.

She hovers, shifting from foot to foot as if she hasn't decided if she really wants to stay or not. Her hand pushes her hair back from her face. Few people would recognize that nervous tick. She always hated it when I would point it out, but she'd smirk and punch my shoulder.

"I came to apologize," she finally says.

"What? Why?"

"For being so short with you the other night. I know you were trying to help. I just... I have a hard time accepting help." She pauses, like she's debating continuing. "And I really didn't want you to be the one giving the help." She shrugs.

Somehow, I understand, though it was little bit of an insult. "You don't have to apologize, Sawyer. There is nothing for you to be sorry for. I'm just grateful I was at the right place at the right time."

"What *were* you doing walking down Main Street at ten

o'clock at night anyway?"

"Leaving work late... and taking a walk to clear my head." I was living a double life. In one, I was trying to stay true to Lily, stuck in a perpetual state of denial that we could possibly work. In the other life, my need for Sawyer and the hope that we could have a second chance kept me in a constant tug-o-war. That night, I was sorting out where to go from there. As twisted as it seems, finding Josh all over Sawyer was exactly what I needed to push me to make a decision.

Sawyer nods without pushing for more of an answer. I'm sure she knows better than anyone else when you want a topic to be dropped. "Thank you, as well," she mumbles.

I shake my head. "No thanks needed."

She bites on her bottom lip and rocks on her heels. She wants to say more, but there's an internal battle going on inside of her, so I take that small window of opportunity. If she can't accept me now, I don't think she ever will.

"Sawyer, can we be friends?"

She pauses and contemplates my question. "Friends, huh?" Her left eyebrow lifts. A smile wants to come, but she's fighting it. Hard. "And how do you think Lily would feel about that?"

I make my decision in that moment not to mention my relationship status. "Lily's opinions don't affect my decisions."

"How very considerate of you," she says wryly.

"She doesn't own me." You do. "We have separate lives. I'm a grown man. I can make my own decisions."

"Must be nice to have such freedom."

I laugh humorlessly. I don't remember what freedom feels like anymore. Sawyer has enslaved my every thought for the last ten years.

196

I don't know why I don't tell her about Lily and me. I guess it's because I know if she's finds out it's over between us, she'll end this mending before it gets a chance to start. She'll know my end game.

The hesitation in her eyes is apparent. She doesn't trust me, whether it's with her heart or my motives or both. The conflict to agree teeters on a fence.

"I don't trust you, Dean."

"I know." I nod. "But I'm not going anywhere. This is my home. You might as well get used to that now."

She nods, but it's not because she's decided to trust me. She knows she has no other choice.

"I haven't forgiven you."

"I know that, too."

She nods again, and I know I really can't screw it up this time. "Okay. Friends."

CHAPTER THIRTY-THREE

Sawyer

ALIX PERCHES ON the edge of my bed and stares blankly at me as I pace my bedroom. I was hoping I'd get a little more of a reaction out of her or at least some advice or maybe a pat on the back for putting on my big girl panties and working to get over the past.

"Oh, c'mon. Will you please not look at me like that?"

"Like what? I'm looking normally at my best friend who just signed her life over to the devil."

"Alix," I groan and look up at the ceiling. "Would you please not?"

"What?" She chuckles. "That's exactly what you just did."

"I did not."

She clears her throat. "Okay. In all seriousness, do you really think it's a good idea to let him back in?"

"Felix, my heart was broken. Not my brain. I'm not stupid. I can stand on my own two feet and make good choices."

She looks at me with a questioning, *can you?* "The heart has a way of blurring the logic in our brains."

"I know, but I'm making nice because I'm tired. I'm tired of hurting. I'm tired of hating. I'm tired of holding a grudge. It doesn't mean I have to completely forgive him. It doesn't mean I'm going to go running into his arms. It only means that when I see him on the streets I'll wave rather than run. I'll smile rather than scowl. It takes so much more energy to stay mad, and I'm so tired."

"Okay."

It concerns me when she says it like that. I know she's not okay with it. "Alix?"

"Okay. I understand where you're coming from. I just know what ground zero looks like after Hurricane Dean lets loose, and I don't want to revisit ground zero, Sawyer. Ever."

"I promise you I'm going to guard my heart like it's the Crown Jewels."

"Where Dean is concerned, you don't have the control to guard anything."

"Dean Preston?" Alix nearly shouts, and I immediately shush her, looking around at everyone near our lockers. "You like Dean Preston?" She says his name as if it's a curse word, whispering it under her breath.

"What's wrong with Dean? He's nice. And cute." I exchange my calculus book for my chemistry book, replacing it in my locker on the stack of other textbooks and old notes.

"He's freaking hot, but that's beside the point, Sawyer. I thought that date was a pity date. He basically cornered you in the hallway. There was no way you could have said no without looking like a complete shrew."

"I wanted to say yes," I retort, trying to defend myself. Though I don't know why I should have to. Alix should trust me. She's my best friend. She should be rooting for me.

"You're serious." She honestly can't understand why.

"Why is it so wrong to be serious about him? What has he ever done

199

to you? It's not like he's a criminal."

"You don't know that," she interrupts me, and I roll my eyes, closing my locker. "You know why you can't date him." She stands in front of me, forcing me against my locker with only one place to look—at her. "Number one: your parents will blow a freaking gasket. They tolerated him for that first date, but there is no way they'll keep cool if he becomes someone constant. Number two: his dad is a psycho recluse. After his wife left it was like buh-bye, Mr. Preston. No one ever sees that guy. Does he have a job? No one knows. It's no wonder people scatter the hallways when they see Dean. But lastly and most importantly," she points her finger at my chest, "that kid has the power to ruin you and your reputation."

I sigh and suppress another eye roll. "I don't think he's who everyone makes him out to be. When we hung out, he was thoughtful and respectful. He held open my doors and kept asking me questions to make sure I was comfortable. It was really sweet." I hug my arms around myself, rubbing away the goose bumps. My stomach flutters when the gentleness in his eyes flashes in my memory.

"Oh gosh..." Alix says dramatically. "You're so far gone. There's nothing I can say to talk you out of this, is there?"

I shake my head with a smile when I see him walking down the hallway. His hands are tucked in the front pockets of his dark jeans. He holds his head with confidence, but not cockiness. The look in his eyes is the way it always is. Stoic in the most heartbreaking way, yet poised like he could take on the world. When he notices me, his eyes lighten as if he's watching the sunrise for the first time. He lifts his chin once, the way guys do to acknowledge you, and I know I'd do anything to make him smile at me like that every day.

For the rest of my life.

"It's different this time. I know better," I tell Alix

200

adamantly.

"Somehow I don't believe you, but it's your life," she surrenders. "I can't stop you. And I understand why you have to do this. Just be careful."

"I don't know why you think I wouldn't be."

"Because I know you, and I know that Dean Preston has the ability to make you lose all good judgment."

"I resent that."

Alix purses her lips. "I didn't say it to pay you a compliment."

When my phone rings a few days later, I pick up without looking. I've just gotten off work, and Alix and Blaine are known to habitually call me around the same time. They are the only ones that call me anymore, if you don't count my mother. I pretty much burned every other relationship I ever had after Grayson died.

"Hey," I say.

"Sawyer?"

When I hear his voice on the other end I freeze. How did he get my number?

"Sawyer?" he repeats.

"Hey," I say as casually as I can manage, but it sounds completely strained.

"I thought I lost you there for a minute." I hear the smile in his voice. So many thoughts run through my mind on how to reply to his comment, but I keep them all to myself.

"No, I'm here," I manage.

"I thought we could go grab a burger or something." He sounds so casual, as if we talk all the time, as if it's completely natural for him to call me and ask me to go out for burgers. I feel both anger and relief. It's an exhausting combination of emotions.

"You want to go out?" I ask, still trying to figure out how I'm going to answer him.

"Friends eat food, right?"

"Yeah, I just..." I want to come up with an excuse. Something, anything to give me a reason to say I can't. And yet, I don't. "Okay."

"So I'll pick you up? In about an hour?"

"Right now? You want to go right now?"

"Well, I'm on my way home from the garage so I can shower, but yes. I'm hungry. Food sounds like a necessity if I want to live through the night."

I can't hold back my laugh. "Okay. I'll see you in an hour."

I hear the words come out of my mouth, and I can't stop them. I hit end and stare down at the phone in my hand. Did I just agree to dinner with Dean Preston?

The familiar rumble of his motorcycle approaches our street. I hear when he stops outside of my house, and I begin to pace. I can back out. I can tell him I'm not feeling well and take a rain check. He doesn't have to know I won't redeem the rain check.

When he knocks at the door, I stop. I could not answer the door—pretend to forget because I have an emergency or a very

202

important errand that absolutely cannot wait. Nope. It can't wait. It's the highest level of importance. I begin to back away from the door.

"Sawyer, are you going to get the door?" Mom hollers from the study.

Gah! He totally heard that.

I take a deep breath and stride to the door. I roll my shoulders back in preparation with my hand on the doorknob. Taking a couple more breaths, I attempt to control my internal freak out.

"Are you going to answer that?" I jump at the sound of my dad's voice. I turn to see him sitting in the recliner in the far corner of the living room with a knowing smirk and a book in hand. It's as if he knows who's on the other side. He's daring me to answer the door.

I flush. He just witnessed my entire inner monologue. I'm about to respond when my mom's voice echoes through the entryway. "What are you doing?" I turn to see her at the end of the hallway. "Why haven't you answered it yet?"

I glare at her. She has no idea how awkward she made this. And then I realize I really don't want her to see me leave with him. I shift and breathe, preparing to open the door with her there. How am I going to explain this? What can I say to get her to walk away right now?

"Oh, for heaven's sake, Sawyer. Answer the door." I want to strangle her. Wrap my fingers around her neck and shake. Instead, I turn away from her and open the door.

Dean stands there with an amused expression on his face. There is no way he didn't hear our entire exchange, and I want to crawl in a deep, dark black hole and die. For real this time.

203

"You ready?" he asks. His lean body is dressed in jeans, a black shirt, and a dark leather jacket. He couldn't be more cliché if he tried, and yet it doesn't matter. He pulls it off flawlessly. My heart flutters.

At the sound of his voice, my mom walks up and peeks out the door.

His face falls, but he recovers and smiles. "Hey, Mrs. Hartwell. How are you?"

"Hi, Dean. What an unexpected surprise." The unwelcoming undertone in her voice is so obvious, I want to lock her in her room to keep this situation from being anymore awkward than it already is.

If I were thinking clearly I would have waited outside for him. *Why didn't I wait outside for him?* Why couldn't I have thought of that five minutes ago? My parents didn't really like him that much when we were dating, so you can imagine how they felt about him after he left me a crumpled mess.

"We are going to get something to eat," I step in. "I'll be home in a couple hours."

She's confused, but she nods. "Don't be too late."

I toss a wave and walk out the door followed by Dean. "Bye, Mrs. Hartwell. It was good to see you."

"Bye, Dean." I don't miss the fact that she doesn't share his sentiments, so I know it can't be lost on him.

I hear her close the door, but I know she'll be watching through the curtains. When we reach his bike, he hands me a motorcycle helmet, and I suddenly feel nauseous. I haven't been on his bike in years. It might be a different, newer, and improved bike now, but it's a motorcycle nonetheless.

"Are you okay?" he asks with a hint of knowing in his voice.

I breathe and realize I'm staring at the bike with a look that says I might puke. "Yeah, it's just been a while."

He stops before putting on his helmet. "If you would rather, we can take your car…"

"No, it's fine." I'm being ridiculous. It's a stupid ride on a motorcycle. I can be civil and mature about this.

"You sure?" He's offering me an out, but I can't take it now. He'll see right through me. I refuse to back down and show him how this affects me.

"Yes." I toss my hand in the air to brush him off.

He throws his leg over the motorcycle, steadying it for me to get on behind him. When I straddle the motorcycle, up against his back, I start to second-guess my answer. Maybe my car would be the smarter choice. He's awfully close. My thighs brush the sides of his hips, and I *know* I made the wrong choice, but I can't back out now. He starts the engine, and I reluctantly wrap my arms around his waist to feel more secure. His muscles tense under my touch, but he tries to relax. He's not overly successful, but then we're off.

Around every turn and curve, I hold on a little tighter and feel him shake with laughter. His enjoyment at my expense is expected, but he's enjoying it a little too much. When we stop at a traffic light his hand drops onto my thigh. It's a natural reflex. I know because that's where his hand always use to lay when we were at a standstill.

It takes a moment, but he finally flinches and removes his hand. He turns his head slightly over his shoulder. I can't hear him, but I know he apologizes. His hands grip the handlebars, and then the light turns green.

Dean orders first at Rita's Diner and without my permission orders for me, not giving me the option to pay. I should be annoyed that he ordered for me, but he got me exactly what I would have gotten myself. I'm more annoyed that he paid for me, making me feel like this was a date as opposed to two old friends catching up. We get the burgers to-go and head toward the park.

When I glare at him he chuckles and asks, "What?" But he knows exactly what my eyes are conveying. "Just thought I'd do something nice for a friend. Nothing more."

"Dang straight it's nothing more."

"I wouldn't dream of it."

We sit on the park bench closest to the pond, near where I first saw him with Lily, and I instantly feel uneasy. She couldn't possibly be okay with us hanging out. Not that I'm all that worried about her feelings. She obviously has no respect for mine. But this couldn't look good to anyone else who passes by. I know I shouldn't care about what everyone else thinks, but I do.

"So, what was he like?" Dean breaks the silence.

"Wow. You're really ready to dive right on in."

He chuckles. "I'm sorry if I overstepped. We don't have to talk about him if you're not ready yet."

I glance over at him to really gage his interest. "You really want to talk about Grayson?" It surprises me how easy Grayson's name falls from my lips when I couldn't say Dean's name during all of those years.

"Yeah." He talks around chewing his burger, trying to cover his mouth to be polite. "He was your husband, Sawyer. You loved him. He was important to you. I want to know how he stole your heart."

My fingertips cover my lips. That last statement was so off base, if I speak now, I'll give away the truth. It's hard to steal a heart when there's hardly one there to take. Grayson patched my heart. He took what fragments he could find and pieced them together to create something barely capable of beating, but that's all it needed. Sometimes, I think if only I could have met Grayson first, things would have been so much different. I might have lost him in the end, but I wouldn't feel this damaged. I wouldn't feel so jaded.

I haven't been able to talk about Grayson since I came back to Willowhaven, but for some reason I feel like I can talk about him with Dean. He makes me feel at ease. He always did—that hasn't changed.

I finish my bite, debating on where to start. "Gray… Grayson always knew the right thing to say to me. I could be fuming mad at him, and he'd find the button to shut it off, and I hated him for it." I chuckle. "I wanted to be able to stay mad, but he couldn't handle that. He'd crack a joke or smile just right, and my anger would melt away."

"Did he keep a manual somewhere? I'd really like the directions to that skill."

My smile broadens, and I look to the ground.

"What else?" he prompts.

"Umm, he used to make these faces that creeped me out, while somehow making me laugh without fail every time." I chuckle again. "My favorite was the goat. He'd pull out his upper lip and bottom lip and 'bah' like a goat." I peer over at Dean who's watching me carefully. "I know it's stupid." I smile, looking back to the concrete. "But he was actually really good at it." A small laugh leaves my lips when I hear Grayson's goat noises play in my head.

"I don't think it's stupid," he says quietly. "He sounds like he was good for you." He pauses. *Yeah, he was.* "Is it getting easier?"

I meet his eyes. "No." I shake my head and take a sip of soda, buying some time. "The pain isn't as fierce, but it hasn't faded. I think it'll always be there. I'll just get used to living with it."

He nods with understanding.

Maybe he does.

I shrug because I have nothing else to add. Not that I couldn't talk about Grayson for hours. I just can't talk about him with Dean anymore. I want to keep him to myself. I don't want to give his memory away. As if sharing things about him could take them from me. I'm not ready for Dean to take him away from me.

"So, Lily." It pops out before I can stop myself. It felt like the progression in our conversation. We talked about Grayson, so now it's his turn. It's not as if I want to talk about her. If we talk about her, I know I'm going to start saying things that I don't want to get into now. I'll say things I'll regret. Not that I'll regret saying them, per se, but I'll regret saying them to him.

He shifts. I should retract it, but the words are out there now.

I decide to approach it more casually. "What's she up to tonight?"

His shoulder lifts. "She's probably at home watching some sitcom reruns. She really likes those detective shows that don't have much of a storyline. The ones you can jump into and try to solve the crime of the current episode."

"I remember that about her." I nod and ask the question that has been nagging at me for months. I'm not sure I want to hear the answer, but I ask anyway. "Does she make you happy?"

CHAPTER THIRTY-FOUR

Dean

THE QUESTION HANGS in the air, and I have no idea how I'm supposed to answer her honestly. In her eyes I see hope. Whether it's hope that Lily doesn't make me happy or hope that she does, I can't be certain.

Does Lily make me happy? Or more accurately, did she ever make me happy? She was good at making me temporarily forget. Was that the same as happiness? Probably not. She was good at making me feel a little lighter, but never in the same way that Sawyer ever did. What I liked most about Lily was that somehow, though they were best friends, she didn't remind me of Sawyer. Nothing about her brought back memories of Sawyer.

I take too long to answer. "You know what?" she says. "I don't know why I asked that. Don't answer that." Sawyer lifts her fingers to brush her waves of hair behind her left ear.

Her wrist flashes the black dandelion on her porcelain skin. I catch sight of something more to it and my curiosity gets the best of me. "Can I see the tattoo?"

She swallows, but nods her head and hands me her left wrist uncertainly. It's a small tattoo, covering about two or three inches of her arm. The dandelion has a patch missing as if it's been blown away. A few specs of fuzz drift up toward her palm and end with a single little black bird. My thumb brushes over it, and I hear her small intake of breath.

"What kind of bird is that?" I ask gently. Just touching the soft skin on the inside her wrist makes me question, Lily who?

"It's a sparrow," she says quietly.

"Why a sparrow?" I ask. "Does it mean anything?"

"The simple answer—love."

I look up at her, cradling her wrist in the palm of my hand. I'll always be gentle with her. "And the complicated answer?"

"We will have to save that for another day," she states, pulling away from me and getting up swiftly. She stands, waiting for me to join her. "You ready?" Her voice is full of false cheerfulness, and I want to call her on it, but I don't.

I should be disappointed that I haven't been able to gain her trust again, or that she wants to leave already, but I'm too grateful that she gave me hope for another day to be truly disappointed.

"Okay," I say and reach for the food wrapper she has balled up in her other fist. After I throw out our trash we get on my bike and I take her home.

I cut the engine when I pull up in front of her house and help her off. She has to be the one to take her hand out of mine because I don't want to let go. She doesn't give me the option to walk her to her door.

"Thanks for the dinner, Dean." She tosses a wave and begins a hurried walk up the stone pathway to her porch.

"Do you think maybe we can do this again?" I call. Even if she gives me a breadcrumb I'll be happy. I can work with a breadcrumb.

211

After pausing on her steps, Sawyer turns around to look at me. "We'll see." She doesn't smile, but she also doesn't glare, nor does she shoot me down completely, so I take that as more progress. She lifts another wave and walks inside of her house.

I remain by my bike, looking up at her house. It hasn't changed. The white paint is curling a little more around the edges of the siding, and the trees have grown taller, but that's the only difference. I see the curtains in her front window flutter, and take that as my cue to leave. Mrs. Hartwell definitely hasn't warmed up to me over the years. But I'm going to have to change that.

CHAPTER THIRTY-FIVE

Sawyer

"DEAN?" MOM QUESTIONS after I close the front door. She's peeking through the curtains, and I'm certain Dean is in an awkward staring match with her.

"I got tired of being angry at him."

"Is that all?"

"What else is there to say?" I really don't want to talk about this with her. Being with him for those couple hours took all the emotional sanity I had for one night, possibly for the week.

I hear the engine of Dean's motorcycle rev to life before he takes off. She finally releases the curtain back in place and looks at me. "He's not good enough for you, Sawyer." Those words hold no meaning to me anymore. She used to repeat them to me nearly every day.

Before I can react she says, "Don't pretend like that boy didn't ruin your life."

"*I* decide that. I decide who ruins my life." I point to my chest. "*Me*. It doesn't just happen. I get to make decisions for my life. If he ruined my life, it's because I let him. And if I want to spend one night with Dean, so be it. You're supposed to be on *my* side."

Her face softens, and she strides over to me. "I'll always be on your side, baby. Why do you think I have such a hard time watching that boy come around again? It was hard enough to see him come back after you left. And now I have to watch him crawl back on his hands and knees, while you stand with open arms. That boy doesn't deserve that."

"What open arms?" I retort. "It's taken me all of this time home to feel comfortable enough to have a conversation with him. You call that open arms? I'm doing everything I can to hold myself together around him. Give me some credit. I'm treading carefully."

Her shoulders sag, and I finally see in her eyes the one thing I can't stand to see. Pity. "Sweetie, you're grieving. You're finally grieving. I don't think you ever let yourself grieve all those years ago. There were tears and heartache, but then you bottled it up and moved away to Seattle. Just because you moved away doesn't mean you moved on. Dean isn't the answer. It's time to let life take its course and then you can heal and move forward."

The tears start to form in my chest, clogging my airway. I swallow them back. "Mama, I want that in the past. Can we please keep it in the past?"

"The past can't stay there if you haven't even worked through it to move forward."

"I've struggled every *damn* day to work through it. You don't know what I've been through. You don't understand half the pain I've felt. I'm doing the *best I can*."

"Then tell me, Sawyer," she urges, walking closer to me. "Talk about it. Let out your anger and frustration. You've been bottling it and all it's doing is piling up and festering. You can scream. You can cry. But at the end of the day, that won't do a dang thing if you can't talk about what you're screaming about."

I grit my teeth. "I'm going to bed."

She sighs. "Okay." There's disappointment in her eyes, and it's too much to look at any longer.

"Goodnight."

"Night, baby."

I walk into my room and lock the door. Before my thoughts are making sense, I dive to the ground to look under my bed. My eyes spot the box pushed to the center. I don't know why I'm going to it now. This box hasn't been touched in over five years. Before I moved away I toyed with lighting it on fire, but in the end, I couldn't bring myself to do it. There were too many memories in this box. And I need these memories now.

I reach for it and drag it out. Taking a deep breath, I lift the lid. All at once, my brain fogs and goes on overload. I immediately slap the lid back on and breathe. *What am I doing?* This is a horrible idea. I don't know what I hope I'll gain from looking in it. Nothing good can come from looking through this box. But in the end, the rational side of my brain loses the fight. I've got to figure out why I'm willing to risk my emotional sanity for the boy who stole everything from me. It's like I have a sick vendetta against myself. As if I have to punish myself for ever feeling that way. I don't know why, but I don't actually want to forget.

I lift the cardboard lid and set it reverently at my side. Delicately placed on top is a plastic bag with a dried up dandelion inside. Some fuzz is still attached, but the rest of it has settled at the bottom of the bag. Not one dandelion have I passed and not thought of him. I take out the bag and gently place it on top of the lid.

215

The box is filled with pictures of us and notes we wrote back and forth during school and traded during passing periods. I can't look at the pictures. Those snapshots tell everything. They remind me of the good. They paint a happy picture of what we used to be in my head. They remind me of how much I loved him. I flip them over and shove them behind my back.

There's a concert ticket to see Novice and movie ticket stubs to every movie we ever went to together all stacked on top of one another. Underneath it all, I pull out one lone folded piece of paper. It looks like he tore off the corner of some notebook paper. I know what it says before I flip it open and see his handwriting in black ink.

Surrender?

Loving Dean is like fireworks when it's not the Fourth of July. It's sudden and explosive and it scares the crap out of me. Not because I don't want to feel this way, but because I know he is my end game.

I look at him, and I know.

We're wrestling in my backyard. He thought he could take a girl, but he'd never wrestled with me before. I don't fight fair. I have an older brother. My strength isn't enough to win in a match. I had to learn how to hold my own.

He almost has me pinned on the ground. I'm facing him, and that's his first mistake. His smile is wide across his face with a triumphant glow in his eyes. He's taken hold of one of my arms and is frantically trying to grab hold of my flailing free arm that I refuse to give up.

I stick my finger in my mouth and shove it in his ear.

"SAWYER!" he hollers, choking on his laughter. I know I really caught him off guard because he says my real name. He sits back, rubbing his ear. "Did you just wet willy me?"

216

I take his moment of weakness and flip him on his back. "I did what had to be done." I kneel on his lean biceps, pinning him to the grass and ruffle his hair as he thrashes his head from side to side. I stick my finger in his ear again. Dry this time.

"You fight dirty!"

"Surrender!" I shout and pause to wait for his reply, calculating my next move.

"No way!" he retorts with a chuckle. "That's my line!"

I raise my eyebrows and bite my bottom lip. "It's mine now."

He shakes his head, but I see him giving in. I see the desire in his eyes to kiss me, but I hold back. I won't give him what he wants yet. I have the upper hand here. Finally.

"Do you surrender?"

He pauses and lets his eyes soften. "Always."

It's there in his green eyes, everything I know that is reflected back from mine. I love him. I don't say it, and neither does he, but we know. It's as if we want to savor the moment, the moment we first realize we're falling… and falling hard.

I shift down his body, hovering over him, and lean in to kiss his mouth. He breathes my name before our lips meet.

All I say is, "I know." Because I do.

Anyone can say it, but knowing that it's true is what makes it real.

CHAPTER THIRTY-SIX

Dean

AIDEN HAS ME cornered in my office. I can't wipe the stupid grin off my face. He knows something is up. There are customers out there that need help, and he's ordered everyone else to handle it.

"Funny," I say, leaning against the wall. "I thought I was the boss."

Aiden closes the door and whirls on me. "Something happened. I know it did." He points at my chest. "Spill it."

"Sawyer and I hung out." I shrug to keep it light.

Aiden throws a fist pump and jumps in the air. So much for trying to remain cool. "Finally!"

"She let me take her to get burgers at Rita's," I say coolly to calm him down. I don't need him adding any false hope. "It's not a freaking commitment, Aiden."

"No, but its progress, man. She would hardly look in your direction before. Granted, it took her like seven months to get this far, but it happened, and that's what matters. Did you tell her about Lily?"

I exhale. I was hoping to avoid this part. After I tell him, I won't hear the end of it. But he has to know so he doesn't slip if he talks to her. "I've decided against it."

"Are you a freaking moron? She'll never let you in. Why would you want to keep something like this from her? What if she hears it from someone else?"

"Then she hears it from someone else, but it's not as if Lily and I are the talk of the town."

"It doesn't matter. You should be the one to tell her. She shouldn't hear it third-party."

"You don't know Sawyer the way I do. I need to ease her back into this. She just needs a friend right now, and if she knows it's over between Lily and me, she'll think too much about it. She won't let me get within a mile of her. I can be a friend. Even if that's all I get to be, I'll take it. I'll be good with that." For now.

"You'll never be good if friends is all you get. Don't kid yourself."

"I refuse to push it, Aide," I retort. "I will accept whatever she is willing to give me for now. We will have to see where it goes from here."

Aiden closes his eyes and shakes his head in disapproval, but he says, "You're right. Take it slow. But don't let the charade of you and Lily staying a couple jeopardize all that you're working toward here. She could completely lose it if she knew you were lying to her the entire time. Honesty is the best policy."

I want to punch him, but I hold back. "I know, but I have to take that chance. She can't know yet. It's not the right time to bring it up."

"Just be smart about it."

"Am I seriously taking advice from a guy that thinks the best way to lure a woman in is through snarky comments and making her jealous?"

"I know women. I've got three sisters." He holds up three fingers and wiggles them.

I toss the rag in my pocket at him. "Get back to work."

He laughs and opens the door. "It's on. May the best man win."

"Are you seriously making a competition out of who will get the girl first?"

"At the rate you're going, I have a much better chance at winning over Alix before you do Sawyer."

I scoff and wish I had another rag to throw at him. "Now who needs a little more faith?"

He flashes a goofy grin and darts out of my office. "Good luck, man. You're going to need it," he hollers, and I shake my head, though I know he's right.

CHAPTER THIRTY-SEVEN

Sawyer

I WAIT FOR my hot chocolate at the counter of Moment In Thyme. I couldn't stand my mom's judgmental eyes this morning. After the other night, I went to bed without saying anything else to her. We haven't spoken since. She watches me. Her words latched on to my heart, but I can't let them sink in yet. I needed to get out, be on my own for a few hours, and get some fresh air.

"You know, if I didn't know any better, I would think you might be stalking me." His voice flows softly over my shoulder. The nearness of his gruff voice sends shivers down my spine.

I turn toward him. Dean's face is only inches from mine, and I flinch, backing into the counter, startled by his nearness.

He laughs. "Didn't mean to startle you."

"Yes, you did." I smirk. My lips want to smile, but I'm suppressing it. Between every class period, he used to hover behind me at my locker, waiting for me to notice him. When the moment was right all he had to do was whisper my name and I'd flail. It would give him enough amusement until the next break between class periods.

"You caught me." He licks his bottom lip and drags his

teeth across it. My eyes instantly zone in on the gesture and butterflies explode into a frantic frenzy. Don't think about it. Think about the color orange or rain. I actually kind of miss the rain in Seattle. *Seattle...* Grayson. No. Think about chickens or dying puppies. Ugh. So morbid.

"Sawyer," he prompts.

"I'm sorry. What?" I blink. *Freak.*

He snorts a short laugh. "You wanna sit? Do you have some place to be?"

"I ..." I hesitate, but go against my better judgment. Today is my day off, so I don't have anywhere I need to be. I just had to get out of the house. "Okay." I nod.

He gets Haley's attention and points to a table we're about to sit at so she'll bring my hot chocolate there.

"It's Tuesday," I say, sitting down on one side of the table. "Don't you have to be at work or something?"

"I own my garage. I'll go in when I need to go in."

"Must be nice to make your own hours."

He scoffs. "It's not as luxurious as it sounds. I like the freedom of running the garage the way I want to run it, but it's a lot harder than it looks and definitely not stress free. But it's something I can call my own."

Haley appears and sets down two cups. "Dean, here's your coffee. Black. Just how you like it. And Sawyer, your hot chocolate."

I look down at the two drinks. Did Dean tell Haley what he wanted? Was it while I zoned out? "Did you even order?" I ask.

"Haley knows I never change it up."

"A regular, huh?"

He stretches back against the booth. "Every morning.

222

Sometimes I come in on Sunday when the garage is closed. She can brew it better than I can."

"That's either really pathetic or true dedication."

"I like to think it's a little combination of both." His green eyes smile above the coffee cup as he takes a sip.

He's a thief and a liar. I shouldn't want to sit here with him. He stole everything when he left—my heart, my soul, my life. But sitting across from him now makes me think he's willing to surrender it all back to me, if I'm willing to let him. *Am I willing to let him?*

"So, how's your dad?" I realize then that I haven't heard much about him since I moved back.

"Well, it's just me now." He bites his full lips.

"What happened to your dad?"

"Died. Just before I came back. Rumor has it he had a heart attack. He was alone in our old house, and no one knew to check on him." He shrugs, and I can't tell if it's because he really doesn't care, or if it's because there's nothing he can do about it now so he's feigning indifference. Probably the latter.

"I'm really sorry, Dean." I don't know why I say it. It's one of the phrases I hate being told. It's merely a filler when you have nothing else to say because there's nothing else you can say. But I realize I am sorry. I know things were never easy where his dad was concerned, but he was still his father. It can't be easy to lose, not just one, but both of your parents.

"Don't be. He was a dirtbag. I hated him, and he hated me, but life happens. I've moved past it." He shrugs, but I see the underlying sadness. "It took a little bit of time, but I've come to terms with it."

I can't say anything back because as harsh as those words

sound, they might be partially true, and there's nothing I can say that will make him feel better.

"Lily's probably worried about you," I comment.

He takes a sip of his coffee and shrugs. "Meh. Doubt it."

I lift my eyebrows. "Oh, I see. You have one of those trusting relationships where you don't have to know each other's whereabouts at all times."

He chuckles dryly and bites his lips nervously. "Yeah. Something like that."

Hours pass by on fast forward. Haley brings over food when she realizes we have no intention of leaving soon. We talk more about Grayson and Seattle. We talk about his garage and Aiden. He asks more about the bakery and where I want to end up.

"The bakery makes me happy. It's the one bright spot in my day. I've spent the last five years trying to figure out what I want to do with my life, and I think I've found it at Sprinkles. It's just fallen into place."

"So why don't you buy it? Take it over?"

Hope fills my heart. "Someday. Polly's not ready to give it up yet and," I clear my throat, "I don't really have the money for it. I'm kind of drowning in debt." He raises a questioning brow. "Grayson's school loans. But it's fine. Someday it'll all work out."

He nods with empathy in his eyes.

We continue to talk about the subtle changes of Willowhaven, and how, though it hasn't changed much, it's a completely different town than the one we grew up in. Every time I bring up Lily, he brushes over the subject. And somehow we manage not to talk about us once. Not where he went. Not what happened. Not what happened to me. It's the elephant in

224

the room, but when six years pass by, I suppose there's more to talk about than the one event that tore you apart.

I'm not ready to talk about it anyway. Though he pretends like he is, I know he's not either. If he were he would have taken this opportunity, but today is about pretending. Pretending everything is okay, pretending we can be friends, pretending our lives haven't gone in completely different directions—two different directions that may never intersect again.

I look at my watch and see it's almost one. We've been here for over four hours. "I need to get home to my mom before she starts to worry. I told her I'd only be gone an hour or two. And that was this morning. I didn't bring my cell phone with me." It was merely one more way for her to get a hold of me.

The corners of his mouth turn up, and I hear myself years ago, repeating the exact same thing to him after we'd been kissing in the bed of his dad's truck for hours. It was definitely a regular occurrence. If it wasn't me worrying about my mom, it was his dad hollering from their front door. We always made sure to stop before *that* happened. Neither one of us wanted to be on the other end of his father's anger.

"Wouldn't want to worry her now, would we?"

My eyes shy away from his. "No, we wouldn't."

"Well, friend," he says as he gets up and stretches. "It was good talking to you. We should do it again sometime."

I bite my lips to conceal my smile as he walks me to the door of the café. My lips betray me. "Maybe we'll bump into each other again around town or something."

"It's been known to happen."

What am I doing here? Flirting? This can't happen. "Tell Lily I said hi." I can't restrain the punch that my words pack. I tried. I

225

really did.

He nods once with a fallen smile. "Will do."

After I wave, I head toward my car. My mind replays the last several hours. My smile can't be stopped until I notice it there. I bite my lips as punishment to make them stop. *What just happened?* With one look over my shoulder, I see he's watching me from the café entrance. He lifts a crooked smile and tosses a small wave. I return the wave and spin back around. Opening up to him is a stupid move. This can't end well.

CHAPTER THIRTY-EIGHT

I DON'T KNOW what's worse. When I knew that I lost her to someone else or knowing that I can't have her because of the turmoil I created, a mess that I can't seem to fix no matter how hard I try. We were making progress today; at least I thought we were. She feels so close and yet so far out of reach. Though she started to open up to me, she was still on guard. She's fighting it.

I used to fight it, too—my need for Sawyer. I used bury myself in whatever job I could find at the time or distract myself with a girl I knew I would forget the name of by the next day. I found stupid outlets for it all. But then, when nothing worked, I would cave to the one temptation I hated more than anything in this world because nothing could satisfy my craving for Sawyer but Sawyer herself. And only one thing could bring her back to me.

I lean over the bar with one hand over my eyes and a drink in the other. I've lost track of time. Who knows how long I've been sitting here. But I'll wait as long as it takes. My head feels foggy and disoriented, the way it should. The music is booming. The TVs are competing. I hate this place, but I can't stay away.

"What are you doing here, Dean?"

Finally. I lift my head and see Sawyer sitting on the barstool next to me. "Hey," I say, sitting up a little straighter. "I've missed you, Jack."

"This isn't you. Why do you keep doing this to yourself?" Her eyes aren't the usual smiley kind. They are sad, and I want to change that so badly.

"Because when I drink, you come. I get to see your face and it takes away the pain."

Her head shakes. "But you know I'm not real. Once you're sobered up I'll still be gone. And you'll hate yourself all over again for doing exactly what you promised yourself you would never do." She levels her eyes.

I didn't dream her up to be lectured. "I'm not my dad," I snap, and she winces. I hate it when I make her do that. "I didn't mean to snap at you. I'm sorry."

"I know." She offers a small understanding smile, but it doesn't rise to her eyes. They remain sad. I want to kiss away their sadness. "But this is what happens when you let it take over you. You're not my Dean."

"I am. I swear I am," I declare adamantly. "I haven't changed."

"Then put down the drink and walk out of this bar. Get a cab or call someone to come and get you. This place is a bottomless black hole that you will never be able to climb out of if you don't clean your act up."

"But it's the only way I can see you," I murmur desperately.

"And whose fault is that?" My eyes narrow, but I know it's true. And I know she's not really here. Somewhere, in the back of my mind, I know I'm having a conversation with myself.

"Hey, handsome," a throaty voice purrs near my neck. She's so close I can feel her warm breath on my skin. Sawyer fades away.

I turn and have to blink to focus in on her. When her face comes in clearly, I see eyes so dark they might as well be black and hair the color of coal. She's a fierce one who I can't seem to escape no matter how hard I try.

"Tiffani," I acknowledge, but she's not the one I want to be talking to. I want Sawyer back. She scared away Sawyer.

"You haven't been back in a few weeks. I was beginning to think I'd never see you again."

My eyes shut because I can't keep them open any longer. If only when I closed my eyes, I could imagine that Tiffani was Sawyer. But there's nothing about Tiffani that's like Sawyer. She's taller and darker. Her hair is shorter, and her voice isn't raspy enough. Her touch isn't as tender, and she has an obnoxious, booming laugh. One might think it's a good thing, but there's nothing good about forgetting Sawyer. She's the only good thing I ever had.

"You all right, Dean?" she asks, placing a hand on my shoulder.

I rub my fingers into my eyes, hoping that will clear some dizziness. I open my eyes to see two Tiffanis. "I need you to call me a cab. Please?"

She's a little miffed, but I'm too hammered to care. I can't keep doing this. I hate drinking. It doesn't solve anything. I'm going to wake up in a world of hurt tomorrow. One worse than this one.

I have to go back. I have to get my Sawyer back.

All I got when I came back to Willowhaven was a town with no Sawyer and a dead dad. Funny how plans work out. Or how they don't. Life never goes as we hope it will. This shouldn't come as a shock to me anymore. Every decision I make blows up in my face. Why should that start changing now?

Making things right with Sawyer is going to take all the patience I've mastered over the years. Patience might be a virtue, but it's a beast.

CHAPTER THIRTY-NINE

Sawyer

"I RAN INTO Lily today." Alix leans over the counter while I decorate some pastries for the display.

"That must have been awkward."

"A little, yeah. I think she wants to be friends again. It seemed like she was trying to apologize to me."

My eyebrow quirked up in question. "For what?"

"I don't know. She didn't flat out say, 'I'm sorry for such and such.' She said she missed me and hoped we could get together sometime."

"How special for you two. What did you say?" I ask, concentrating again on the task at hand.

"I said, maybe. But it was weird, Sawyer. She's probably trying to cozy up to me to know what's going on with you and Dean."

I stop decorating and give her my full attention. "Nothing is going on with me and Dean, so there won't be anything to tell."

Alix shrugs. "Maybe. But if there was something going on, I wouldn't tell her and she knows that, so I guess that doesn't make any sense."

I set down the icing bag. "What are you getting at, Felix?"

She throws her arms in the air as if she doesn't want to take the blame for anything that comes out of her mouth. "I don't know. It was just strange how she suddenly surrendered. She's been avoiding me for three years—nearly as long as Dean has been back—and all of a sudden she wants to be friends again. It's fishy."

"Maybe she finally realized by taking Dean she lost her true friends, and now she's left with all her fake ones." The bite in my voice is irrepressible.

"That's possible, too. But why now? Why after all this time? What changed?"

"When you get that all figured out let me know," I say, turning my attention back to decorating. Not that I care terribly about the fate of the friendship. She's made no attempt to rectify ours, though I doubt I'd be all that welcoming to the thought anyway.

"I will, but I'm out. Got to pick my brother up from school."

"Okay. Ruffle his hair up for me."

"Will do," she hollers as she walks out of the bakery door.

My car makes a funky clinking noise when I start it the next morning. I groan and lean my head against the steering wheel. I don't have time for car troubles right now. I'm late for work as it is. I call Polly and tell her my dilemma, explaining I'll be even later. As much as I don't want to ask him, there's only one place I know won't jerk me around, or make me any later than I already am.

I pull up to Dean's garage and, thankfully, he's already out front, so I don't have to go searching for him. The place looks pretty busy. He's talking to a customer and pointing out some of the new bikes he has on the lot. When he notices my car he smiles but finishes up his conversation. I get out and lean against my driver's side door to wait. After a couple minutes, Dean gestures for the man to keep looking and tells him he'll be back in a little bit.

As he walks up to me, I notice how fresh and clean he looks. He probably hasn't done much of the garage work today. He's dressed in black jeans and a form-fitting gray t-shirt. Dark stubble along his jawline makes him look incredibly rugged. Inhaling, I struggle to control the urge to run my fingers over it. Would he fight me if I were to drag him into his office and—

It's such a ridiculous thought I cut myself off. Yet it's the only thing I can think of as he makes his way over to me.

"She's knocking a little bit," he says as a way of greeting.

"I know you don't normally take care of cars," I say apologetically, "but I was wondering if you could take a look and see if it's something major, or if I'm just being a girl and could fix it with something simple like an oil change."

Dean lets out a throaty chuckle. "What's the issue? What kind of other noises has it been making?"

I explain the noises it made when I started it and how it's driving. I repeat the noise, trying to get it right. Dean looks at me as if I'm giving him his entertainment for the rest of the day. "Okay." He laughs. "Okay, you can stop. I heard it when you pulled in. I know what it means. I just wanted to hear you do it."

I step forward and punch his shoulder with enough force that he grabs his arm. He laughs harder. "I'm sorry I couldn't resist."

I bite down on my laughter. "Well, can you fix it?"

"Yeah, give me a few minutes." He holds out his hands for my keys, and I hand them over. "Just hang out. I'll bring her out when I'm done."

At the end of the garage is an open bay that he backs my car into. Though I've been to Dean's shop before, I've never really looked around, so I decide to do some exploring. The tin roof shines underneath the sunlight. The garage is bigger than I imagined a motorcycle repair shop would be. It looks like he bought a regular auto repair shop and converted it. When I stroll by one of the open garage doors Aiden waves at me from inside, motioning for me to come to him.

"What's up, Sawyer?"

"Hey, Aiden." I smile.

"You here to see Dean?" His greasy hand lifts for a high five until he realizes how dirty it is. "Sorry," he says and wipes it on a rag.

It throws me a little, the way he asks if I'm here to see Dean. As if I would be here for more than car troubles. "I had some issues with my car this morning. He's taking care of it for me now so I can get to work."

Aiden grins impishly. "Ah. I see. Sure."

I arch my eyebrow, silently questioning what he's insinuating.

"You can hang out in his office if you want," he offers. "It's through the main office." He points to a door on the other end of the garage. "Just that way."

My curiosity is piqued. "Okay. Thanks." I nod and walk past a few other guys I don't recognize working on bikes. A

233

couple of them look to be around our age. Some look a little older. They nod politely, and eye me all the way as I cross the open space.

The walls of the main office are covered with rims and posters of different kinds of motorcycles. Some other automotive posters hang on the front counter. Past the counter is another door that leads to a smaller office—Dean's office.

I hesitantly enter, feeling a little bit like I'm intruding on his personal space. But Aiden was the one to tell me to come and wait here.

I tell myself to sit down in the chair in front of his desk to keep me from snooping, but Dean has a couple frames on his desk. I can't help picking them up one by one. The first picture is of him, Aiden, and Josh standing outside the garage. Aiden has his arm thrown over Dean's shoulder, and they're both flashing a thumbs-up. Josh stands on the other side of Dean with a straight face like he's trying to appear tough. I hadn't realized Josh had been a part of the garage, too. He looked different back then, not nearly as affected by the harshness of the world.

It could be the opening day or just after Dean first opened the garage. Dean looks a little younger with not as much scruff on his face. He appears happy, but there's a smidge of something else in his eyes—a distant sadness that I don't think most would pick up on. My fingers brush gently over the face that looks more like the Dean that left me behind. A piece of me fills with disappointment and envy, a gut-wrenching bitterness that I missed such a big moment in his life. Lily was probably here. Knowing her, she was most likely the one to take the picture, not willing to miss a moment of the action.

I set down the picture with a sigh and lift up another frame with a one-dollar bill mounted in the center.

"That was my first dollar."

I twirl around to see Dean leaning against the doorframe, and his arms folded over his chest. My first thought is, *how long has he been standing there?* My second, *dang, he looks good in black.* The contrast of the dark against his skin makes the green in his eyes even brighter. I attempt to shake thoughts of kissing him right here and now, but they hit me over and over like a jackhammer.

Setting down the frame, I point to the picture of him with Aiden and Josh. "That's a good picture of you guys." I swallow.

"I had just gotten the keys to the place." A reminiscent smile forms on his lips. "It was one of the best days of my life." All I want to do is stand here and watch him with that content aura in his eyes. He looks so satisfied with life, and I wish I could feel the same way.

"Josh used to work here?"

He nods grimly. "But he became too unreliable. Over the last few years he became someone I didn't recognize. I should have cut him out of my life a long time ago, but he was my best friend, you know?" He clears the emotion from his throat, the building tears. "He was like a brother to me, the brother I never had."

I did know. I never understood it, but I did understand the depths a friendship could go. Alix was the sister I never had. If she were to change like that, I don't know how easy it would be for me to turn my back on her.

"I'm sorry."

Pushing off the doorframe with his shoulder, he walks into the office to stand in front of me. He shakes his head. "There's nothing for you to apologize for. He made his bed. It's time he

235

lay in it. Unfortunately, it took me watching him hurt someone I really care about to realize that."

Dean's eyes unhurriedly glide over mine, making me lose myself. If I just lean in a little more... His hand rests on my upper arm, and I freeze. His touch brings me back to reality. I have to get out of here, and I really have to get to work.

"Is it all taken care of? Did you find the problem?"

Dean takes a moment, blinking. He nods once and drops his hand. "You needed some oil. You were running low. That's what that knocking noise means."

"Really? That's it? Are you sure?"

He can't hide his amusement. "I realize my expertise resides with the motorcycles, but yeah. I'm familiar enough with the sounds your car was making to know how to fix it. You're good to go. You brought it to me just in time. Driving with low oil will burn up the engine. So, make sure you check your oil regularly."

"Okay. Thank you. What do I owe you?"

"Nothing." Dean shakes his head adamantly as he steps back.

"No, seriously, Dean. How much?"

"It took me ten minutes," he says, coming around on the other side of his desk. "I looked around a little and poured in some oil. I'm not going to take your money for that, Sawyer."

"And I'm not leaving here until you let me pay you." Standing my ground, I fold my arms across my chest. I don't want him to do me any favors, nor do I want to feel like I owe him.

He merely shakes his head with a humored expression and sits down.

"Well," I sigh. "I don't feel comfortable with you doing it

236

for free."

"All right," he agrees. "Then how about in exchange for taking care of your car, you make me a batch of your famous Reese's Pieces cookies."

"Seriously?" *That's it?*

"It's been ages since I had them. I think I've been patient for long enough."

I hadn't made Reese's Pieces cookies since I last made them for him. It was the only thing I could make in high school. What could be better than peanut butter, chocolate, and cookies? Nothing. And Dean agreed.

A chuckle escapes as I shake my head at him. "Okay. Sounds simple enough. One batch of Reese's cookies coming right up."

"Deal." He holds his hand out over his desk for me to shake, and I take it.

The handshake should feel completely platonic and all business, but the moment our hands touch, I swear fire shoots up my arm. I attempt to cover the shaken look in my eyes, but when Dean's eyes turn heated, I know I'm not the only one who feels it. I yank my hand back, unable to remain cool and unaffected. It's so obvious that he made me nervous, I feel like a total idiot.

"Well," I say, "I'll drop some off tomorrow. I've got to get to work now."

He nods once, but doesn't say anything more as I race out the door as fast as my feet will carry me without breaking into a full out sprint.

CHAPTER FORTY

Dean

A WEEK LATER, I sit with a stack of invoices an inch thick piled on the side of my desk. Business has really started to pick up since Jerry Drake came to the shop. Soon I'll have to hire more mechanics and only be able to handle selling the bikes and running the business end of things. There won't be time for much else, which almost makes me second-guess my answer to Rob. I thought it was the right decision to make. I know he was disappointed when I shot him down, but I couldn't sell my garage. This place is more of a home than the house I live in. But the look on Sawyer's face when she talked about the bakery... I'd sell my garage for her. I'd sell my garage to get that bakery for her.

I take a bite of one of the cookies Sawyer dropped off the other day. It bummed me out because I didn't see her. I was in the garage with Aiden, and when I came back to my office, the cookies were in the middle of my desk, plated perfectly with no other sign she was here. If she was back to completely avoiding me, she had another thing coming, because I wasn't about to let that happen.

The cookies are as good as I remember, if not better. It's

very possible that she's gotten better at baking. She's always had a knack for it, which makes her working at Sprinkles so fitting. That place is perfect for her.

"Hey," Aiden prompts from the doorway of my office. "Sawyer is sick. We should bring her some flowers."

"How do you know?"

"I finagled it out of Alix. She's over there now." He lifts his shoulders with a smug grin.

"Alix still hasn't agreed to go out with you," I say suspiciously. "Why did she tell you about Sawyer?"

"It passed in conversation, and I knew it would be a perfect opportunity for you to make a nice gesture. It doesn't have to be romantic. Just that you heard about her being ill and were thinking about her. Chicks eat that crap up."

"If I had known, I would have brought her something anyway, but thank you for the heads up." I look back to my computer screen.

"No." Aide steps in. "I'm basically handing this competition over to you. Sawyer. Platter. Take it. Now."

"First of all, there is no competition, and you know it. Second, I will go. I just have a ton of crap to do first. I'll be done in a couple hours, and then we can go."

"You're killing me, Dean. We have to go now. Alix is there. It's a perfect opportunity for me to run into her."

"So the truth comes out." I narrow my gaze at him and grunt a chuckle. "You're using me."

"Yes. Shamelessly, I am."

"Just let me finish this report real quick." I tap my keyboard, attempting to get my numbers in.

"There's no time for that." He places his hand over mine,

239

stopping me. "I don't know how much longer Alix will be there. You can finish the report when we get back."

I laugh. It's not a secret that he likes Alix, but it really sets in now. If I push him hard enough, he might get down on his hands and knees and beg. It's really tempting. "You've got it so bad, Aide."

"And I'll have her eating out of the palm of my hand before I'm done with her."

"Please tell me you're just spewing out crap, and that you don't actually believe the words that are coming out of your mouth."

"Yeah." He grins. "She'll totally walk all over me, and I'll love every minute of it."

My amusement continues as I save my documents on my computer and get up. "All right. Let's go, cupid. I've got a sick girl to visit."

CHAPTER FORTY-ONE

Sawyer

MY THROAT IS on fire, and my head has little dwarves crawling around inside, throwing a rave. Someone knocks on the front door and rings the doorbell. If my mom hadn't been expecting a package I needed to sign for I wouldn't have answered the door.

When I peek through the peephole and see who's on the other side of my front door I tug my robe a little tighter around myself.

Dean and Aiden smile when I crack open the door.

"Hey," I greet, brushing the dingy hair from my face. "What are you two doing here?"

"I wanted to stop by to make sure you were okay," Dean says. "We heard you weren't feeling well."

I swallow. "Oh, thanks. I—"

"She's great because I'm here," Alix chimes over my shoulder.

"Alix," Dean acknowledges with a close-lipped smile and purses his lips in a way that tells me he's waiting for her snarky response.

I peer back at her, and her expression changes as soon as she realizes Dean isn't alone. Her haughty smile turns into a frown.

"Preston," she says. "Ballard." Her voice lowers with annoyance, but I see right through her.

"Hey, Alix." Aiden beams. He's so asking for it.

"We didn't mean to interrupt." Dean sounds apologetic.

"Dean wanted to bring these." Aiden holds out a bouquet of white lilies. A little ironic if you ask me.

"Aiden insisted we couldn't come empty handed," Dean adds.

"Oh... well, thanks, you guys." I almost bite my tongue, but the words come out before I can think twice. "Do you want to come in?"

Aiden shoots a smirk behind me so I assume Alix is shooting him a death glare or daring him to take one step closer. Dean's eyes shift between Alix and me, but then he finally decides. "It's all right. Just get some rest, if Alix will allow it. We'll catch up later."

"Okay."

"What's that supposed to mean, Preston?" Alix snorts.

"Nothing. Just having the two of you together is never a quiet environment." He glances at me with a knowing smile. I know he's referring to anywhere Alix is, but we only share the look.

I thought it would be more awkward to see him here than it is. I'm actually disappointed he said no. Though Aiden and Alix seem to take some of that edge off. They're like a buffer.

"I'm an amazing caretaker, I'll have you know," Alix says. "She'll be begging for me when I leave." She crosses her arms, daring either of them to say otherwise. Only Dean knows better.

"Or begging for you to leave. Bye, ladies." Aiden winks, and

I know Alix is going to blow a gasket when I close the door.

"See ya," I say.

Dean waves timidly as I shut the door. I bring the lilies to my nose and inhale.

"He's such a tool!" Alix screams and I laugh.

"I think he's charming. And I'm almost positive he heard you."

"Hold on. We are talking about the same guy here, right? Though, I'm not okay with you calling either of them charming."

I roll my eyes and walk to the kitchen to put the flowers in water. "I was talking about Aiden."

"I don't know if that's better or worse," she scoffs.

"He likes you, Alix. Just give the poor guy a break."

"Just like you're giving Dean a break?" Her eyebrow lifts, calling me out.

"I'm not giving anyone a break. Dean has Lily. We're friends."

"You don't want to be *just friends* anymore, Sawyer. I'm not blind. And you know what, if that's what you want I won't stop you. But he's always had trouble written all over him."

I exhale and arrange the lilies in a clear vase before setting them in the center of the counter. I head for the living room. "Alix, what part of 'friends' don't you understand? Give it a rest."

"I won't give it a rest, Sawyer, because I know you love him. You're lying to yourself if you don't see that you still do. And as much as it scares me to see you give your heart to him again, I don't think he ever really gave it back."

I collapse on the couch with my hand across my eyes to block out some light... and to block her out a little bit. The

243

dwarves are pounding with a vengeance. *Can't they go mine for coal somewhere else?* "Alix, please stop. It's not going to happen. There's too much between us. He's with Lily now, and I don't think I could ever fully forgive him." And he deserves better than a broken me.

She's silent for a moment, and I know I'm not going to like what's about to come out of her mouth. "Sawyer," she pauses. "You can lie to yourself all you want, but you were a goner the moment you realized he was back."

I drop my hand from my eyes and glare at her. She looks earnestly back at me. "You might have been angry and hurt at first, but we all know what he means to you. It was only a matter of time."

"I can't do that to Grayson."

"Do what? Sawyer," she sits down on the couch by my feet, "I don't mean to sound insensitive, but he's gone. And if you ask me, I know this is exactly what he would want for you. As much as he drives me crazy, Dean makes you happy. Grayson would want you to be happy."

"Dean doesn't know," I murmur, tears filling my eyes.

"Then *tell* him," she presses, rubbing my feet. "You can't hold against him what he doesn't know. That's probably half of the reason why you can't completely forgive him. I won't promise that giving him a chance is a good idea, but it's time to be honest with him. He knows he betrayed you by leaving, but he doesn't understand how deep it runs. If you two would talk about everything, there wouldn't be *too much* between you. You're both tiptoeing around each other. I don't know how you can stand it."

"Lily," I say simply.

244

"Screw Lily. She's not you, and he knows it. There's no way he's with her because he wants to be. He's biding his time until you realize that he's the only person you could ever be with."

"You say that as if you talk to him about this." I sit up on my elbows. "Please tell me you haven't talked to Dean behind my back, Felix."

"Heck no. Sawyer, it's like you think I haven't been around for the last twenty-five years of our lives. I know you and what kind of a person you make Dean. There's no way he is going to let you walk out of his life without a fight this time. But he's not stupid. He doesn't want to scare you. He wants to give you time, as he should."

I want to give in, but as soon as I think of giving in, I'm reminded of everything he's put me through, and it's so hard to sit here and be okay with it.

Alix pats my feet and stands. "At least talk to him, Sawyer. You deserve more answers, and he doesn't deserve to be left in the dark anymore."

I can't get Dean out of my head. The lilies he gave me eventually die. They were my only connection to him for a week. He hasn't come to the bakery. I haven't gone to his shop. We haven't seen each other in passing while running errands or at the grocery or at Moment in Thyme. Before I would have been counting my blessings, but something in me has changed. I find myself scanning the streets and watching every passerby in front of the bakery window. My ears perk up to exhaust backfiring on a truck or the rumbling of a motorcycle engine in the distance, but it's never him.

I walk outside to the trashcan near our garage to throw the lilies away. Before I dump them all, I think twice and save one. It's wilted and probably won't even dry nicely, but I want to keep it. It's a pleasant night, so I settle onto the top porch step and peer up at the starlit sky.

My brain keeps reminding me that I shouldn't be thinking about him, that he's with Lily, and I should forget him, but my heart has other plans. My heart should know better. It was the one that took the real fatal blow, but it doesn't remember that he was the one who broke us—either that or it doesn't care.

But I care. I owe it to Grayson to be a stronger person, to live the life I promised him I would. Letting myself fall for Dean again could be the end of me.

Or just the beginning.

A flash shoots across the sky and my heart jolts with excitement. It doesn't matter how old I get. Shooting stars make me feel like a child seeing Disneyland for the first time. Every time I'm awestruck and amazed.

The blanket shifts underneath me as I scoot closer to Dean, and he arranges his arm beneath my neck like a pillow, cradling my head in the crook of his shoulder. The bed of his dad's truck isn't the most comfortable place to lie down, but we can remain undetected here—unspotted by the rest of the world.

Dean lives far enough away from town that there are no streetlights to disturb the glimmering sky above us. When I look up, I see nothing but stars for miles and miles. The night encases us. We are a part of the sky.

Dean's hand shoots up, pointing into the darkness. "There! Did you see it?" he asks excitedly.

246

My eyes dart to where he's pointing, but I'm obviously too late. "Dang! No, I missed it," I say.

His fingers wrapped around my shoulder idly play with the ends of my hair. "Next one. You'll see the next one." I feel the touch of his lips on my forehead. "I still can't believe you've never seen a shooting star before," he murmurs into my hair.

"I guess I never took the time to look for one before."

"Well, we've got all the time in the world."

"But what if the world ends tomorrow?" I question him wryly.

"You're right. The sky could fall down on us right now," he says seriously, but I hear the hint of sarcasm.

"That would be really tragic."

"It would be," he says. "But you know what? Even if the sky were falling, and the world as we know it was crumbling to the ground all around us, everything would be okay because I have you. You make me feel safe, Jack."

I peer up at him and kiss his clean-shaven jaw. "You make me feel safe, too, Dean. I trust you. I know that you'll take care of me no matter what."

"Did you know that I love you?" His green eyes blink down at me.

"Yes." I nod.

"But I've never said it before."

"You didn't have to." Deans presses his lips to mine once. And again. "You know I love you, too, right?" He smiles. And again.

"I do now."

When we stop kissing, we lie under the stars in silence. And I'm okay with that, because doing nothing with Dean is better than doing something with anyone else.

A flare of light fires across the sky and I gasp. "Did you see it?" Dean asks.

247

I nod into the arc of his shoulder. "It was beautiful."

"Sawyer," Mom startles me. "It's pitch black. What are you doing out here?" I whirl around as she flips on the porch light. "Are you trying to catch a cold? It's freezing out here."

"It's not freezing, Mama. It's perfect. I'll be in in a minute." I turn back and face the stars.

"Are you okay?"

"I'm fine. Will you please turn off the light? I can't see the stars with it on."

"All right," she says, resigned. The light goes out, and the front door closes. I exhale. Lifting my face again toward the night sky, I wait and listen for something in the universe to tell me where I'm supposed to go from here.

There's only one place I want to be. I just have to decide if I'm willing to let the universe take me there.

CHAPTER FORTY-TWO

I'M SITTING ON my porch swing, waiting for the sun to set when I see a figure walking up the dirt driveway. When I stand up against the railing, I see that it's Sawyer. Though it's only been about a week since I've seen her, it amazes me how much pressure has built up in my chest. The sight of her immediately relieves it. She smiles timidly when she sees me and lifts her hand in a hesitant wave. My lips curve up in response.

"Hey."

"Hey," she says, a little out of breath.

I wait until she's closer to ask, "What are you doing here?" I'm not complaining, but it's nearly a five-mile walk from her house.

"I just... I went on a walk and found myself here." She looks up at my house, the house I grew up in. The house that holds so many memories I wish I could forget. I ask myself every day why I haven't sold it. I still can't answer that. "It looks different."

My eyes remain on her. She's wearing cut-off jean shorts and a yellow sweater. If I didn't know better, under this light, I would have mistaken this Sawyer for the teenage, full of light and life Sawyer. I know she's in there. Somewhere.

"I cleaned it up a bit when I took over," I say. "Replaced the siding and gave it a new paint job. It just needed a little love."

"The blue looks nice," she says. "It's got a little gray in it."

"Thanks." I nod and pause. "Do you want to come in? I could get you some sweet tea. Got a cold pitcher of it in the fridge."

"Nah, I was just getting some fresh air." She looks behind her with a look of uncertainty in her eyes. It's possible that she regrets coming here. But I can see something is bothering her. Flat-out asking her won't go well. She doesn't work that way. When she wants to talk about it, she will.

"Take a breather then." I sit down on the top porch step and pat the seat next to me. I'm pleasantly surprised when she accepts.

"I love this time of year," she sighs. "When the nights have cooled down enough so that you can be outside without it being too hot or too cold. It's the perfect weather for walking."

It felt a little cold to me, but I agree anyway. "It is a nice night." We watch the sun in a comfortable silence as it begins its descent, painting the sky a pinkish-orange. If I close my eyes, I can almost imagine that the last six years never happened, and we're back to the way it was always supposed to be. Whatever wars are raging in my head quiet down when I have Sawyer by my side.

I hear her breathing and feel the tension wafting off of her, but it doesn't seem to have anything to do with me. She exhales. It's coming.

"People don't really know how he died." She pauses and touches her fingertips to her lips. "It was internal bleeding."

There it is.

"They knew not even surgery could fix it. Too many vital organs were damaged. He would have died on the table. His body wasn't found fast enough after the attack. If it had, they might have been able to save him. I fought with the doctor for like ten minutes. He finally snapped at me and told me I could argue with him or spend the last few minutes I could with Grayson." She swallows. "He drew his last breath during our last conversation."

I keep silent because I can't speak. If I open my mouth, I might cry, and I haven't done that in years. I have to stay strong for Sawyer.

"Did you know it wasn't supposed to be him?" She pauses, peering over at me from under her thick black eyelashes. I can tell she's not really asking me, because I don't know what she's referring to. Her hands run up and down her arms anxiously before she looks down at her feet resting on the wooden steps. "They beat up the wrong guy. The guy who they meant to beat up lost in a game of poker and didn't pay up. The other guys were too drunk to really recognize him, but they saw Grayson and thought he was their guy." She lifts her eyes slightly and stares off with an emptiness I crave to fill.

"Sawyer," I breathe.

"He shouldn't have died," she says blankly, like she's not feeling what she says. I know if she felt the words she would drown and maybe never surface. "They got the wrong guy."

"That's... I... I'm so sorry." I grit my teeth, clenching my jaw so tightly as if that will fight off the tears. I want to reach out and touch her so badly. She carries this pain with her every day. I want to hold her and make it all go away.

251

She takes a breath. "I know there's a reason for everything, but I can't figure out why it had to happen to him. He was everything good in this world." She pauses. "Is it my fault? Because I was never supposed to leave Willowhaven? Fate was pushing me back here and losing him was the only way I'd do it? Or was it my punishment for..." she chokes on her words, shaking her head, unable to finish.

"No. Stop it." I grab her shoulders and force her to look me in the eyes. Her eyes are filled with tears. I wipe them away with the back of my fingers as they fall down her cheeks. "Sometimes bad things happen to good people. It's not a punishment. It's not fate. It just happens. And it sucks, but we can either let it bring us down and consume us, or we can learn from it. It can make us stronger."

"When?" she whispers, her wet eyes search mine for answers I can't give. I want to kiss her so badly it hurts. I want to heal her with my touch, to bring her back to life. It's the only way I know how. "When will it make me stronger?"

"With time," is all I can give her.

"I'm through with time. I want to be stronger now."

"You *are* strong. Don't you see?" I shake her shoulders, urging her to understand. "After everything that has happened to you, you're still breathing. You talk about being broken, but you're not broken, Sawyer. You have a few scars. That's all. I've seen the transformation you've made in the last few months. I know it hasn't been easy, but you've done it." I motion my hand between us. "Even now. Would you have been able to tell me that all those months ago?"

Her head shakes back and forth, and the light that I've been waiting so long to see starts to flicker faintly in the depths of her

252

dark brown eyes. My hope grows.

"You are stronger than you know. You have to start believing it."

"When life keeps knocking you down it's hard to believe anything," she utters.

"You have to know that I understand that," I urge. "I understand that more than anyone."

"Then you have to know losing someone like that can destroy a person." She turns her gaze away from me. "I've lost too much to be as strong as I once was."

"You've survived, Sawyer. You've continued on with your life. You've picked up the pieces and carried on. That's what makes you strong, even if you don't feel it." She's so close to me. All I need to do is lean closer and her lips would be mine. It hits me then that she doesn't know how I felt about her when I left. She doesn't know how much I wish I could take it all back.

"Sawyer—"

"I'm going to head home," she cuts me off. It's obvious she cut me off on purpose, so I hold my tongue. "It's a long walk back. I should probably start now." She stands, brushing away the tears and wiping them on her shorts as she walks down the steps.

I shake my head and get to my feet. "Let me take you home. It's getting cold, and it'll be dark soon. You shouldn't be walking that far in the dark."

"I'll be fine, Dean," she attempts to reassure me. "I like walking."

"I wasn't asking you. Let me get the keys to my truck."

It surprises me that she doesn't fight me. She nods and waits at the bottom of the steps for me to come back. On the drive over, we don't say anything, but the silence doesn't drag. It almost feels the way it used to. Sawyer looks out her rolled down window, the wind blowing her waves back. Her smooth jawline is more flawless than I remember. I'm grateful her eyes are focused in the other direction, giving me the opportunity to really take her in. Though her appearance is the same, the curves of her features have subtle changes, matured changes. She's not the girl I fell in love with. She's a woman now. A woman who lost that girl somewhere along the way.

I put my truck in park when we get to her driveway.

"Thanks for listening," she says to the floor before she peers over at me from across the bench. "I haven't really been able to talk about it with anyone. I don't know why I felt like I could talk about it with you."

I reach over with the possibility that she'll brush me off and touch my hand to her arm. She tenses, but she doesn't pull away. I've missed the touch of her soft skin. "I'm really glad you did. I miss talking to you."

Her eyes trail from my hand touching her and back to my eyes. Our eyes hold their stare for a short moment, but all I need is that moment. I can tell what she's thinking before she immediately grabs the door handle and briskly utters, "I have to go."

She's out of the car before I can reply or attempt to stop her.

CHAPTER FORTY-THREE

Sawyer

I'M SO STUPID.

My head shakes as if that will clear it from my ridiculous thoughts of him—thoughts of actually kissing him. *Ugh!* I disgust myself. I can't do this with him again. He doesn't want me in that way. Why am I letting myself feel for him again?

I hear Dean's car door open and slam shut. "Sawyer," he calls. "Sawyer, wait!" But I don't. The only thought raging through my head is that I have to keep moving. *Don't turn around. Don't you dare turn around, Sawyer.* I nearly reach the steps up to my house when he grabs my hand. "Sawyer, *please*," he pleads.

I turn to him, knowing I'll regret it, but I don't have it in me to resist him right now. He doesn't let me go. He holds tighter to my hand, curling his fingers around mine, fitting the contours perfectly. I don't know what it is about the feel of my hand in his, how it can be the simplest gesture and yet the most intimate. I never want him to let go again.

"I regret leaving every day," he breathes. "Leaving you was the worst decision I've ever made. I wish I could take it back. I wish I could take it all back."

Lies. That's what he does. I have to remind myself of that

when he looks at me the way he's looking at me now. The tears start to form in my chest, drowning the oxygen. "Dean, I can't do this with you." I beg with my eyes for him to go, to stop while we still can, though everything inside of me is begging me to shut up. I can't think with his hand touching mine. He holds on tighter as if he couldn't survive if he let me go. The contact is more than I can bear.

He shakes his head, and his eyes change. I know this change. I'm all too familiar with this change. How can I possibly deny him? They fill with need and tenderness as he steps closer with resolution. His mouth covers mine, and I don't stop him. His hands cradle my face as the tears start to prick my eyes. I don't know how to explain that this kiss is both painful and alleviating. Cracks start to fill and break all over again with each passing second.

He sucks in a heavy breath and deepens the kiss, thrusting his hands behind my neck, tilting my face even closer. My hands rest on his chest, pushing him away and clenching his shirt, unable to entertain the thought of letting him out of my grasp. I want it to end and last forever. But I can't let this happen. There's too much between us. So much that hasn't been said. So much that will ruin us. And as much as I don't understand it, I care about Lily's feelings.

I push him and stumble back. "I can't." My head shakes at the ground. "I can't do this again."

"Sawyer, please," he begs, reaching for my waist, but I maneuver out of his grasp. "Sawyer." There's a trembling in his voice that I nearly give into. I don't look back as I rush for the front door and close it behind me. I collapse on the cold wooden floor, letting the tears take over me.

"He did what?" Alix freaks, and I have to pull the phone away from my ear.

I hiss out a sigh as I pace my room. After waking up the next morning, the realization of what happened the night before comes crashing down on me. "I know. I know. I don't need a lecture to top off the guilt and shame. I just don't know what to do now."

"I just... I can't... Did he... I mean, I knew..."

"Alix!"

"Okay. Okay," she amends. "I knew this was coming. I just didn't realize how soon it would happen. What did you do?"

The feel of his lips on mine invades my thoughts, their gentle eagerness consuming me. I break the connection and breathe. "I started to cry and shoved him away before running inside my house."

"Abort. Good tactic. I probably would have done the same thing."

"Felix, this isn't helping." I attempt to stifle my chuckle.

"Well, I have you laughing, so I'd say it's a success. You needed to calm the heck down."

"Me? You're the one screaming in my ear and having difficulty finishing your sentences."

"I'm fine now. I can function in this conversation. When did this happen?"

"Last night. I went over to his house and talked to him about Grayson. We had a moment—a *stupid* freaking moment of weakness. He told me leaving here was the worst decision he ever made." I sigh and fall back on my bed with the phone attached to my ear. "What does that even mean?"

"I think it means leaving was the worst decision he ever made."

"Thank you, Einstein." My fingers pinch the bridge of my nose in an attempt to calm my oncoming headache.

"What are you going to do?"

"I'm going to pretend it didn't happen. It was an impulsive mistake. He's with Lily. I'm not over Grayson..."

"I'm sorry to break it to you, sweetheart, but I don't think you'll ever be over Grayson. That's one you're going to have to live with for the rest of your life. There is no such thing as closure. It doesn't exist."

"I was afraid you'd say that." I curl onto my side and bring a pillow to my chest.

"It's not a bad thing, Sawyer. Grayson was your husband. He was a part of your life for four and a half years. He didn't just pass away peacefully. He was taken from you. If you tossed him to the side and forgot about him, I think that'd be a pretty disrespectful thing to do. I think you'll learn to live with his loss. To be honest, I think you've already learned to live with the loss, and that's okay."

"But what do I do about Dean?"

She hesitates. "What do you want to do about Dean?"

I groan. "I have no idea."

"Then don't do anything reckless now. Just think about it, and remember what I said. As much as you want to keep it to yourself, he deserves to know the truth."

CHAPTER FORTY-FOUR

Dean

SAWYER IGNORES ME at every turn. The kiss was impulsive, but I know she felt it, too. I know she wanted it as much as I did. No one can kiss like that and not mean it.

I've tried calling her and texting her with no response. I nearly catch her outside the café on Monday morning, but she darts away in the opposite direction, pretending she doesn't see me. The feeling I get when our eyes meet can't be ignored, and I know she can't ignore it either.

We're back to her avoiding me, though, this time it's for a different reason, so I don't feel so dejected. I want to go to her house, but I fear that's bordering on stalker-ish. Plus, I really look like a jerk since she doesn't know the truth about Lily.

I wish I thought about that before I kissed her. To her, I'm probably more than a cheater. But I don't want to tell her that over text or in a voicemail. If only I could get her to look at me.

For a week, I do nothing but work. I keep my mind as focused on the bikes as I can. Though it's a little escape, it doesn't help completely. I finally spot her coming out of the drug store the following Tuesday. She's walking down the sidewalk toward her car wearing black leggings and an oversized sweater. It hangs off of one of her shoulders, baring her flawless skin. Her hair is piled on top of her head in one of those messy buns that, even though she doesn't put any effort into it, makes her look incredibly beautiful.

I rush to the opposite side of the street, avoiding an oncoming car and somehow come up close behind her undetected.

"You know, you've really mastered the power of invisibility."

Sawyer spins around with her hand pressed to her chest. "Holy crap, Dean. You nearly gave me a heart attack."

I chuckle under my breath. "It never fails."

Her fist darts out to punch my shoulder. I move, but she's quicker than she looks and clips me just right. "Ouch." I laugh.

"That's what you get, punk. You scared me half to death."

"You would think after all these years you'd be more prepared." I wink and she glares, but it's playful enough. And then it's as if it dawns on her what happened when we saw each other last and she shifts uncomfortably, her eyes looking around at everything but me. If she had ruby slippers, she'd be clicking them together right about now. She needs me to pretend the kiss never happened, so I do.

"No Sprinkles today?" I ask.

"I'll be going in a little later," she responds casually. "I needed to run a few errands this morning, so Polly is having me close. It's Tuesday. It's usually not too busy to handle the bakery alone."

I think about the last time she closed and grit my teeth. "You really shouldn't be closing that place all alone that late at night."

"That was a fluke night, Dean. Normally, I'm out of there by eight. We had a lot of prepping to do that day for a big order for following day."

I don't care. If that happened once, it can happen again. "On nights like that, will you call me, please? Let me either walk you to your car or take you home. I'd feel much more at ease if I knew you were safe."

"Dean, I'm fine. I doubt Josh will try anything again."

"I'm not talking about Josh. I know he knows better. But there could be others. This town isn't free of creeps."

"You're ridiculously paranoid."

"I don't care, Sawyer." I can't stand the thought of anything happening to her. "Promise me."

"Okay, okay," she finally concedes. "But I don't think you have to worry about that for a long time."

"Nevertheless, promise me you'll call me."

"I will." I nod, grateful she forfeited this fight so easily. "I need to get home to get ready for work."

I can't figure out what she would possibly need to change about her appearance, but she fusses with her hair self-consciously. "All right. Have a good day. I'll see ya later."

She lifts her hand to wave. "Okay. You too." Sawyer walks away, and I watch her the entire way.

CHAPTER FORTY-FIVE

Sawyer

"HEY THERE, SWEET girl. Long day?"

I offer my dad a small smile and collapse on the adjacent couch with a sigh. "Yeah. You could say that." I reach for the TV remote on the ottoman.

He lifts his foot, resting it atop his other knee and sets down his book on the side table. "You know this old man's a pretty good listener. Now that I'm retired, I've mastered quite a few arts. Something on your mind?"

Everything. Hence the TV. I want it to drown out my thoughts, be a mindless distraction so I don't have to feel. I want to stop feeling so much, stop feeling everything. I want it to all go away. Grayson, Dean, how everything unfolded…

Before I can turn on the TV to avoid this conversation, he says, "Sometimes avoidance can be the worst kind of self-destruction." I tilt my head to look over at him. His eyes are saturated with worry. "I know you're coping with a lot. You're coping with more than anyone should have to, but when you don't handle problems head on, they fester and escalate."

"It's not that easy, Dad," I mumble.

"It can be. It'll be hard initially, but once you give yourself the opportunity to heal, once you let yourself be open to the idea of moving forward, life will fall into place, as it should. But in order to do that, you need to deal with the problems at hand. You can't keep your feelings inside, sweet girl. They won't go away by avoiding them."

I think he's talking about more than Grayson, and I want to know how he knows, but I don't ask. I don't want to know what he knows. It's not that I don't agree with him, but it's so much easier said than done.

"I'm trying, you know?"

"Are you?" he asks. It's such a loaded question that I don't answer. His eyes shift and land on my hands resting on my stomach. I realize he's looking at my wedding ring. The sadness in his eyes mirrors mine. "Just think about it, sweet girl. I miss our Sawyer."

I do, too.

The bakery door chimes. "Sawyer? You here?" Dean hollers.

"Back here," I call, reaching for a new bottle of oil on the top shelf. Why Polly insists on putting the oil on the top shelf is beyond me.

The stool wobbles beneath me, and I know it's going to give way, but I don't have time to latch on before I fall. *This is going to be bad,* I think before steady arms catch me.

Dean grunts, placing me upright. "Looks as if I got here just in time."

I turn in his arms to say thank you, but I didn't realize how close we would be. Our lips are a breath away, but we don't move. I can tell he's as surprised as I am. The air thickens the longer we remain still, but neither of us is able to step apart.

"Polly should probably make the placement of ingredients more accessible," he says softly.

"I was thinking the same thing." My tone matches his.

His eyes drift to my lips, and my breath hitches. I watch him lick his lips before his eyes slowly travel back to meet my eyes. *He's really trying to kill me, isn't he?* I hate that I want him to kiss me again. I know that will make things so much more complicated. My fingers tremble with the need to curl into fists of restraint, but when they clench, they tighten around Dean's biceps, revealing my desire. His eyes widen.

The front door chimes, and I jump. He reluctantly lets go, and I race to the front of the bakery. I'm startled when I see who's up front. "Lily."

"Hi, Sawyer."

Dean follows me out of the back, and I know how bad this must look. I look back at him briefly before turning my attention to her. Nothing happened. I need to look less guilty. "What... what can I do for you?"

"Dean," she says, caught off guard. She clearly didn't know he was coming to see me. *Oh, this could be bad.*

"Hey, Lily." He sounds calm. *How can he be so freaking calm?*

"I was coming in for some cupcakes. My mom needs a dozen for Juliette's twelfth birthday."

"Right. The fourteenth. It's your sister's birthday today."

There's an awkward pause, and I don't know how to fix it. We weren't doing anything wrong, but there's an unspoken conversation going on between them. "Umm... what flavors can

I get you?" I ask, grabbing a box from the shelf behind the counter.

Lily's eyes speak volumes, but all she says is, "Juliette wants the black and whites."

"Coming right up."

"Can I talk to you for a minute?" Dean asks. I think he's talking to me until I see he's looking at Lily.

"Sure."

They walk outside, and I'm worried I'm about to witness a private fight. Though I'm not really that worried. I try to peek over the glass countertops inconspicuously, but it's a difficult to remain hidden behind glass. I decide I don't care and stare, ready to avert my eyes if they look inside. They are facing one another on the other side of the window. She's nodding while he does all of the talking. For some reason, I thought it would be the other way around with Dean looking officially scolded, but Lily just looks sad and a little hurt. Even now, watching them fight, I feel a twinge of jealousy. She gets to fight with him.

He steps forward, reaching out to hug her, but she lifts her hands to ward him off. She's definitely not happy. He says one word that I can't decipher, and her hands withdraw back to her sides. Dean leans in and kisses her cheek. He hovers for a moment, and I can't look any longer.

As soon as I've put the last cupcake in the box, they're walking through the door. I try to act as if I haven't been spying on them, grabbing the closest rag to wipe down the countertops.

Lily walks up to the counter and pulls out her wallet. "How much for a dozen?"

"It's thirty dollars."

She hands me cash and smiles weakly. "Thanks. Have a

265

good one." She says, "Bye, Dean," and walks out of the bakery. To my surprise, she leaves without him.

"Is she okay?" I ask. I care a little bit.

"She's fine, but I should probably head back to work," he says swiftly. "I can only trust Aiden there by himself for so long."

I offer a soft laugh, but I know the trouble in paradise threw a wrench in our friendship. Or whatever it is we have going right now. "Did you need something?"

"What?"

"Well, you stopped by, but then Lily came so I didn't know if you needed anything."

"Oh, right." He rubs the back of his neck. "Just wanted to say hey."

"Oh." I know I sound dejected, and I hate that I let my tone slip. Nothing is going on between us, and nothing will ever go on between us. I have to accept that completely now. Seeing him with Lily confirmed that. He loves her. "Well, hey."

He nods and gestures to the door. "I'm gonna go." He salutes me. "I'll see ya later."

"Okay. Bye." I lift my hand to wave and watch him leave.

I'm not stupid. Alix nailed everything right on the head. I'm still in love with him. But he has Lily and obviously doesn't have any intention of breaking things off with her. I can't forget that he doesn't feel the same way about me anymore. But sometimes it really doesn't feel that way. So, we kissed. It was rash and thoughtless. It obviously didn't mean anything to him or he wouldn't have pretended it didn't happen.

I have to know one thing—one thing and I will let this go. For good this time.

CHAPTER FORTY-SIX

LEANING MY HANDS on my desk, I hover over it, staring at nothing and breathing through my frustration. Lily has the worst timing ever. Of course she had to walk into the bakery while I was there. If I were thinking straight, I would have stayed in the back. As soon as Sawyer said her name, I knew I was a dead man. She didn't deserve to see Sawyer and I together so soon. I had to apologize to her. Not that anything happened. Well, something almost happened. Sawyer and I were *this* close.

And the look on Sawyer's face said it all. I compromised her morals, made her think we were doing something wrong behind Lily's back. That was exactly why I had gone in there in the first place. I wanted to finally tell her about Lily. It couldn't have been timed any worse. After work. I'll go tell her after work. She deserves to know, no matter the consequences.

Sawyer walks into my office after we close. I wasn't expecting her, especially after I left the bakery earlier. We hadn't made plans, I don't think. Although, this is my opportunity to set things straight. I step out from behind my desk into the main office.

"Hey."

"Hi." She looks nervous.

"What's up?"

"I just have to know something."

The tone in her voice automatically makes me uneasy. "Anything."

"Why did you pick Lily?" I can hear in her voice how much she hates to admit that this hurt her. "Of all people, why her?"

"Sawyer," I sigh and look to the ground. My mind tries to formulate the best way to answer this.

"Did you choose her because you knew she was the one person that would get to me? Or were my feelings not a factor at all?"

I blink. There was no good way to answer that. "It had nothing to do with you." I shake my head and step closer to her. "I forgot how much that bothered you in high school until the day you saw us at the park."

"Oh, c'mon." She exhales, waving her hands in the air. "We used to fight about that all the time."

"Okay, so we fought about it nearly seven years ago. I was lonely. She came along and made me feel wanted so I let her. She helped me with my dad's death and reminded me I wasn't worthless. Along the way, my feelings grew for her. What's so wrong with that?"

"Obviously nothing. You disregarded everything else we built up in those two years. Why stop there?"

Something snaps inside of me. "Look, Sawyer. I know I hurt you. I know I left, and it was hard, but I think you've

268

punished me long enough. I thought we were getting past this."

"You don't know anything," she snaps back. "You think because you left me that I became a pile of depression and misery. I've been playing nice, Dean, because I was tired, but I can't do it anymore. Lily deserves better. You deserve better. I deserve better."

"Then tell me," I urge. "Tell me what I'm missing so I can fix it. I know you're hiding something, I just can't figure out what. I'm so done with these games. Just tell me how to fix it for once rather than throwing it in my face!"

Her teeth clench. "No. I'm not doing this with you. I don't know why I tried, why I thought this could possibly be a good idea. Mend it and move on. That's all I wanted. Alix warned me, and I didn't listen. Let's end this, once and for all, Dean. We've been beating around the bush for long enough. I want to be done."

"No," I say with firmness. "Jack, c'mon."

She takes a determined step toward me. "Just because my name is typically a guy's name doesn't mean you can call me whatever guy name you feel like," she says vehemently. "Jack is not an acceptable replacement for Sawyer. So stop. Just stop already!"

She doesn't know. I can't believe I never told her. How could I possibly have kept that from her? "I never told you, did I?"

The irritation on her face is wearing on me. I want to see her smile again. It's been so long since I've seen that smile. A smile from Sawyer is like a gift. If she flashes it your way, you treasure it—hold onto it for as long as you can because she doesn't hand them out to anyone.

269

"Told me what?" she fires.

"Why I call you Jack." She waits for me to continue, and her expression perks up with interest, but she tries to remain neutral. "Do you remember our first date?"

She scoffs, but it holds a hint of a smile. Though it isn't the one I'm waiting for, I latch onto it. "Like I could forget."

I let the corner of my mouth rise. Aiden and Josh were so sure I'd end up the punchline of the biggest joke of the year. "Aiden, Josh, and I were talking about you one day. We saw you walking down the hallway with Lily and Alix as if you owned the school. Aiden said something to the effect of, *'It's a shame none of us will ever know what it's like to be with a girl like that.'*

"So I took them up on a bet. I bet them I could get you to go out with me. They thought I was insane for trying, but I didn't care, and after that first date I knew something they didn't. With you, I'd hit the jackpot."

She blinks and doesn't respond.

"I figured calling you jackpot was a little over the top."

Tears well up in her eyes, and I don't know what I said wrong.

270

CHAPTER FORTY-SEVEN

Sawyer

I HATE THE fact that he still has the power to make me cry. I don't want him to have any power over me anymore. I don't want to cry in front of him. He's taken enough of my tears. I want to unhear the story because I want to keep my distance. Hating him is so much easier. I have to hold onto the anger. Without the anger, I'll crumble, and I can't crumble in front of him. He can't keep seeing my weaknesses.

"You can't say stuff like that to me." It's not fair. It's so unfair because it makes me hate him less. So much less.

"You had to hear it. I need you to know your name isn't replaceable. Neither are you."

I scoff to hide how much the comment stings. "Does Lily ring a bell? Or do I have to remind you that *you* left *me*? You decided I wasn't good enough, and you up and left." Rehashing this, reliving the day over and over—I can't do it anymore. I turn and start to walk away, but he won't let me. He grabs my hand, holding it as if it were a lifeline and the touch of his skin against mine shoots a current up my nerves.

"I lied." He swallows. I don't turn back, but I stop. "That night when I told you I was leaving... I lied."

I should keep walking. This is dangerous ground to cross, talking about that night. I'm too close to him, too close to giving into the kryptonite he is. "You didn't leave?" I give in to the need to see his eyes and peer over at him.

"No." He chuckles lightly, but I don't find it very funny. "No, I lied about not wanting you."

"Why would you do that?" I breathe.

"I was never good enough, but you loved me anyway. You made me feel like I was worth something and it scared me. You were right. I was scared. You fell for me, and I was going to bring you down. I was going to tear apart every good thing about you, and I couldn't let my poison be the end of you."

"You left because you didn't think you were good enough for me?" His silence gives me my answer. "You stomped on my heart and left me bleeding on the ground because you were insecure?" I clench my teeth, taking in breaths, trying to calm the anger rising. "You should have let *me* make that decision. I don't know why everyone thinks they know what I want or need better than I do! You made decisions that affected me. You should have let me decide what I wanted—how I wanted to live my life. You took that away from me that night. You took my *life* away that night, Dean!"

"I know, Jack," he exhales, reaching for me.

"No!" I step away. "You can't call me that! You lost that right the day you said goodbye."

"I came back. I know I was late, but I came back."

"Why did you come back?"

"Isn't that obvious?"

"No!" My head shakes adamantly. "It's not. Nothing you do is ever obvious. Nothing you do ever makes sense to me."

272

"You! You, Sawyer," he says firmly and then lowers his voice. "I came back for you," he whispers.

My shoulders sag as the weight of his answer sets in. "And you thought, what? That I'd still be around? Just waiting for you, pining for you? How long did it take before you returned, Dean?"

His face falls. "Does it matter now?"

No. Yes. Yes, it does. "If you're going to throw coming back in my face to redeem yourself, you better believe that the timing matters. The timing is everything. I want to know exactly when you came back."

He sighs, barely able to meet my eyes. He hates the words as he says them. "You had just gotten engaged."

If he had come back after a few days or weeks, I would have been begging for him to take me back and pleading with him to never leave me again. If he had come back after a few months, I might have reconsidered taking him back. If he had come back, groveling on his hands and knees, after a year, I may have listened. But nearly three years? Without so much as a phone call or text?

I can't speak. I shake my head, grasping for words that will suffice. But nothing does.

When he's answered with silence, he continues. "Sawyer, I regret it. I regretted it every single day. Every damned day."

My shoulders weigh down. "I loved you so much, Dean. But you broke me. All those years you waited to make your gallant return… it took all those years for me move on, to recover. I couldn't stand this town where every corner and crevice held a memory of you. I waited for months and months, thinking maybe it was another one of our fights. For an entire

273

year I didn't live. I listened for rocks at my window and motorcycle engines. But you never came," I choke. "You *never* came."

His head shakes from side to side. "I knew coming back was anything but gallant. I was coming back with my tail between my legs. I didn't dare to believe you'd still be around, but a man could hope."

It's too much to keep looking at him, to see his green eyes plead with me. They have the power to wear me down, but it's too late. "It's time to bury that hope. Lily loves you. She'll take care of you better than I can." I walk to the door. "We need to let this go once and for all."

"I'm not with Lily anymore."

All of the air leaves my lungs, and I slowly turn back to him. "What? Since when?"

"I haven't been with Lily for almost a month."

My chest feels light with… relief? "You what? Why didn't you tell me?"

"Because I didn't want to scare you away." He slowly approaches me. "Sawyer, Lily and I worked because you weren't here. She filled a space, but the void was never filled. I've never stopped loving you, and I didn't want you to pull further away from me just when I was getting you back. I don't know how to not love you." He pauses to take a breath. "I knew I'd scare you away if you thought I was trying to win you back."

"And were you?" I pause, "Trying to win me back?"

He exhales. "How could I not?"

I rest my hand on the door handle to leave. "I have nothing left to offer anymore, Dean. I'm not the same person you fell in love with in high school. I gave the last piece of myself to

Grayson, and it died with him. So, let's stop trying to fix this. It can't be fixed. We're too broken. It's time to move on."

The door shuts behind me as I walk out.

"I bought you some Reese's Pieces." Grayson tosses the bag into my lap, but I don't touch it. "I always see you eyeing them at the grocery, and you've been extra quiet recently so I thought you could use a little pick me up."

It was such a considerate gesture, but the thought of eating Reese's Pieces still churns my stomach. They're tainted by the past. Grayson notices the look of unease on my face that I'm not quick enough to conceal.

"Do you not like Reese's Pieces?"

I swallow the emotion because I can't lie to him. "No, they're my favorite. Thank you." I move them to the side table next to the couch, trying to avoid eye contact.

He exhales, and I know what's coming. "I know there's something you aren't telling me, S. Something you don't think I can handle. Or maybe you can't handle telling me, but I don't keep secrets from you, and I feel like your life is made of secrets."

I bury my face in the novel I'm reading, trying to get lost in the another world. Grayson knows he's missing something, but I don't have it in me to tell him. "Gray, I don't know what you want from me. I'm always honest with you. You know everything you need to know."

"Obviously not. Why don't you trust me?"

"I do trust you!" I insist, sitting up straighter and meet his eyes.

"It doesn't feel like it. I'm your husband, Sawyer. Nearly three years ago, I vowed for better or for worse, I promised to stay by your side. I give you all of me. I always have, and I always will. Are you really not going to do the same in return?"

He's right. He's totally right. I didn't want it to hurt him. I didn't want him to feel any less important or special in my eyes. I've covered up the past because I couldn't handle it, not because I didn't trust him with it.

I take a deep breath, prepping my heart, and scoot over on the couch. Tapping the empty cushion beside me, I start from the very beginning. When I'm finished, Grayson embraces me as I cry and doesn't hold my past against me.

He numbs the pain, but he doesn't make it go away. And I don't expect him to or blame him for being incapable of making it disappear. I know only one person can do that.

CHAPTER FORTY-EIGHT

Dean

MY FIST MEETS the wall as soon as the door closes, and I drop to the ground behind the counter with my head in my hands. I lean back against the wall below the hole in the plaster I made and cry like a damn girl.

I lost her all over again, but this time it's worse. I laid my feelings on the line this time. I gave myself to her and, in the end, she still rejected me, like I knew she would eventually.

I knew better. I was smarter at eighteen. I should have stayed away. I should never have come back and tried to redeem myself, as if that was possible.

I wasn't going to say goodbye. I was going to leave after sneaking out of her window earlier that morning, but she deserves more than that. Even if it kills me to see her one last time. I need one last look at her face—for the long road ahead of me.

I call her cellphone and ask her to come outside. I have to make this brief—short and to the point—but she can't know the truth. I'll have to lie to her. She'll hate me, but she needs to hate me. It'll make it easier to leave if she hates me. If she hates me, she won't miss me.

She walks down the steps of her porch to the pathway that leads to the

277

end of the driveway. I don't leave the side of my motorcycle. I keep my helmet in my hands as a reminder to keep me from touching her. When the sun touches her eyes, they sparkle. I've noticed that before, but today, rather than the lightheaded feeling I normally get. it makes me feel like I've been punched in the stomach. She lifts on her tiptoes to kiss my cheek, but I don't move.

When she pulls back and looks at me, she knows something's off. "What's wrong?"

I do my best to get rid of any emotion in my voice and say, "I'm leaving."

"Leaving? Going where? I'll get my stuff and go with you."

I clench my teeth and force out the words. "You can't come with me."

"Why? Where are you going?"

At least I can answer this question honestly. "I haven't figured that out yet." I shrug.

"Wait." Her rosy cheeks go pale. I see the understanding set in her deep brown eyes. "You're leaving, leaving... like not coming back leaving." Her voice is hardly audible on her last words.

I nod once because I can't actually say yes. The word gags me when it finally hits that I'm leaving. How cowardly am I?

"Dean, don't leave." Tears build in her words. I expected anger. I wasn't prepared for sadness or begging. How could I leave her now? "Or let me go with you. I don't have to stay here. I would go anywhere with you."

"You can't go with me, Sawyer," I say sharply.

She flinches when I call her by her name. I never call her Sawyer. She knows something has changed. "What about us?" she asks earnestly, and I realize this is it. This is where I have to make her hate me. I don't have another choice.

"What about us?" I counter, emotionless.

She doesn't get it. She flinches, but it's in confusion not pain. I'm trying to keep my face blank when her expression contorts from confusion to

278

sadness to anger. She finally gets it.

"So that's it?" she asks with more force.

The cruel things I have to say hurt when they come out of my mouth. "Did you really think more would come out of this? Did you really think we were going to get married and have kids and live happily ever after in Willowhaven?"

Her face falls. Of course she did. I did, too. But those were pipe dreams. I must have been delusional to believe that we could have been possible. How could I possibly deserve that kind of happiness? I can't trust myself to give her what she needs, what she deserves.

"You can't leave. You're crazy if you think I don't know what you're doing. You're scared and you know it!" Tears stream down her cheeks, and she steps toward me to call my bluff. She knows me so well. I hate to see her tears, especially because I know I've caused them. I know I cringe, but as soon as my brain kicks back in, I make my face blank. I have to be a better liar. She has to believe I don't want her, that I don't love her.

"It's over, Sawyer. There's no way I can stay in this town one more day." My voice sounds so bleak. "I don't want this. I don't want this town. I don't want you."

And that seals it. The searing pain that flashes in her eyes is instant. It's so fierce that it burns through me and scorches every last nerve ending.

"Fine!" Her hands shove my chest with all the force she can muster, but I don't budge. "Leave! If that's what you want! Go! What we had was obviously a huge joke. I don't want to see your face ever again. I hate you!" Another shove. I grab her hands to pull her against me. I want one last kiss, but I know that will make this worse and contradict everything I accomplished. So, I push her hands to the side, away from me and it sends such a sharp pain to my chest that I nearly drop to my knees. If I get on my knees, I could ask for forgiveness.

I take a deep breath to collect myself. "I promise you never will." I throw my leg over my bike before starting the ignition. I hear her hollering at me, but I put my helmet on to drown her out. If I hear her, begging me not to go, I won't be able to leave. But I can't stay. It's not possible.

This is for the best. She will find someone better than me. She will find someone who can give her so much more than I can, who will actually deserve her, and who will treat her the way she deserves to be treated. And she won't get the chance to toss me to the side in the process.

The farther I drive, the more it hurts, a life altering hurt—one I know that will leave a scar on my heart forever. But I tell myself the pain will lessen. I will move past this, and so will she.

What I didn't realize was that I would have to repeat those words over and over every day to keep me from going back. I would have to repeat those words to make myself believe that our lives were better apart.

I learned how to live away from Willowhaven before. It shouldn't be too hard to start over somewhere else again. I could try and get Rob to reconsider buying the garage, and with that money, I could start over in a new town, a new state, somewhere completely different. Sawyer did it. She somehow found happiness elsewhere. Why couldn't I?

When I calm down, I get up and turn the corner of my office to see Sawyer standing inside the door of the garage. She shifts from foot to foot with a confused look in her eyes as if she doesn't know how she got there. Everything inside of me screams to go to her, to grab her and hold her and never let her leave again.

When she sees me, there is resolve. She has a purpose.

"I was pregnant, Dean."

CHAPTER FORTY-NINE

Sawyer

I KNOW WHY I came back, but I'm not sure if I'm making the right decision. Do I want to cross this line? Do I really want him to know? Having him know will change everything. It will make it real.

Yes. Alix is right, as much as I don't want to admit it. It's important for him to know that it was so much more than losing him. I lost a piece of myself, a huge piece of myself, and I never got it back.

Dean appears from the back with bloodshot eyes. He looks pathetic. *Was he crying?* It takes everything I have to keep from rushing to him and wrapping him up in my arms. I've taken on a lot over the last few years. I could handle his pain, too. I want to make his hurt disappear, and yet I know I'm about to be the one to intensify it.

My heart beats once... twice... three times. "I was pregnant, Dean."

My heart beats once more.

"What?"

I take a deep breath, reining in the courage to repeat it out loud. Only a few people know. I want to keep it that way. The less I talk about it, the less it hurts. "After you left I found out I was pregnant."

"How? How is that possible?" he says, breathless. "Did you cheat on me?"

The fact that he thought me capable of that shoots a bullet to my heart. "What? No!"

"But we only did it that... that *one* time." He's grasping for a reasonable explanation, but there isn't one.

We hadn't planned it. As soon as we did it, I felt instant guilt and regret. Not because it happened with *him*, but because I always promised my parents and myself that I would wait. We weren't ready. It took one time in the heat of the moment, and we lost control. It felt right at the time. But that didn't last—especially since the following week he was gone.

"It only takes one time, Dean," I try to explain calmly. "We weren't careful."

The color drains from his face as he realizes what a pregnancy means. "I'm a father? Do we...?"

The tears rise and fall without my permission. "No." I shake my head. I'm not ready to say the words I know I have to say to him. Please don't make me say them.

"But you just said—"

"I miscarried," my voice breaks. I feel that word deep in my bones. I've never had to say that word out loud before. Everyone that I confessed to knew, when they saw my face and the words I couldn't speak out loud, that I lost him. I lost my baby. "At almost twelve weeks."

"Well, that's..." He doesn't have the words, and neither do I. His face contorts. I see tears filling his eyes, but he angrily blinks them away. His arms latch around his torso, and I see his hands curl into fists. His fists only clench when the emotions are too much for him to handle. It's the only way he can cope. "I guess that happened for the best, right?"

"You don't get it." I choke on my tears. "Do you know what it's like to be pregnant at eighteen and not married? Do you realize how scared I was? I could hardly tell my mom."

His head shakes, trying to dispel the words from his mind. He sucks in a breath of air as if it will help his words flow more smoothly. "I... I'm so sorry, Sawyer."

"No!" His apology makes me angrier. "Do you know how guilty I felt? I not only learned what true loss feels like after having another human being inside of me taken away, but that miscarriage was combined with relief." I gasp through the emotion taking control over me, and look to the ceiling, trying to find oxygen. Even after all these years, it guts me. I can still feel the cold tile of the bathroom floor on my cheek as I breathed through the pain. I still feel Alix's hand stroking my back as my body slowly rejected the baby inside of me.

"I felt relief because I knew I wouldn't have to do it alone," I confess and shift my eyes back to him. "I wouldn't have to look at the face of a child who would remind me of you every day for the rest of my life. How could I feel relief? How selfish is that?"

"It's not selfish," he softly reassures me, stepping closer. "You weren't ready for that kind of responsibility yet. And I wasn't here the way I should have been. I *should* have been here," he says, gritting his teeth. I see his anger toward himself. "Of course, you didn't want to do it alone. No one could blame you for that."

I don't know why I can't leave it alone. Why can't I walk out? Why do I feel the need to tell him everything? I don't want

283

to tell anyone everything. "Every day there are women who yearn to get pregnant and try over and over again to have a baby and can't. I wished mine away. What kind of a mother does that?" I choke. "And now... now there isn't a day that goes by that I don't ache for that baby—our baby—who never got a chance. Because I wished it away," I sob. "I wished it away, Dean."

At some point, he strides closer to me and pulls me into his arms. I resist at first, pounding his chest for him to release me. I can't stand his caring touch. I don't want his sympathy, but the more I resist, the tighter he holds me. Finally, I relent. For the moment, I want to pretend his touch can heal me. "I needed you there, Dean, and you weren't there. I needed you so badly."

"I know." His hand runs over my head, combing through my hair over and over. "I know, Sawyer." I cry for everything. For everything I lost over the last six years. For everything that could have been. And it's crushing and liberating and it might all consume me until I fade away.

CHAPTER FIFTY

AFTER A WHILE of holding her as she cries, she calms down. I pull back and hold her tear-stained face in my hands. Her eyes stay closed—looking so brokenhearted I can't hold back any longer. I kiss her cheeks and her nose. I kiss her eyelids and her forehead. I kiss away every tear, and between every kiss, I tell her how sorry I am. I pour my remorse into every word and touch. My mouth memorizes every curve of her face and when I find her lips she gasps, but doesn't pull away, and that's all I need.

Our lips meet with a fierceness I've never known until now. We kiss for every day missed, for every kiss lost. We kiss as if it's the last kiss we will ever have. And I know that I will never let another day go by without kissing her. For as long as I live, my lips will belong to her.

Sawyer breaks away, and I know if I don't say what I need to say, I'll explode, because it so desperately needs to be heard. "I love you, Sawyer." She blinks her tearstained eyes at me. "If I had known... I swear, if I had the slightest idea, I *never* would have left. I hate that I didn't know. Knowing you had to do that alone kills me. I hate that you hurt so deeply. I hate that I hurt you at all."

She nods, closing her eyes, and more tears fall down her cheeks. "I know," she says in a raspy, drained voice.

She draws her left hand back from my face to wipe her eyes, and I catch sight of the patch of black. My eyes narrow in on the sparrow. She follows my line of sight. When I look her in the eyes the tears are back, glistening ever so slightly.

"The sparrow," I say reverently.

Her eyes hold the sparrow. She looks at it tenderly. "I loved that baby, and I wished him away. This is my reminder to never go a day without thinking of him."

"Him?"

She shrugs, blinking her wet eyelashes up at me. "Just always felt like a boy to me. I hated referring to him as an 'it.' He was so much more than that." Looking back down at her wrist, her shoulders sag.

I kiss the corner of her mouth to try and bring her back to me, but I already see I'm losing her. She's slowly slipping away.

With crestfallen eyes, she peers up at me. She shakes her head, and my hope plummets. "I'm sorry. I shouldn't have…" she says. "We shouldn't have…" Sawyer backs away out of my grasp with one step.

"Sawyer," I say softly.

"This. Us. It's a fatal disease. We're never going to be able to work. I'm not the same person I was in high school. I don't think I could ever put complete faith in you to never leave me again. We could try, but we'd only fail. Our relationship is already destined to self-destruct. There's just too much that's already broken to fix it, Dean."

I drop to my knees and my vision clouds with tears. "No," escapes my lips.

"I forgive you. Okay?" She nods, peering down at me. "I know that's what you need to hear me say. And I do. But this… this is never going to happen again. This can never happen."

"I'm so sorry," I say gruffly. "Please don't do this. *Us.* That's all I know. We are what makes life bearable." My arms wrap around her waist.

"We don't make sense anymore," she says gently. "This will be better for the both of us, Dean." Her hand rests on the back of my head. As she speaks, her fingers tighten in my hair. "It's a fresh start at life. We've been through enough. Don't you want a life that doesn't continuously bring us back to the past? I do. Being together would be a constant reminder of what we lost. I can't do it."

I choke on tears rising, reality slowly closing in. I don't agree. I don't agree at all. "This can't be it."

"Please stop." Her voice is wrought with emotion. "Please, let me go." I tighten my grip because I know this is the last time she will ever be in my arms. "Dean," she begs.

I don't want to, but I release her from my arms and bury my head in my hands. The sound of the shop door closing is the sound that will always remind me of our story ending.

CHAPTER FIFTY-ONE

Sawyer

ALIX AND I lay side by side on my bed. I didn't respond to her texts or calls all day, so she finally came over and saw me lying here. Without a word, she crawled onto the bed next to me and joined in staring up at my blank ceiling. It's blank now. I can't make out any of Grayson's features. I probably never could.

"I told him." Warm tears rolls off my cheeks, soaking the pillow beneath me.

I feel her head shift on my pillow to look at me, but I can't make eye contact yet. I don't have to explain myself. She knows I told him about the baby. "And?"

"He feels guilty." I exhale. "And I thought that was exactly what I wanted. I wanted him to hurt as much as me. But Felix, seeing the torment and regret on his face… I've never wanted to take away someone's pain more."

Alix pauses. "You love him," she says softly, simply.

I nod, not taking my eyes from the ceiling. "But it doesn't change anything. He loves Sawyer from six years ago. I'm not that person anymore. He deserves more. And on top of that…" I breathe. "Every part of me is so sad we lost our window of happiness because he left. I can't let that go. What if he stayed?

What if I hadn't miscarried? What if I stayed? What if all of this heartache could have been avoided?"

She stays silent for a moment. "If nothing ever happened to us, how would we grow? What would make us stronger?"

"That's what we say to make ourselves feel better about the despair we have to endure. How is it supposed to make me feel strong when I feel so damaged? I would rather stay weak if it meant I didn't have to feel this way anymore."

"You don't mean that."

"Sometimes I do."

She pauses. "So what are you going to do?"

"I told him it was over. Even though I promised Grayson I'd move forward, I don't feel like I have the right. And I miss Grayson. So. Much. He was my constant. He was everything," I whisper. "I don't want people to think I'm trying to replace him."

"No one is ever going to replace Grayson," Alix says gently. "Just like Grayson couldn't replace Dean. People judging you should be the last thing on your mind. I don't think they would. And who cares if they do? It was always Dean. And Grayson has been gone long enough. No one could blame you for moving on. It's not like Dean is just anybody. I think Grayson would understand, don't you?"

I decide to wait to tell her about the end of Dean and me. I'm already feeling every bit of that loss. Once I tell her, it will demolish the last piece of my heart I've been clinging to so tightly. "Grayson knew everything."

I wait for her to ask. "You told him about the miscarriage?"

I nod.

Grayson pulls away from me after I pour out my soul. Though I finally feel free, I worry how Gray really feels. His hand brushes back my hair and wipes away my tears. His hazel eyes gloss over with unshed tears and tenderness, and I know without a doubt he must really love me if he's able to look at me that way when he knows the darkest parts of my soul.

"Sawyer, I want you to be happy. Whether that is here with me in Seattle or whether it's back in Willowhaven. You need to decide. But I can't look at you every day knowing you left, not because you were moving forward, but because you were running away."

"Wherever you are I will be happy. You make me happy."

"Do I?" he breathes, his eyes searching my face.

"Yes." I touch his cheek, and he offers a sad smile. I want to be honest with him. I can't look him in the eyes and give him a partial truth. That's all I've ever given him. "But... but I think there will always be an ache in my heart for everything I lost in Willowhaven." The ache never goes away. I've learned to live with it by pushing it away. We can only coexist because I ignore it.

"Do you still love him?"

I feel the air leave my lungs. That isn't fair. He doesn't really want the answer to that question. I can't answer him right away.

"I don't expect you to say no, but I do expect you to be honest with me."

Lie. The thought rushes my mind. Lie to save him. I want to say no, I want to say no so badly. "I love you, but there will always be a piece of my heart that will keep Dean." I can't be rid of him no matter how hard I try. He holds a connection to my greatest loss. He was my first love, and one doesn't forget that kind of love no matter how elusive it might have been. It was always real for me.

"Do you want me? Do you want to stay here with me?" Grayson chokes out the last word and then recovers. "Or do you want to go back

290

home, Sawyer?"

"No," I answer too quickly, and he shakes his head. "There's nothing for me in Willowhaven." I know he'd go back with me in a heartbeat, but that's not what he's asking. Our life is here. Not in Willowhaven. I could never have a life in Willowhaven with Grayson.

"There are answers there. You can't find your answers here. You can't find your answers by running from them. You will never be happy if you keep running from your past, Sawyer. I've tried looking past it. I thought if I loved you enough... but there's always a distant look in your eyes like you're somewhere else. I can give you time. But I can't wait forever."

In my gut, I know what I should do, and it makes me sick. I'm not ready. I don't want to face everything yet. "I don't want to go back. I want to stay here with you. I can work through it all here."

He nods. "You know I would understand if you didn't. I wouldn't like it, but I would understand."

"I know."

"I just want you to be happy."

"I know that, too."

"I told him everything about Dean and the baby the day before the incident. He was the one who was encouraging me to come back. He basically told me our marriage couldn't last if I couldn't figure my crap out. I didn't want to come back, but he told me I couldn't move forward if I was running away."

"Did you ever make up your mind? Did you choose between him and Willowhaven?"

I finally look over at her. "Yes."

"Did you get to tell him your answer?"

CHAPTER FIFTY-TWO

Dean

"DEAN, IT'S AFTER midnight. What are you still doing here?"

The brick wall of my office comes back into focus, and I look up to see Aiden's shadowed figure standing in the doorway. "What?"

"You look horrible." He snickers, but there's a nervous edge.

Running my hand down my face, I blink and try to make out the time on the clock on the back wall, but I can't focus. I'm not sure I want to be able to focus on anything ever again. When I do, my broken life will become clear. "What time is it?"

"It's a quarter after midnight."

"Already?" *How did I lose track of five hours?* "What are you doing here?"

"I was driving by, and I saw the light on," Aiden explains. "I wanted to make sure it was you."

I pinch the bridge of my nose and take a deep breath, leaning my elbows on my desk. Sawyer's words have been running through my mind all night and my body is finally catching up. I ache everywhere.

"Oh man," Aiden sighs, moving forward. "What happened?

Did you tell Sawyer about Lily? Is she going to forgive you?" He pauses, but not long enough for me to answer any of his questions. "What did she say? You didn't lose her for good, did you? Throw me a bone, man."

All the air leaves my lungs. I can't tell him that yet. I can't bear to say the words. "Sawyer was pregnant when I left."

Aiden's steps halt in the middle of the room. "I did *not* see that one coming." He falls back into the chair on the opposite side of my desk. "And…"

"She lost it." My eyes follow the wooden grooves that branch out across my desk. I'm hoping they will lead me to answers to end this intensifying agony.

He exhales. "Yours?"

I want to snap at him for thinking otherwise, but that would make me a hypocrite. I merely nod, keeping my eyes down.

"I realize I don't know a lot about women, Dean, but I know that must have messed Sawyer up." I want to agree, but for some reason I can't say the words. I don't want to believe my Sawyer is gone. I know she's not. There have been enough glimpses throughout the last few weeks for me to know she's not completely lost. Even if she were, I would have found her. I would have brought her back to me. If she would have let me.

The silence lengthens between us before he speaks again. "My sister has had two miscarriages. She's changed a little bit with each one. We don't get it. My sister once told me, that when she's pregnant, it's on her mind every minute of every day. Every little change in her body, every cramp or shift makes her wonder if something is wrong or if the baby is okay. It's not the same for us. Her husband said he didn't feel like a dad until he first saw their son, but my sister felt the change as soon as she saw her

293

pregnancy test was positive."

I choke back a sob. I can't figure out why I'm so sad about this. I should be grateful I'm not a dad. I should be grateful I didn't obliviously miss the last five years of our baby's life. But right now, I wish for nothing more than to have that connection with Sawyer. I want that for us. It hits me that I want that more than anything.

"You okay, Dean?"

"It's over, Aiden. She told me it's over." My jaw tightens, and my fists close shut.

Aiden doesn't say a word. All I hear is the sound of our breathing filling the room. "I... That can't be... What can I do for you?"

"Nothing." I shake my head, unable to meet his eyes.

"Will you be okay?"

"Yeah," I grunt, dragging my hand under my nose. "I'll be fine."

Aiden can sense I'm about to fall a part. "You want me to go?"

"Yeah, I'm right behind you," I say as calmly as I can.

He reaches over and clasps his hand on my shoulder with a knowing look. "I love you, man." I nod to acknowledge him before he leaves.

Aiden isn't gone for more than a minute when I break down. The loss draws me forward, doubling me over with its force. For hours, the knowledge of losing that baby took its time setting in, seeping into the crevices of my heart and mind. Now that it's soaked in, it's taken hold of me. It's a part of me just as it's a part of Sawyer.

I drive myself home—though it's probably not the smartest

294

thing to do—rubbing away tears from my eyes to keep them from blurring my vision. I want to sleep and forget what she told me. I want to forget that she's had to carry this around for years without me. She might have had Grayson, but the baby wasn't his. It was mine. The wave knocks me down again.

It was mine.

When I crawl into bed I lay there with my eyes shut tight, trying to smother the tears, wondering how it's possible to mourn the loss of someone I didn't know existed. Tonight I lost more than just Sawyer. I lost everything.

CHAPTER FIFTY-THREE

Sawyer

I'VE MADE UP *my mind. Grayson deserves so much more from me. I made a vow. He's given me the world and more. I owe him to be better. Our marriage deserves better.*

I get in my car and head to the school to find him. Because finals are coming up, he's studying late at the library, but I can't make him wait any longer. I want to tell him now. He needs to know now. He needs to know that I will never leave him. He's my husband, and I will be loyal to him until the very end, as I vowed.

When I near the school, I see red and blue lights flashing. They blur and blink under the night sky. A sick feeling pools in the pit of my stomach. There are cop cars and ambulances and yellow tape blocking off the parking structure. Crowds of people gather on the border of the barricade. My heart sinks, and I know. I just know. I don't know how, but I know all of this commotion is for Grayson. I leave my car in the middle of the intersection, with car horns blaring at me, and run to the scene.

"Ma'am, I need you to step back." An officer holds up his hands to stop me from barreling through. His voice gives no room for civility. "You can't cross this line."

"What happened?" I say, catching my breath. "Please tell me what's going on."

296

"There was an incident regarding a student. No one is allowed in the structure until we clear the area. Now please step back."

"My name is Sawyer Jones," I hurriedly say. "Was the student Grayson Jones?"

"Ma'am, I can't give out any information," he says routinely. "I need you to step away now."

"Please tell me if my husband is okay." I know I'm hysterical, and soon someone's going to haul me away, but I have to know. I have to know if my husband is okay. "He's a student at UW. Please tell me!"

Another officer approaches us. "What's your husband's name, Miss?" he asks calmly. His voice holds a little more courtesy, but it's clear he wants to contain the situation and ask me to leave.

"Grayson," I nearly choke. "Grayson Jones." The officer's eyes fall. He didn't actually believe I would be of any importance. "Please, is he okay?" I know the answer. Of course I know the answer. If he were okay, there wouldn't be a thousand cop cars and ambulances and fire trucks lining the streets. People wouldn't be crowding the area to get a peek at the scene of the incident. If he were okay, the officer's eyes wouldn't be looking at me with pity.

"Come with me," the officer says quietly and lifts the yellow tape.

Grayson lies in a hospital bed, bandaged from head to toe. I hardly recognize him. An IV pierces his wrists and tubes feed into his nose. They've taken his glasses from him. His face is swollen and bruised. He's motionless. When I drag a chair across the linoleum to his bedside, it thumps, and his eyelids flutter.

"Hey," I croak, swallowing back tears and brush my fingertips across his partially unbandaged jaw.

His eyes open as much as they can. "Hey," he rasps.

My heart clenches at the weakness in his voice that sounds nothing like

297

him. The doctors are surprised he's still conscious. I don't know what to say. I want to say everything and yet nothing at all.

He licks his lips before he speaks. "I waited for you," he whispers.

I can't force back the tears. I collapse across his chest. "There is so much I want to tell you, and yet I don't know where to begin." His hand slowly brushes down my back.

"Some way to go, huh?"

"Stop it," I hiss, looking up. "That's not funny, Gray."

"Sawyer, you need to go back to Willowhaven." His voice is so gruff I can hardly hear him. "You need to go back home."

"No." I shake my head. "What are you even saying?"

"Sawyer, promise you'll go home. Be with your parents," he utters. "Fix whatever it is you need to." He pauses, then says, "Find him. Have babies. Grow old. Live your life."

"No, I'm staying here with you. I've already made that decision. I was coming to tell you before," I choke as the tears stream down my cheeks. "I want this to work. I. Choose. You."

His head feebly shakes once. "You know it doesn't matter anymore."

"It does matter. You have to stay with me. I choose you!"

"Stop it, Sawyer. I know the doctors…" he pauses to catch his breath, "spoke with you."

I shake my head in frustration. "It wasn't supposed to happen like this."

"I know." He tries to lift his hand to touch my cheek, but he doesn't have enough strength. I grab his hand between mine and bring it to my lips. "I love you." His words make me cry more. "I love you so much."

I kiss his palm and cup it against my cheek. "I love you, too. So much."

"Promise me. I couldn't fix this. You have to do that for yourself." I clench my jaw and try to breathe. "Promise me," he presses.

298

"I promise."

He nods once and relaxes, closing his eyes.

"Grayson?" I ask, fearing he's already gone.

"I'm still here, S."

I swallow. "Please don't leave me. Please. Please stay."

"You know I'll never leave you."

Tears pool in Alix's eyes. "Sawyer," she murmurs. And then she pulls me into her arms because she obviously can't bear to look at me in the eyes anymore.

"You don't look surprised," I whisper.

"Of course you picked him." She pulls away. "He was your husband. Your loyalty runs deep. Why would he think there was any other option?"

"I think he wanted to hear me say it."

"And you did. Whether you did it because that's what your heart wanted or because of loyalty, it doesn't matter. He knows you loved him. You had a good life together, no matter how short. It was good. Great, even."

I nod and feel the tears taking over me again. It *was* great. It was *really* great.

Her fingers brush through my hair. "Do you not want to be with Dean?" she quietly asks.

"I do," I confess. "I just... I can't. We would never work. I don't understand why he felt like he had to leave, why he thought that was what was best for us. He said it was because he was afraid, but that doesn't sound like him to me. I've never seen him do anything but face life head on. With everything and everyone against him, he always believed in himself. If he really loved me, he would never have left."

Alix speaks into my hair. "Everyone has their reasons and, as much as it pains me to say it, I'm guessing even Dean Preston had a good enough reason. But in the end, it's your choice." She lifts my left hand gesturing toward my wedding ring. "Though before you can ever move on with life, Sawyer, other things need to happen."

I nod, gazing at the diamonds. "You're right. Just not tonight. Okay?"

"Okay."

CHAPTER FIFTY-FOUR

Dean

WITH RESOLVE, I dial Rob Dillon's number as I sit at my desk.

"Rob Dillon," he answers.

"Rob, hey. It's Dean Preston."

"Dean, what an unexpected surprise."

I shift the phone between my shoulder and ear. "I was hoping that I'm not too late."

"Having second thoughts?"

"More like I'd like to do a little renegotiating. Is it possible that your offer still stands?"

He clears his throat. "Well, I've had some other promising options, but nothing is set in stone. What do you have mind?"

"I'd like to sell the garage to you, business end and all. Everything."

"You wouldn't be staying on board?"

"No, I, uh, I'll be moving out of Willowhaven in the next couple weeks."

Rob exhales. "Well."

"I know before the offer included me, but I'd like to just hand everything to you. My friend, Aiden, knows this garage almost as well as I do. I think you'd be just as happy with him at

301

the helm as you would me. He's been a part of this business from day one. I know he'd be a perfect asset for you."

Rob is silent for a moment, and I say a silent prayer. If this falls through so will everything else. "You sure about this?" he asks.

"I've never been more sure of anything in my life."

"Can I ask you what made you change your mind?"

That was an easy answer. "There's something in this world I care more about than this garage, and I can't have both."

"Well, all right."

Rob and I discuss the final business transaction. The final price was renegotiated. I don't get as much as he originally offered, but it's enough. It doesn't take more than ten minutes to essentially sign my life away.

"Well," Rob says, "if you ever change your mind, I'd be happy to have you on board."

"I won't, but thank you, sir."

"I'll have the papers drawn up. All you'll have to do it sign on the dotted line."

"Thanks, Rob."

"Thank *you,* Dean. I hope everything works out for you."

I do, too. "Eventually it will."

It wasn't as hard as I thought it would be to give up the garage. That's how I know I made the right decision. I thought it would feel more like a loss, but losing Sawyer drowns that out. This is the only way for me to move forward.

It only takes about a week for everything to finalize. Rob

wasn't kidding when he said he'd pay cash. Thankfully, he made everything really painless. The garage has officially been signed over to him. By the end of the week, I'll be on my way out of Willowhaven. For good this time.

"I can't believe you're really leaving, man. You sure about this?"

"It's got to be done. I can't stay here. If I have to stay in Willowhaven and watch Sawyer fall in love with someone else, marry someone else…" I can't finish the thought. It's too much to let my thoughts go that far. Clenching my teeth, I keep my emotions in check. I shake my head and continue. "I know you'll take good care of the garage."

"It won't be the same without you there. Who am I going to go to about my Alix drama now?"

"I'm sure you'll find someone," I chuckle dryly.

"Well, at least you're giving me the chance to say goodbye this time." Aiden smirks and punches my shoulder.

"Well, I'll need your help, so I had to tell you."

"You have underlying motives. I see how it is. You're just using me."

"It's all a little impossible without you, Aide."

Aiden agrees to help me sell the house. I put it on the market, and he's agreed to keep me posted as buyers approach. It's not really a seller's market right now, but with the mortgage already paid off, I'm not too worried about it.

With Aiden's help, I'm boxing my life away. I've decided to sell the majority of what my father left behind. His things only hold memories I want to forget, and it will be easier to move with less to worry about. There's just one thing that I don't want to sell.

303

Aiden's mouth hangs open as we stand in my bedroom, packing up my dresser. "Why are you giving me this?"

"You need it more than I do."

He looks at the open ring box in his hand and tries to give it back to me. "I can't take this."

"You can and you will. I don't have any use for it anymore." I shove it back to him. I don't want it.

"But this was meant for Sawyer."

My wall shoots up. I can't think about that. "And that's not going to happen. So, take it." I shake my head firmly. If I can't give it to Sawyer, I don't want to give it to anyone else. "Someday, Alix will get her crap together. Now you can be prepared."

Aiden chuckles humorlessly, but nods. "You really do have faith in me."

"Always have."

Through a little detective work, I found out when Sawyer wouldn't be at Sprinkles. Pushing her out of my mind hasn't been easy, but it's the only way I'm still functioning. I've done everything I can to avoid running into her over the last week. It's a lot easier not seeing her face and I know she doesn't want to see me. I will respect that.

The door chimes as I walk into the bakery. Polly appears from the back, wiping her hands down the front of her apron. Her gray hair is tied up on top of her head.

"Dean Preston, how are ya, son?" She smiles.

"Ms. Polly, I'm doing well. How are you today?

"I'm blessed." She nods. "If you're here to see Sawyer, she's not here today. She has the day off."

Taking a step toward the counter, I say, "I actually came here to talk with you. Do you have a minute? I have an offer for you I'm hoping you'll consider."

CHAPTER FIFTY-FIVE

Sawyer

WITH THE MORNING light shining through my bedroom windows, I sit on the edge of my bed with trembling hands. Today is the first day of my fresh start. It's been three weeks since I told Dean it was over. In order to really begin anew though, I have to start with this. My head bows forward as I gaze down at my right hand clutching the other in my lap. I spin my wedding ring around and around on my finger, watching each facet sparkle under the rays streaming in. The reflection dances on my yellow walls. It's time. I know it is, but this diamond-encrusted band hasn't left my hand in five years. I've never taken it off. Not once.

I remember the way it felt when he first put it on my finger. How the cold band warmed instantly, fitting perfectly in place, like this ring was always meant for my finger. I remember the look in Grayson's eyes whenever he saw it. The way his eyes would light up every time as if he was reminded that I said yes.

I grasp my ring, still circling my finger, and close my eyes. With a shaky breath, I imagine Grayson with me. I can't do this without him. His hand rests atop mine. When I peer into his face, he offers a tender smile. A lock of hair curls in the center of his forehead. I have the urge to sweep it back. His hazel eyes gleam behind his dark-rimmed glasses and then he nods. A tear escapes my eye, but I know I'm ready. I breathe in. Pulling the ring gently off, I breathe out.

"Sawyer, you headed in to work?" Mom asks while I'm grabbing an apple from the fridge with my naked left hand.

"Yeah, I'm opening for Polly today."

"Will you bring home a dozen red velvet cupcakes? I need a dessert for pikino tonight with the ladies."

I nod. "Shouldn't be a problem."

"Also, when you talk to Blaine, will you ask him to come home for Christmas? I think you have a better chance of him saying yes."

I grunt out a laugh and head toward the front door. "I'll try, but we haven't been able to get him back out here in how many years? I doubt this will be the first year."

She follows me. "It doesn't mean a mother can't dream. He might surprise you. This year has been quite a year. I think he just might make an exception. For you."

Offering a small smile, I turn back to her. "I'll call him later today, but I'm not making any promises. Christmas is barely a month away."

"Thanks, darlin'."

When I open the front door to leave, someone is jogging down our walkway, away from my house. The broad shoulders and blond hair give him away instantly.

"Aiden? What are you—" I step out onto the mat and close

307

the door behind me. Something crinkles under my foot. Looking down, I notice a manila envelope on the doormat. "Did you drop this off?" I pick it up and turn it over. It's blank.

Aiden looks over his shoulder with an expression full of guilt, like someone caught with his hand in the cookie jar, but he doesn't respond.

"What is this?" I press.

"I... I..." Never in the ten years that I've known Aiden Ballard has he ever been at a loss for words. He shifts uncomfortably and my stomach drops. *What is going on?*

I open the envelope and pull out some paperwork. Something clinks on the porch. I squat down to pick up a brass key. *Huh.* Standing back up, I scan over words I can't compute: BILL OF SALE - TRANSFER OF OWNERSHIP. Polly's name is on it. My name is on it.

"Aiden, what in the world is this?" I ask, breathless.

He curses under his breath. "You weren't supposed to see me."

My shoulders sag as I read further over all the legal mumbo jumbo. "Aiden." I exhale.

"He didn't want you to know, which is ridiculously stupid. Of course, you would have figured it out. You're not an idiot."

My hands begin to shake. *What is he trying to tell me? Why is my name at the top of a deed for Sprinkles?*

"If you couldn't get it out of me, you would have made Alix try to pull the information out of me—"

"What did Dean do, Aiden?" I demand. I have to hear him say it to understand. Tears distort my vision as I clench my fist over my heart.

Sighing, he says, "He bought it for you."

"He what?" I wrench my eyes away from the paperwork to look up at Aiden.

"Dean bought Sprinkles for you. It belongs to you now."

My head shakes in disbelief. *What did he just say?* "Where is he, at the garage? Why would he do this?" I can't control the volume of my voice. "I need to talk to him."

Aiden walks up the porch and touches my shoulder to keep me in place. "He's gone, Sawyer. He sold the garage last week. He left earlier this morning. He's gone."

"What? No. He did *not* just buy me Sprinkles and leave!" I push past Aiden and sprint over to my car in the driveway. "He can't be gone."

"Sawyer!" Aiden calls, but I ignore him as I slide into the driver's side.

On my way over to Dean's house I call his cell phone, but it goes straight to voicemail. I throw my phone onto the passenger's seat without leaving a message.

My tires peel into Dean's driveway. A FOR SALE sign is planted next to his mailbox, confirming my nightmare. Dirt clouds my car as I pull up the road. The house already looks deserted. The truck is gone, as well as his bike, but I bolt up the steps to his house anyway. My fists pound on the front door.

"Dean! Dean Preston! Open this door!" I bang, but there's no answer. I know he's gone, but I don't want to believe it. "Dean, you open up this door right now!" This can't be real. "Dean!" My fists let out their frustration, repeatedly beating the door over and over until they throb.

This is really it.

My pounding slows, and I fall to my knees. "Dean." His name is a distant cry. He's gone. Again. That freaking man left

309

me *again*. But how could he actually leave me when there was no *us* to leave? I told him it was over. This is my fault.

Leaning my forehead against the door, I try to breathe through my tears. *How dare he do this?* Buy me the bakery and then leave without saying goodbye, as if I would just accept it graciously. *Why would that be okay? Why would I be okay with that?* But he isn't leaving me with any other choice. He's going to force me to accept this.

I try to calm myself. Taking a deep breath, I bring myself to my feet and turn back to my car. Dean is standing at the bottom of the porch steps, blinking. I gasp.

"What are you doing here?" he asks.

"Are you kidding me?" I laugh humorlessly and wipe away my tears with the backs of my hands. He stands casually in a fitted white t-shirt and worn jeans, waiting for me to continue, as if he didn't just catch me having a mental breakdown on his front porch. "What are *you* doing here? I thought you were gone."

"I got a flat tire a little ways up the road. I forgot my spare in my garage." He motions to the side of the house. "Are you okay?"

I hold up the crumpled deed in my hand. "What is this?"

"It looks like a trashed piece of paper."

"Why?" I demand. I don't want to play games. He knows exactly what I'm holding.

He works his jaw and sighs, averting his gaze from me. "You deserve happiness."

"So, what? You were just going to buy me Sprinkles, leave town, and everything would wind up in happily ever after for me? You sold your garage?"

310

His chest rises and falls without a word spoken. He was full of information the other night, and now he has nothing to say for himself?

"You sold your garage for me," I say with less vehemence.

The shrug of his shoulders makes me want to shake him or kiss him, but I decide against both.

When his eyes meet mine again, he says, "Sawyer, even if I can't have you, it doesn't change the fact that I want you to be happy. You deserve to have the bakery. It's your future. I've accepted that I'm not. Please just take it. After all that I've put you through, let me just do this one thing."

"How am I supposed to accept this? You sold the one thing you love most in this world to make it happen."

Dean snorts and shakes his head. "The one thing in this world I love most is standing in front of me. I would sell that garage a thousand times over if it meant you were happy. Hell, I'd give it away if it meant I got to keep you."

My arms go limp at my sides. The thumping of my heart echoes in my ears as his words reverberate in my mind. There's no way to stop the tears from streaming down my cheeks. Tiny fractures form in my resistance, breaking down my walls.

Dean strides up the stairs to meet me at the top. His hands clutch my shoulders as he dips his head, compelling me to match his gaze. "Please don't cry. I can't bear to see your tears anymore." His thumb brushes across my cheeks.

"You only have yourself to blame," I say, and he chuckles softly.

"Tell me what to do, Sawyer. Tell me what to do to fix this, and I'll do it. I will do anything."

I want to ask him to stay. That realization strikes a chord

311

because I know how selfish that would be now. With his house on the market and his garage gone, I know I've let this go too far. He's moving on just as I asked him to. *Why did I ask him to do that?*

"Why are you doing this to me?"

"Doing what?" he asks earnestly. "I thought this is what you would want. You told me to move on. I'm only doing as you asked."

"I didn't ask for the bakery."

"You didn't have to."

I exhale and close my eyes. "Why did you stay in Willowhaven?" I ask. I need answers before he's out of my life for good. Now is all I have. "When you came back here you didn't have to stay. I was gone. Your dad was gone. It's not like you ever wanted to stay in Willowhaven, but you did."

His gaze caresses my face. After he lets out a deep breath, he gestures to the bench on the porch. "Can we please sit?"

I nod and follow him down the wooden porch. When we sit down side-by-side he continues. "I hoped you would come back, too." He pauses and averts his eyes to his front yard as he bites his bottom lip and groans. "Sawyer, I wish you had come back for different reasons, under different circumstances. Even if it meant I never got to have you, I would never have wished for Grayson's death." His eyes peer over at me. "If I had to blow away a thousand dandelions to make it all go away, I would. I would do anything for you."

My shoulders fall. "You stayed and waited for me."

"I had to make something of myself. If you ever came back, I had to be good enough to deserve you. When I heard you were engaged to some big shot in Seattle, I knew I would never win you back with the life I led. Alix not so delicately dropped hints here and there about how *amazing* Grayson was and how *unbelievably* happy you were." I nearly choke over her exaggeration. "So, I started the garage, and it wasn't much, but it was more than what I had before. It was the only thing I knew how to do, and I had to be someone deserving of you."

I blink, unable to understand how he could possibly feel that way. "You were always deserving of me, Dean."

When his head shakes I want to hold it still and force him to understand what I've always seen when I look at him. "It's hard to believe that when you're repeatedly told you're not," he says simply.

I wake up in the middle of the night to a warm body wrapping around mine. I smell Dean's familiar scent as soon as he buries his face in my neck, so I don't shy away from him. Though he'd snuck in my room countless times, he had never crawled into bed with me before.

Wetness trickles down my neck—across my spaghetti-strapped shoulder, and I hear him sniff as if he's crying.

"Dean?" I shift beside him to look at his face. "What's wrong?" His green eyes shine with unshed tears. He blinks them away with embarrassment.

"I just need to lay here with you for a little bit, that's it. I'll be gone before your parents wake up," he murmurs.

He closes his eyes and buries his face in my neck again, reaching around my waist and forming me tightly to the curve of his body.

"Dean, you're scaring me," I whisper, trying to shift in his arms to face him.

"Please, let me lay here, Jack." He breathes, squeezing me closer as though he's trying to meld us together, keeping me in place. "I just want to be

near you."

I don't want to question him further. The desperation in his voice is enough for me to give him what he wants. I relax and press my lips to his temple.

"I'm here, Dean. Whatever you need. I'm here." I shift to wrap my arms around him, cradling his head to me, brushing my fingers through his hair. "I'll always be here," I murmur, and we fall asleep.

True to his word, he was gone before I woke up the following morning. And later that day he walked out of my life completely. I hadn't thought about that night in years, but for some reason Dean's words send a memory flooding to the forefront.

"What happened that night, Dean? The night before you disappeared. You left Willowhaven because of something that happened then, didn't you?"

314

CHAPTER FIFTY-SIX

SAWYER'S VOICE BREAKS through my thoughts. I hoped she had forgotten about that night. It was a moment of weakness. I wanted one last piece of solace before our worlds were torn apart. That moment of weakness nearly changed my mind. If only I let it change my mind, none of this would have happened. I would have been there for the loss of our unborn child. She never would have met Grayson. She never would have had to deal with all the misery that resulted from the day that I left. But I know it's pointless to play the what-if game now, so I finally aim for the truth.

I sigh, rubbing my fist across my forehead. "My dad happened that night." Her eyes show understanding, but she doesn't know. We'd skimmed over the topic of my dad and his drinking habits when we were together. I didn't want to taint her world with mine, so I kept my dad to myself the best I could. It's exactly the reason I never wanted to bring her into this house. Every wall was tainted.

"He told me I didn't deserve you, which wasn't news to me," I chuckle, but it's completely without humor. "I knew it was true. But he flew off the handle that night." I close my eyes tightly. I can see him, raising his fist in the air, shouting in my face.

"You'll only drag her down! You'll never be able to be what she needs!" A glass beer bottle flies by my head and shatters against the wall, splashing beer on my clothes as the shards fall at my feet. I've learned not to flinch. I stand my ground, preparing for the punch that's sure to follow.

"I'll spend every day trying!" I shout back to keep from recoiling. I'm done cowering. It's my time to fight back. *"She loves me. She believes in me and what we have."*

"You think?" he scoffs, his head tipping back as he bellows. *"You're a fool! You're just a toy now. You'll never amount to anything worthy of her! You're a useless waste of space in this world. And if you think anything different, you're more stupid than you look!"*

"Sawyer believes in me," I insist, but my confidence is fading fast. My eyes remain focused on him.

"No one believes in you!" He rushes me and grabs the collar of my t-shirt, spitting in my face, pinning me against the wall. *"You hear me? No one!"* He shakes me like a ragdoll. I choke back my cry.

"She does," I utter, but my belief in her is slowly depleting. I avert my gaze so I don't have to look him in the eyes any longer. I don't want him to see me cry.

"Okay, you little piece of crap." He tightens his hold on my collar. *"Let's say she does decide to stick around and marry your sorry mug. It'll never last. She'll eventually leave you. Women like her don't stay around for Preston men. It's in your blood. And the day she realizes you're not good enough you'll end up just like me."* I look up, and he lifts his index finger that's not gripping the neckline of my t-shirt and thumps my chest to the point of pain. Every thump stings. *"If you listen to any advice from your old man, hear this: you're better off alone. And she's much better off without*

316

you."

"That's not true," I say softly. "We're better together." I have to believe that that's true. It's the only thing I believe in this life.

"If you stay with her, I'll make sure she doesn't live to have your children. No one deserves a lifetime committed to you."

His threat shoots needles through my veins. "What did you just say?"

"She's better off dead than living a life with you," he growls. "You will destroy her just like you destroyed your mother. I would be saving her from a lifetime of misery. She. Would. Thank. Me." He punctuates each word, the alcohol saturating his breath as it wafts across my face.

The darkness I've suppressed for the last year envelops me. Our living room becomes one big distortion, and my fists take over. I've never fought back before, but that ends tonight. No one threatens Sawyer. No one. All I see is red. It blurs my thoughts and controls my actions. When it ends, the only thing I see is blood and my father lying on the wooden floor. He groans and rolls to his side, too drunk to pick himself up off the floor.

I peer down at my bloody, shaking hands—hands that don't resemble mine. This isn't me anymore. I don't fly off the handle. My temper is supposed to be controlled. How could I lose it like that?

"You," he grunts. "You will never know happiness."

Shaking my head, I walk away from him. "You've made sure of that," I say as I slam the front door behind me.

"DEAN!" he shouts, and I find it ironic that this is the time he chooses to call me by name. I don't remember the last time he ever called me by my real name.

I never look back.

I swallow the ugly feeling I get when I think of him and take a cleansing breath. "I got out of the house as fast as I could. I had to see you." I take another moment because reliving that day means reliving a nightmare. Except it wasn't a nightmare. It was real. Things like that used to happen nearly every day of my life, but that night he went too far. "The closer I got to you the more solidified my decision became. I had to feel you against me one last time before it was all over."

She peers over at me with tears brimming in her eyes. I've seen her cry hundreds of times, but these tears aren't for her. They are for me, and I hate that no matter what I do I can still make her cry.

"Why didn't you tell me?" she whispers.

I shake my head. "I was eighteen and naïve, and I believed him. I couldn't let him hurt you and staying with you only gave him more fuel. I had to protect you. Every part of my life was toxic. If I stayed with you, or let you come with me, my poison would disintegrate any goodness you had. You deserved someone so much better than me. You deserved someone like Grayson." Sawyer presses her lips together to fight back more tears. "But that wasn't completely it. What if you did stay with me, or we ran away together? What if I became like my dad someday? His temper is in my genes. The thought of hurting you that way makes me sick. I could never do that to you. I never wanted to hurt you. *Ever.*"

She presses her fingers against her lips the way she always does when she's trying to keep her emotions at bay. "Dean," she exhales and reaches for me, but holds back, keeping her hand on her thigh. "I never knew it was that bad. If I had known… if you would have trusted me with that… we could have avoided the last six years. I would have taken you away from him. I never would have let you leave me."

I nod. "But I was so afraid I'd turn into him. I was so

318

ashamed. That kind of anger runs in my veins. My temper isn't the most controlled, and I couldn't end up like my father. If I ever did to you what he did to me, I wouldn't be able to live with myself. So I had to cut the ties. I'll never forgive myself. I'll never forgive myself for the time we lost. I know now I'm not my father. I would never, *ever* lay a hand on you."

"You've never been like your father, Dean. I always knew that." Her hand lifts and presses against my chest, over my heart. "I could have told you that."

I look up to fight back tears. *What is happening to me?* "You know, it took me all that time away to realize he was talking about himself every time he told me how worthless I was. I know now that my father had a choice. He let the grief of my mom leaving consume him, rather than letting me be his reason for living, rather than finding help and a healthy outlet to grieve."

"You're not worthless, Dean." Sawyer's deep brown eyes gaze up at me with sincerity. "You've never been worthless."

CHAPTER FIFTY-SEVEN

Sawyer

IT NEVER OCCURRED to me that Dean could be just as broken. I've been so wrapped up in the wreckage that is my life, I never took the time to really look at him and see what he's gone through. I never wanted to believe that anything could be wrong with Dean, because he's always been so perfect in my eyes. Even now, as he sits with his emotions bare, I see how beautifully broken he is. He's still perfect—so perfectly imperfect.

When Dean looks at me the way he's looking at me now I have hope that the pieces of my shattered heart have a chance to be picked up off the floor. For the first time in all of these years lost, I feel I might be able to piece them back together. To make something whole. Together. It's possible Dean and I could do this together.

"I was so stupid, Jack." When he calls me Jack this time, I don't feel bitterness or pain. I feel comfort and serenity. "Please forgive me. Don't make me go another day without you. Let's stop this. I'm so tired of not having you in my life." He shifts, taking hold of my arms, curling his calloused fingers around my biceps. "Just seeing you here at my house." He swallows. "I want to see you here with me. You fill this place of painful memories with light. I need more light in my life, Jack."

I blink and finally feel relief. "You should know... I never stopped loving you. I loved Grayson, and for a time I belonged to him, but my heart always belonged to you." I shrug. "Always."

Dean bridges the gap between us and takes my face in his hands. He releases a breath when he looks at my mouth, and then his lips are against mine. There's no way to explain how I feel the kiss all the way down to my toes. Though I feel his urgency, he remains tender. His tongue explores my mouth, and I'm brought back to every good memory, where we learned how to fit together seamlessly with every kiss and every caress.

One of his arms tightens around my waist, drawing me closer to his mouth, devouring me in a way he never has before. My name is a whisper on his lips—not Jack, but Sawyer. It's more intimate. He makes me feel like I could survive on purely this—him, breathing life into me.

Life is worth breathing for again. Every bitter thought that has tried to swallow me whole vanishes. Through his touch, I can be mended. His hands move to grip my hips and his kisses slow.

"Even after all this time," he whispers heavily against my mouth. "You taste the same."

"I hope that's a good thing," I reply.

He pauses and smiles against my lips. "You know... I kept thinking the longer I was away the easier it would get, but I missed you more and more every day. I missed this." He inhales and kisses me deeply, filling the parts of me that have been empty for so long. I know this is only the beginning, but it's a start. "It hurt so much some days I thought it might kill me. If I wanted any chance at survival, I knew I had to come back and make you forgive me," he breathes.

321

I press my forehead to his. "And then you came back, and I had moved."

I feel his head shake from side to side. "You didn't just move, you moved on." He leans back. "I lost you. You were engaged, and Alix made sure I knew how happy you were and to leave you alone."

"So, you heard I was happy and engaged and you gave up? Why so easily? That doesn't sound like you."

"No." He shakes his head again, trailing his fingertips up and down my arms, leaving goose bumps in their wake. "I *saw* how happy you were, so I let you go."

The air escapes my lungs. "What?"

"I went to Seattle." He shrugs as if this isn't the most important detail of all. "I was able to get that much out of Alix. I didn't know how to find you. I searched in phonebooks and online through social networking. I was in Seattle for weeks and weeks. It wasn't like I hadn't learned how to survive without a permanent residence over the years.

"Then one day, I saw you. The heavens finally opened up for me. You were in a tiny coffee shop soaked to the bone and laughing. Your hair was dripping down your back and the brightest smile lit up your face. I was still drawn to you. That smile... oh, that smile." His fingers stroke my parted lips. "And then I saw him, the one who was making you so happy, and I knew it was selfish of me to try and steal you back. I stood there for a solid twenty minutes fighting with myself. You know which side won. So, I left."

"Soaked to the bone," I repeat.

"Yeah," he says with a chuckle. "Sopping wet. I couldn't understand how you could look so comfortable when I knew

322

how miserable you must have felt."

I can't breathe. With closed eyes I utter, "I couldn't have been engaged…"

"What?" he says it as if he didn't hear me, but he's merely processing.

I open my eyes and look at Dean who looks more confused than ever. "If I was soaking wet, that was my first date with Grayson. We weren't engaged."

Dean's head is shaking, trying to understand what I just figured out. He pulls away from me and leans back against the bench, running his hand down his face, grazing the scruff on his jaw. "Are you saying—?"

"How long did you wait to come back?" I ask to clarify, just to be sure. Alix couldn't possibly have gotten the details *that* wrong. "Give it to me in years."

He scratches the back of his neck. "About a year and a half."

"Not long after I left for Seattle," I mumble and stand. I need a minute of not looking at him. *I'm going to kill Alix.* My stomach ties into tighter and tighter knots until I feel bile rise in my throat. After all of this time, thinking he deserted me for *years*… She could have taken away all of the not knowing, all of the pain… *Why would she do that to me?* My back finds the railing to lean against for support.

"Alix lied to me?" The realization finally sets in for Dean. "She said you had been gone for almost as long as I had." I swallow and shake my head to answer him, taking in deep breaths as I put myself inside Alix's head.

"I'd only been gone for six months."

As angry as it makes me, my mind tries to formulate why

she would have done what she did. I realize she was trying to save me, so I looked like I had moved on rather than wallowed pitifully in my depressing life for the last year.

"That little—"

"Dean," I stop him from saying something I would make him regret. "She was trying to protect me. It was a thoughtless decision on her part, but her intentions were honorable enough. And there's nothing we can do now. If I've learned anything from this entire mess, it's that holding a grudge and mulling around the what-ifs will only cause more heartache. What matters is that you came back, and so did I. I don't want to waste any more time. I'm done wasting my life."

He looks at me hesitantly. "Are you saying…?"

I put one foot in front of the other and slowly sit down beside him, our legs flush with one another. My fingers run through his hair, brushing it back from his eyes. "I surrender."

He wraps one arm around my waist, splaying his fingers on my stomach. His other hand reaches up to cradle my face with the gentlest stare forming in his emerald eyes. A crooked smile creeps across his face. "You do? You promise?"

I nod. "I can't promise I'll be the same. My heart has been shattered too many times to be put back together and be unchanged. I will give you all I have, but there's not a lot left to give."

"Then I'll make up the difference. I don't need a lot." He reaches for my left hand tangled in his hair and brings my wrist to his lips and kisses my sparrow. "Let me fill the cracks. Let me make you whole. Isn't it clear by now that I'm not whole without you?"

A tear rushes down my cheek, and he kisses it away.

"What do you say we go find some dandelions?" he asks. "I know this really great park. It has a pond and some really cool willow trees." The smile tugging my lips spreads across my face, and I lean in to kiss him. "We could lay down a blanket and watch the clouds go by. I hear its pretty relaxing," he says between kisses.

"I think this plan gets better the more I hear about it."

"There might be some Reese's Pieces involved, but only if you'll share with me."

"I'm not very good at sharing."

His arms wrap tighter around me as he says against my mouth, "Me either."

Epilogue

SPRING ALWAYS BRINGS a fresh start. When the leaves on the trees sprout light green and the first flower blooms I feel renewed. Willowhaven is the most beautiful in the spring. If it could stay this way year round I would live contentedly forever, but I suppose it's harder to appreciate the good when there's no bad to compare it to.

A new season makes me revaluate life. I can see now that Dean couldn't fix me. Neither could Grayson. I had to say goodbye to my anger. I had to let go of my bitterness. I had to dig myself out of the deep, black abyss that was my life on my own. You have to want it badly enough. There's no easy solution to healing a broken heart. It took will power and an inner strength I didn't think I possessed, but I made it out on top. Somehow after it all, I'm still standing.

I've taken a few tumbles, some unavoidable nosedives. There have been times when I have had to let life carry me some of the way. At times, I let myself stay down. But, today I'm standing. And that's all that I can ask for.

After I leave my bakery, I head for Timberpond Park. I spot Dean making his way down the pathway. His shorter brown hair is disheveled, flickering with the breeze. He peers over at the willow tree along the bank of the tranquil pond, and a smile turns up the corner of his lips. When he looks up and sees me the smile grows. His entire face brightens and I know everything is right in the world.

I was never able to see myself without Dean. I know why now. I couldn't walk away from him if I tried. He's made me realize I don't have to do this alone. He'll stand by me through it all. I heal a little more every day with his help.

I've made peace with losing Grayson. My heart misses him, but it copes better with losing him than I thought it ever would. He wasn't the one I was supposed to spend my life with. He was a scenic detour along the way. We may not always understand the reasons why things happen, but things fall into place when it's their time. This is our time. Dean's and mine. And I'm going to revel in every moment we have together because I know now how easily those moments can be taken away.

"Daddy!" Abigail bolts from my side, making a beeline through the grass, straight for Dean. He squats down to his knees and captures her in his arms.

"Hi, baby girl," I hear him murmur into her long, dark curls.

I wouldn't be able to do it without Dean. Every day he pushes me to be stronger, to believe in myself. He's helped to mend my broken past, our broken past. And every day I try to be the light he so desperately wants—that he so desperately needs.

Dean stands with our daughter in his arms and rests her on his hip as he makes his way over to me. She grins and kisses his stubbled cheek, securely wrapping her little arms around his neck.

"Mommy, I found Daddy!" She beams.

"I see that."

Dean takes my hand and softly kisses my sparrow. "Hey, Jack," he says, and I smile. He kneels down with Abigail in his arms and rubs my belly before kissing it. "Hi, baby." Gentleness caresses his voice.

Not a day goes by that I don't think of you. That I don't miss you and the life we never had, the life you never got the chance to experience. It would be impossible for me to forget you. Though I only knew you for a few weeks, and though those few weeks were terrifying, I loved you all the same.

I know life happens. We can't control what is thrown at us, but we can decide how we're going to respond. I choose to stand with hope. In the end, hope is all we have, but as long as I have that, I know there will be better days. I know I will be able to withstand anything.

We live. We learn. We endure.

So I guess this is me.

After you.

ACKNOWLEDGEMENTS

Writing acknowledgements for my fifth book feels like a dream. But if I didn't have the support team that I do, I wouldn't even have a fifth book to publish.

Thank Madison Seidler, my editor, for the time and effort you put into each and every one of my manuscripts.

To my Alix, for letting me pick your brain and for caring about this story as much as I do, if not more.

A ginormous thanks to my Heartstoppers: Brittany B, Vicki, Lyndsey, Brookelyn, Amy, Laura, Brittany S, Kelli, Morgan, Mary, and Cheri. Without your enthusiasm I don't know that I would have the courage to keep writing. Thank you for being who you are and loving my stories.

Amy Van Wagenen, I appreciate you more than you know. Thank you for always being willing to be my extra set of eyes.

To Starla Huchton and CL Foster, for always being there for moral support, levity and laughs. I know I can always count on you, ladies. Thank you.

Jessica Surgett and Michele G. Miller, you girls go above and beyond what I deserve. You're the brainstorming queens. If I didn't have you I'd be rocking in a corner somewhere with an unfinished manuscript. I can't imagine the book world—or my world, for that matter—without you.

As always, thank you family for supporting me, reading my stories, and spreading the word. I love you.

My Readers: I can't believe I can even start an acknowledgment like that. I have readers! And I'm so grateful for each and every one of you!

And finally, my husband, Ryan, whose endless patience still amazes me. Thank you for supporting this crazy adventure. I love you.

ABOUT THE AUTHOR

MINDY HAYES is the youngest of six children and grew up in San Diego, California. After graduating from Brigham Young University-Idaho, she discovered her passion for reading and writing. Mindy and her husband have been married for ten years and live in Summerville, South Carolina.

Visit Mindy Online:
Website: mindyhayes.com
Facebook: facebook.com/hayes.mindy
Twitter: @haymindywrites

Made in the USA
Monee, IL
12 December 2021